AWAKENED

A Clandestine Citadel Press Book

Published by Clandestine Citadel Press, LLC
Bryan, TX 77807
www.clandestinecitadelpress.com

Printed in the United States of America.

Shielded Citadel is a registered trademark
of Clandestine Citadel Press, LLC.

Our books may be purchased in bulk for promotional, educational, or business use. Please contact your local bookstore or the Clandestine Citadel Press Corporate and Premium Sales Department at (979) 637-5539 or by email at support@clandestinecitadelpress.com.

The Library of Congress Cataloging-in-Publication
Data is available upon request.

ISBN: 979-8-9917894-0-0 (eBook)
ISBN: 979-8-9917894-1-7 (paperback)
ISBN: 979-8-9917894-2-4 (hardcover)

Cover Design | Interior Formatting
Enchanted Ink Publishing

The text type was set in Garamond Premier Pro

First Clandestine Citadel Press Edition: 2025

To my family-

The ones who didn't play favorites. The ones who cared enough to support me and my girls. The ones who tried to fight even through the worst times. The ones who stuck through the struggles. Thank you.

To my girls-

Shoot for the stars, my little loves. You can achieve all that you put your minds to, be it writing, swimming, gaming, baking, you name it. The world is your oyster. Your voices are worth hearing. Be loud and proud and never be scared to be yourselves.

To my friends-

The ones who cheered me on. The ones who keep in touch. The ones I can talk to after months of life being busy and pick up like nothing happened. You rock, keep being you. I love you.

To my BEST friend-

You are a rock. You supported this endeavor and pushed me not to let my chin fall. You've been one of my dearest friends for over 10 years now and I adore you for that. Please never change. You're amazing.

To the readers-

Buckle up. Phoenix, Alison, and Ben are about to take you on a heck of a ride!

To those I lost along the way...

I made it. I miss you every day, and all I can do is try and make you proud.

TRIGGER WARNING

Awakened is a story of magic, love, and redemption,
but it also explores themes and situations that may be
sensitive for some readers. This book contains:

Explicit sexual content and intimate scenes
Graphic depictions of violence
Themes of death, rebirth, and personal loss
Dark magic, necromancy, and supernatural elements
Emotional and physical trauma

We value your well-being and encourage you to read
at your comfort level. If any of these themes may be
triggering for you, please proceed with caution.
Thank you for embarking on this journey with us.

THE SOULBOUND SERIES
• BOOK ONE •

AWAKENED

ARTEMIS GORDON

CLANDESTINE
CITADEL PRESS

Your heart is mine throughout time...

PROLOGUE

All that is gone is not lost

-PHOENIX-
GLASTONBURY, ENGLAND
459 A.D.

"P HOENYX! *RUN!*"

Benjamin's hands grabbed Phoenyx, turning him as Nyx cast another spell out at the two necromancers following them. Behind the two, a woman clad in black strode forward, her hands quickly moving, resurrecting whomever had already been stricken down. Her eyes, a vivid violet shade, locked on them... and she called out to them, laughing.

"Come out... thine art the last of the Followers of the Light... England is *succumbing*. Look around you!"

She wasn't telling falsehoods.

Kingdoms were in a state of unrest. The plagues had come, causing so many to lose their lives needlessly to disease and pestilence. Mothers were pulling their children indoors before the sun crept below the horizon at night out of fear that they might be stolen from their homes. It was a terrifying time to be in. On top of it all, magic was being chased from the world, causing those who practiced the arts to either flee, be killed, or take a last stand.

A flash of light from the woods caught their attention. A few of the necromancers were sent scattering, all of them yelling out in anger and annoyance. A woman, covered in a pale cloak with her hood pulled up, stood atop the ridge. She tugged the hood down as her brown curls gleamed and the amethyst at her neck glittered brightly. The pale blue of her dress shone in the light, her deep brown eyes taking in the surroundings like a hawk. She glared from the upper ridge of the trees, her hand out from her previous spell and her eyes glowing a pale white. "Still thy tongue, Abaddon! We have yet to lose our fight!"

She was quick, her hand moving to pull her bow and arrow out, shooting the freshly risen men in the heads, where they would be unable to be brought back to life. Abaddon hissed with anger. "You foolish shrew!"

Phoenyx, snorting, grasped his blades and swung, felling one of the necromancers behind them with a grin. "Alyson is far from a shrew, Abaddon," he chuckled, taking the arm off of a necromancer as the man let out a howl, grasping his arm before stumbling back. "...She has yet to resort to your ways to invigorate her lifespan like you have."

"Focus, you fool..." Benjamin barked, his eyes on the men coming from behind them as Alyson darted from the woods, coming from her vantage point. "...You remember your vision... is this how it went?"

"My visions have been wrong," Phoenyx muttered, swinging his blades as Benjamin growled, his trident's sharpened ends angrily swinging for the head of another necromancer.

"Phoenyx! Is this how your vision went?!"

"...Yes," Phoenyx admitted, biting back a scowl as Benjamin nodded, panting.

"We are prepared, Phoenyx. Do you understand?"

"Shut up," Phoenyx hissed, shaking his head as Benjamin smiled slightly. "My visions have been wrong, fool. Our actions can change our-"

Benjamin simply shook his head, his trident going up to block another long-range attack. "Phoenyx, you do not have long. You saw us all being overtaken within minutes! My chronal control, Alyson's kinetic ability, your soothsaying, none of it is enough together right now. You two must run to get away." he said. His eyes grew damp as Phoenyx's ash-grey eyes met with Benjamin's blue ones.

"You will be unable to fend them off alone..."

"If this is my time, then it is my time," Benjamin said firmly, nodding before he pressed his forehead to Phoenyx's. "We will find one another again, Phoenyx... and I will always look over you and Alyson... always with you both. You are my greatest allies, and the best friends that a man could ever ask for."

"...I am scared, Benjamin..." Phoenyx said, his eyes leaking over. "I do not want to be alone, Benjamin... I do not want to die alone..." he murmured quietly, his hand twitching for his alchemy bottles latched to his belt, grasping at one as Benjamin shook his head. "...and in the end, I am alone..."

"...We are never alone. Not anymore. We have each other... We have the three of us, always. Now... you get Alyson... and you kiss her goodbye for me. Tell her that she is still as beautiful as the water lilies that she loves so much..." Benjamin chuckled, a hand going out as he muttered under his breath, a blast of light magic leaving his palm. "...I care for you both... so very much..."

Phoenyx's hand went through Benjamin's soft, black hair... and his face crinkled. Heartbroken, he simply nodded. "We love you..."

With that, Phoenyx simply let his hand move down to clasp Benjamin's as he nodded, then turned, his trident held out.

"Go!"

Turning, Benjamin let their hands come apart and let out a roar, darting forward quickly. Phoenyx turned and rushed for the edge of the woods, meeting Alyson there and wrapping his arms around her waist, her eyes widening as she yelled with fright.

"P-Phoenyx?! B-But...!"

"He says to tell you he will always care for us," Phoenyx muttered, the light flashing through his curly, deep brown hair as Alyson gripped his arms, trying to break his grip on her as he tugged her away.

"No!"

"We must go, Alyson!"

"Benjamin!"

"Move!"

Benjamin's howl of pain moments later caused Alyson to bring her fist to Phoenyx's face, then to yank away from him as his grip on her slipped. Panting, he darted after her, his eyes wide, dreading what he knew they were to find. He was hoping to buy them time, get them away from Abaddon and her minions and make it so that they didn't have to see their lover fall.

Alyson's enraged scream and her hand raising moments later caused Phoenyx to wince. The flash of light that blasted from her palm was enough to scorch away anything demonic within miles. The group of necromancers attacking Benjamin was burned to ash from the power of the light magic, their remains scattering in the wind. Abaddon let out a howl of pain, a bright blue light flashing as she used a portal to retreat for the moment. Alyson bolted down to Benjamin, watching as he knelt, the prongs of his trident run through him, and she whimpered, trying to use her robe to staunch his blood loss.

"...Benjamin, no." Alyson moaned, her eyes locking on Benjamin as he sighed and smiled slightly, focusing on her.

"...you...were supposed...to go on ahead," Benjamin muttered, then glanced at Phoenyx, who knelt with her and cupped Benjamin's face, his own eyes wet.

"She hit me."

"...she... does that."

He coughed, a wet, pained cough, and the two watched as the light began to dim from his eyes. Helping him to the ground, Alyson lay his head into her lap, her eyes on him as he peered up at her, smiling.

"...why... are you... so sad?"

"You are leaving us, my love." Alyson said softly, her eyes dripping onto his face as he sighed wetly. "We won't be complete... without you. You are a part of us."

"...and we will find...one another...again, my dearest Alyson..." Benjamin smiled, his eyes on her face as he brought a shaking hand up to stroke her curls. "...it...is why we linked... our souls... because we knew... this was coming..."

"...Benjamin..." Phoenyx wiped his eyes, then brought a hand to cup at the other man's face, shaking his head. "...we can't without you..."

"...you can... and you will..."

"How?"

"...because...I..." Benjamin's eyes dulled slightly as he peered up at Alyson, struggling to take a breath, her hands stroking his hair as she sobbed. "...believe... in... both... of... you..."

His mouth hung open and his air left him, the hand that had been trying to stroke Alyson's curls dropping to the dirt.

Both Alyson and Phoenyx let their heads drop, their eyes full of anguish.

"He's gone." Alyson's voice broke as Phoenyx nodded, wrapping her into his arms, pocketing the crystal again.

"Not forever. Come on, it's time. We know their plan, that's why they were after us, Ali. They didn't want us there tonight. If we get there, we can end this..."

Alyson nodded but glanced back at Benjamin's body, and she shook her head. "I refuse to leave him like this, Phoenyx." She said, moving from him. She pushed her hand into a satchel on her hip, and tugged out the last of the seeds she carried on her. She let out a small sob, closing her eyes, her hands outstretching as she began to mumble spells under her breath. The plants and flowers themselves began to move below them, vines trailing around them. They moved Benjamin, pulling the trident from his chest, out of his body, and placing his arms across his chest. His trident was placed into his hands, the vines encircling him, flowers covering him. With a tired groan, dropping to her knees as they buckled, Alyson coaxed the vines and flowers to entomb him, to give him a resting place. As she opened her eyes, she peered at the various bloomed flowers on him and the water lilies that encircled his head, like a crown of white.

Taking a deep breath, Phoenyx wrapped his arms around her and helped her up, nodding and kissing her neck, sniffling.

"It's beautiful, Alyson. He would have adored it."

"He always brought me water lilies..."

"Because he knew how much you loved them, and thought you were as beautiful as they were... more so, even."

She nodded, her eyes flowing freely, then the two turned.

"Phoenyx, we do not leave that damned ritual tonight without ending this in some way," Alyson said, her face firm. With a nod Phoenyx took her hand, kissing it as they glanced at their lost loved one. They moved down the path, Phoenyx wrapping an arm around Alyson's shoulders, and began to plan their next move, the sounds of nature surrounding Benjamin's now peacefully resting body as their footsteps faded in the distance.

"Are you ready?"

Alyson stared out at the gathered necromancers, watching as the portal opening around them glowed an eerie violet shade, and she nodded.

"Yes. The spell I cast will enhance the power of our arcane abilities to us for a short time. Not long, Phoenyx. We must be swift."

"I know, Alyson. We must find Abaddon fast, stop her damned Armageddon rituals." Phoenyx said firmly, then smiled, leaning down to kiss her deeply, his eyes locked on her as tears went down her face. "For Benjamin."

"For Benjamin."

The two, their faces set, rushed out. Palms out, they muttered fast spells, the darkness threatening to overtake their every move. Alyson's bow rose, firing arrows laced with enchantments at necromancers that spewed the unholy from their mouths. Her hand rose, flinging multiple necromancers back just to give her the opening she needed to shoot them in the chest, then the head, as damage to the brain was the only way to kill them permanently.

Holy energy and light flowed from the two, both trying to put an end to the death and carnage that the Order of the Necrotic Flame had been canvassing across the country. Every step the three had made, the Order had been there with a sidestep, and finally Benjamin had succumbed to the darkness.

The loss was simply too much for them to bear.

The portal the necromancers were summoning opened a portal directly to Shamayim, a place where no mortal being could survive the trip. At least, that was what they had been taught. Benjamin had studied the portals, he had told them that the energy was able to be destroyed with arcane light magic, but it would take more magic than the abilities of one to end a fully opened portal. No, it would take all three, which was why Abaddon had come after them this afternoon. She knew they would come for their ritual, to stop them and end her madness, send her to the depths, even if it meant their own demise.

Phoenyx stared at the portal, his eyes widening slightly as he ran another necromancer priest through. He noted that the circle of violet would be almost beautiful, if not for the demonic entities trying to crawl from the depths of it. The energy coming from it was overwhelming, causing the two to cringe, but their attacks went on. They had to.

Alyson slipped into the fray as Phoenyx, his face set, slashed through another necromancer priest, the last they could see, then glanced towards the main altar. "Where are you, Priestess?" he called, his eyes set as the wind howled, seeming to come from the portal itself.

"I am right here, my little apprentice." Abaddon chuckled, slinking from the shadow of a half-destroyed building to throw a wave of darkness at them, knocking Phoenyx off his feet as he yelped. "The son of the fallen, you come from nothing." She sneered, her eyes on him as he rolled, dodging another attack. "You ARE nothing. I made you all that you are today, and all that you will become will be because of me."

"He does not need you to make him become something more, wench," Alyson hissed, her bow coming up as she stood behind Abaddon, about to let her arrow fly.

"Do it, Ali!" Phoenyx called, his eyes widening as Abaddon smiled, then quirked her brow. "End it!"

The sound of a squelch caused them all to pause, and Alyson's arrow went to the side as her eyes widened. Abaddon's hand clenched at her side, a chuckle leaving her as she moved at an unholy speed to bring her other hand up and stroke Alyson's cheek.

Phoenyx stared, confused, then moaned as he saw the darkness surrounding Alyson's torso, weaving through her body.

"No."

"Dear, sweet girl." Abaddon smiled, leaning forward and pecking her lips as Alyson's eyes leaked tears. "He was merely a distraction." She smiled serenely as Alyson choked, looking up, focusing on the stars, her face broken. "You have always been the one who is my greatest foe. When it comes to our arcane talents, the two men can use the skills, but you... You have perfected it. You caress it like it is your lover, as I do. I had to sever your ties to it, by breaking your ties to your body," she said quietly as Phoenyx panted, coming to his feet. "Your spine is destroyed. You will choke in your own body. If your lover is at all kind, he will take your head off of your shoulders." she glanced at Phoenyx before setting Alyson on the ground, her body laying at an awkward angle as she gasped and made small noises, her eyes wide.

"...Y-You..." Phoenyx spat, about to rush her, but Abaddon snorted.

"You are no true threat without the other two. You are an alchemist and a soothsayer. The pure arcane is your weakest element. My spells have already sealed away your more powerful forms. That was done well before the fall of the water dweller." Abaddon scoffed, her hand waving dismissively as she moved to the altar. "Be with the woman as she dies, it is the last kindness I will give you." Abaddon gave a dark smile, moving to the portal, then beyond it as Phoenyx dropped to his hands and knees, moving to Alyson and cradling her, his eyes on hers as she leaked tears, her eyes half-unfocused.

"...Alyson..."

"...I...s-see..." Alyson choked, then wheezed, her eyes widening as she blinked fast. "...B-Ben...ja...myn..."

Phoenyx stared, then shook his head. They had one other option. It was blood magic, something that the alchemists studied, as it used blood itself as the catalyst for the arcane. This made it intensely powerful, but it often came with a heavy price. "Alyson! Listen to me! I have one idea to close the portal! Okay?! Blood magic! It will kill us. The blood I would need, it would drain us completely."

Alyson simply wheezed, then choked one word. "...y-y...es..."

His eyes wide, Phoenyx gripped her, pulling her to the portal as his eyes got wet, muttering apologies the whole time for what he would have to do. As soon as he cradled her there, he tugged his dagger out of his sheath, swallowing heavily, then grasped her arm as she peered at him.

"...I can't, Ali." He moaned, his eyes wet as she nodded.

"...d-do... it..." Alyson croaked weakly, gasping for air. "...set... u-us... free..."

With a sob, Phoenyx brought the blade to his own arms first, dragging the metal down along the skin and flesh, opening deep wounds as he groaned, then began muttering the only spell he knew that could end this. Finally, his hand trembling, he ran the blade down her arms, letting blood pour from her as she moaned and looked up, then smiled.

"...I... see... you... Ben..."

He set Alyson into his lap, watching as her contented eyes grew duller, her hands limp, their arms more and more wet, and as he muttered the last words of the spell, the red light of the blood magic forcing the portal to implode, a wave of energy sending them sprawling back.

Silence.

Once the spell flickered out, Phoenyx blinked in the aftermath, glancing around and seeing Alyson staring up, a small smile on her ghostly-white face. Tiredly, he crawled to her, her eyes still locked upwards, and he could swear, he could see them in the distance, even as he gripped her to him, held her for some comfort as he felt the chill of the reaper coming for him next.

'I knew... I would be alone... in the end...' he thought, curling around Alyson's body as he stroked her curls, her mouth hanging open. "...We did it," he said tiredly, nodding. "...In the end, we managed... to do it... stop her..."

"...You..."

Abaddon...

Phoenyx turned weakly, his eyes exhausted as she snarled down at him, her eyes livid. "...Yes... me," he said, sighing as she glared, stepping forward, her robes billowing around her.

"...Why? You would have lived. You'd have gone on..."

"Life... is not life... without them," Phoenyx chuckled, kissing Alyson's cooling forehead once more, a sigh leaving him. "...Something... you will never understand..." he said weakly, his eyes fluttering.

As she glared, moving forward to find the dagger he had used, Phoenyx peered forward, still clutching Alyson to him...

'*So, this is what it is like to die...*' he thought, taking a shaky breath as he ran his hand through Alyson's curls. '*...Were you scared too, my beautiful Ali?*' he asked, his breath shaking as he heard the metal of his dagger scraping on the ground as it was lifted by Abaddon.

'*Phoenyx!*'

'*Come home, beloved!*'

He choked... Benjamin... Alyson... he could see them, both with arms out, smiling, waiting to take him from this wretched, painful existence... His hand outstretched, a smile on his face as he beamed at them, trying to take their hands...

He never felt the blade go through into the flesh of his neck, slicing his throat open...

'*By the nine hells, I missed you both!*' Phoenyx sighed, his eyes wet as Alyson kissed his cheeks Ben nodded, his arms crossing in front of his ethereal form.

'*I missed you as well... and Alyson also... but next time...*'

'*We will stop her for good next time.*' Alyson nodded, curling into them as Phoenyx sighed.

'*Next time...*'

CHAPTER 1

Look for me in the moonlight

-ALYSON-

BOSTON, MASSACHUSETTS
1986 A.D.

SILVERLEAF UNIVERSITY, FALL SEMESTER, FIRST DAY OF classes.

Chatter erupted around the campus. Excited students walked around in their stylish jeans, their nice shirts, and polished shoes. Teased hair and well-done makeup flashed all around, because you see, this was Boston, and this was where the people who had the most money came to study. This wasn't some small-town college where you paid your own way in. If you were here, you likely had family money, or the talents to get yourself through with a scholarship.

That was how Silverleaf University worked, and it was utterly daunting, especially for someone who wasn't one of the blue-blooded rich people.

She simply stared at the vast buildings, her eyes widening as she bit her lip and whimpered slightly, utterly overwhelmed. She knew no one, she had yet to make any real friends here, and her damn father, well, he wasn't worth discussing, to be fair. He certainly had done nothing to get her here.

But we're getting ahead of ourselves...

Her name was Alyson Clara Walker, and right now, she was completely exhausted.

You see, she had been hunting for the music and dramatic arts building here at Silverleaf University for hours, and not a soul had seen fit to help her. She wasn't sure if it was her makeup, perhaps she had overdone the black liner a bit, maybe it was the slightly ripped jeans.

It might be the dark black, leather bomber jacket that she kept tightly pulled over her less-than-high-class *Metallica* shirt.

The smooth, black leather had been her first gift to herself, so she really wasn't going to lose that. She loved that jacket, but, she did know that other women tended to have a lower view of girls who wore leather for some reason. She had no idea why, it wasn't like she smoked or drank.

At least, not much.

She had transferred all of her paperwork to Silverleaf University's School of Fine Arts over the summer, and today was her first day of classes. She had meant to get acquainted with the campus last week, but to be honest, she had been far busier in her new town thirty minutes away. Something about the quiet town of Salem had drawn her near, made her curious, and a small little joint called The Black Cat had piqued her interest all weekend, the one bartender slipping her cocktails and bringing his hand down her jaw as he playfully flirted with her.

He had said his name was, oh, she was so focused on his curly deep brown hair and his ashy-grey eyes, that she couldn't remember his name, if he had even mentioned it. He had asked her to the movies for the next weekend too, but she hadn't thought about asking him to write his name down.

Silly girl.

Her shoes clacked on the pavement, a frown on her face as her curls bounced on her head. She had a class to get to, one that was causing her to risk a tardy on her attendance record because she simply couldn't find the building. "I'm going to be late!" she huffed, stomping a foot to the ground furiously as she spun in place, her eyes taking everything in. People glanced at her, staring and frowning.

Not very ladylike.

Like she gave a damn.

"Whoa! Hey!"

Someone grabbed her shoulder and she whipped around, her eyes widening as she let her arm come out towards her assailant with a punch. The figure behind her yelped, dropping his books as he grabbed her forearm, then peered at her, the two staring each other down.

"W-What?!" Ali asked, her body stiffening as he chuckled, his face slightly entranced at her expression.

"Hey there! Sorry, I spooked you!" he said with a small smile, his black hair falling into his blue eyes.

"That's my fault. I heard you getting upset about being late, where you headed?" he asked as she bit her lip and tugged her schedule out, her eyes wary. He quickly picked his books up off of the sidewalk and she relaxed a hair, letting him release her arm as he grinned. He leaned over, peering at her jotted-down schedule, and smiling at her.

"I know where that is, it's on the way to the medical buildings, where I go. Come on." He laughed, shaking his head as he offered his arm and smiled impishly at her. "Do I look that untrustworthy?"

'Yes, like an imp waiting to catch prey...' she thought, her eyes on him as she stared, then let her hand come up, touching his arm tentatively. She swallowed, then let him lead her down the pathway, her eyes down as he grabbed a medical journal and flipped to a page, reading to himself as they walked.

"Excuse me...?" she asked, her eyes darting to him as he blinked over to her, a broad smile on his face. He was the typical looking 'rich boy' from here, nicely pressed tan pants, white shirt, light brown suit jacket that was as neat and perfect as the pants, and he smelled like some kind of fancy cologne,

He looked and literally smelled like he rolled in a bed of money.

"Yes?" he asked, his eyes lighting up as he glanced at his spot in his journal, then made eye-contact with her again, grinning. His teeth were as clean as the rest of him, causing her to blink at how damn clean he was. He could be a prince for crying out loud.

"I'm sorry for almost hitting you." Ali muttered, gazing up into his eyes as he chuckled, marking his place and closing his journal, setting it with his books again as they walked, her hand tucked in his arm still.

"No, no, that was my fault. I was heading towards the medical department and overheard you, then saw you turning in place, you looked lost and confused," he said, smiling as she nodded. "I'm sorry I frightened you, miss...?"

"...Walker. Alyson Walker." Ali said nodding as she tucked a stray curl back behind her ear. He grinned, his eyes on her hair as she looked up at him, her eyebrows knotting together with slight concern. "What?"

"You don't look like the other ladies on campus, that's all."

He wasn't exactly lying, Their perfect clothes, nice shoes, well-done hair, teased and pinned and tucked perfectly into place...

She was having none of that.

"If you don't like what you see, buddy..." Ali muttered, tugging at her hand, but he grinned, shaking his head.

"No, you're misunderstanding me..." he chuckled, his eyes on her hair as she frowned. "...You're lovely."

She went scarlet. *'What's he playing at?'* she thought, her eyes widening as she held her breath, then looked up at the building they'd walked to.

"Right here, Miss Walker."

She nodded, staring as he let go of her arm and patted her arm, waving and turning to leave, opening his journal again, but then she gasped, biting her red-painted lip. "W-Wait!" she yelped, her eyes widening as she moved forward a few steps, chasing after him as he turned.

"Yes?"

"Your name?"

"Benjamin Hancott, Miss Walker."

Ali nodded, her eyes on him as he smiled. "It's... a pleasure to meet you, Mr. Hancott." she said quietly, grasping her books as he turned, facing her fully once more and closing the medical journal again. He got a thoughtful look on his face, his eyes on her. He seemed to be inspecting her every detail, almost on the prowl, like a wolf searching for his prey would be, and like a doe, all she could do was sit there, waiting for him to finish sniffing her out. Her eyes traced his prim and proper white shirt, catching traces of pale brown chest hairs poking up from the top of the fabric as she forced back a flush.

'Don't you dare get all hot and bothered over a stranger, Alyson Clara!'

"Miss Walker, what're you doing after classes let out today?" he asked carefully as she blinked, toeing the ground. "Not to be too forward, but, I'd love to talk, get to know you, maybe take you out for coffee or something."

"I would very much enjoy that," Ali said, nodding and giving him a smile as she let her eyes lock on his. Impish sapphire locked with serious chocolate brown, and he smiled, his head tipping slightly towards her.

"Fantastic."

The two stared at one another, then both blinked in surprise as the bell in the fine arts building rang, causing her to let out a shout. "Oh, shit! I'm late!" Ali yelped, her eyes wide as she turned, then blushed red. "I-I'll see you later!" she called as he chuckled, waving.

"See you later!"

She bolted into the building, and he simply turned, shaking his head and laughing quietly as he flipped back into where he had left off in his journal, murmuring to himself as he read.

You see, Benjamin wasn't very interested in many of the women on campus, or the women of 'high society' either.

-BENJAMIN-

FOR YEARS AND YEARS, HIS MOTHER AND FATHER HAD shoved the 'belles of the balls' at him, and Ben had snubbed his nose at them time and time again. He had told them over and over that he didn't like women who were more interested in money or their appearances. He preferred to have an educated woman, one that would be able to hold her own in an intellectual debate while also having an emotional connection with him Benjamin had told his parents many times that he'd planned to go into medicine, to be a healer and help those less fortunate than himself, but they had always insisted that he marry before he leave.

He'd never found a wife.

They wanted him to find a woman who belonged in Victorian England, not in the 1980s. He had seen more women in corsets and fluted skirts than he ever cared to admit. He'd had girls with the palest of skin thrown at him, girls who had been taught to treat their skin using arsenic to achieve the bluest of tones despite medical advancements disputing the practice. Hell, there was even concealer and foundation that could do the same thing now, but no, actual death-toned skin was what was in to them. He had pointed out to his parents that it wouldn't be the best choice to take a wife that had the life expectancy of a houseplant because she had paled her skin tone with toxins in order to be more appealing to a man.

They had begrudgingly given him that round.

Finally, Ben had gotten into a screaming row with them a few years ago. Allow him to leave Rhode Island and live on his own. Let him have access to the family funds, and he swore to not squander them, and in return, he swore to actually do what they asked and look for a suitable woman while furthering his education. A woman who would make handsome little baby Hancott heirs and pretty little Hancott heiresses, while not being a total embarrassment to the family name. Someone they can paint into their precious portraits and show off at all their little functions.

He had to admit, though, that he had been slacking on that front.

Instead, he had enjoyed being a bachelor.

He had gotten a flat on his own in Salem, enjoying the quaintness of the place. The place was on top of a former speakeasy-turned-nightclub called The Black Cat, and he had enjoyed the solitude there. He had slipped into the place on a whim one day, and fallen for the atmosphere and entertainment, the beauty, and the mystery. He had noted the flat atop the night-club, and that the place could use some sprucing up, so, he had asked the owner if he could possibly help with both parts of the building. He'd rent the flat above the nightclub and, with some of his funds, he'd be a patron of said nightclub, funding them for their needs as long as he had some input on some judgment calls. He wasn't about to fund gaudy green curtains on a pink backdrop after all.

On the weekdays, he spent the time in Boston, driving to the University, doing his studies, maybe flirting here and there, then heading home. The weekends?

He had those to cut loose at The Black Cat.

You see, The Black Cat was the perfect place to bring women for a date, then the flat directly above was just the icing on the cake if he was hoping to have sex with said lovely la-dies, Keep them interested and all that. Benjamin had brought many a woman first to the nightclub, then back up to his flat, and each and every one of them had stared at him the next day, expecting more from him than the proffered breakfast and a second romp.

Never had he once said there would be more involved in his offerings, and he never understood why they expected more.

Things had changed slightly in the last year when a man had come into The Black Cat with a cockeyed grin, his deep brown curls ruffled and a helmet in his hands, hunting for work. He had claimed to be a bartender, that he had slung drinks in New York in the speakeasies before the prohibition laws had been repealed and bartenders had become a dime a dozen up there.

Ben had put him to the test, having him make some of the classics.

He had asked him to make a Gin Rickey, which the man made easily, even adding the dash of simple syrup to keep the drink from getting tart. He had asked for an Old-Fashioned, watching as the man carefully made the drink in a separate glass, then skillfully made a whole new glass with new ice, pouring the concoction over the fresh ice and sliding it over with a cocky smirk. Ben had grinned in response, asking the man to make a Sidecar, and getting impressed as the man had mixed it flawlessly, making sure to cut back the Cointreau to be sure that it didn't overpower the drink.

So, with a chuckle, Benjamin had nodded and told the nightclub's owner, Lewis, to hire the guy.

Later on, the guy had come up and spoken to him, sitting with him and talking about how he had just moved into Salem. The man, Phoenyx Coleman, he said his name was, said that now that he had a job, he could find a place to live, and just laughed. Snorting, Ben had just shaken his head at him and asked him why he would move to Salem without some kind of plan in place.

Nyx, as he had told Ben to call him, had said that he had felt drawn there.

Ben had simply waved to Lewis, moving to the indoor entrance to the flat, then led Phoenyx up with him, past the aged wood barrels and the scent of alcohol. As soon as they had gone up the stairs and opened the door, Ben had nodded towards the bedroom doors, then pointed at the kitchen area.

"There's a kitchen there. Living room there. You can watch the TV whenever you like when I'm not home, but if I'm home and studying, I'll need you to keep it down. If you bring a woman home, bring her to your room, and if you make her see the light of God, try and have her bite a pillow, for fuck's sake."

he had said, stretching as Nyx had blinked, then given him a confused look.

"I'm not following..."

"You need a room. I have a room. You can pay rent every month, I think about half would be, well, just give me $170 and we'll call it even," Ben said, shrugging as Nyx stared, his eyes wide. "My rent's $345, but I'm too lazy to split the last fiver, I'll get that."

"Why?!"

"I was where you were a while ago. New here, didn't know a damn person and had nowhere to stay. Now, you know someone, and you have a place. Welcome to Salem."

Ben chuckled, his mind wandering off of the memory as he shook his head and refocused on his walk to the medical buildings, his eyes twinkling. "If that asshole has a date tonight, I'll boot him from the damn flat."

"If who has a date?"

Nyx's voice echoed from behind him as he bolted up from behind him, grinning as Ben snorted, shaking his head. "I have classes you know," Ben grinned, his eyes darting to the darker-haired man as Nyx snickered, his weathered dark-brown pants and white t-shirt contrasting against his deep blackish brown leather jacket, a helmet weaved into a loop to hold it to him as he walked.

"Oh, classes? You attend the fine arts school now, instead of the medical university?" Nyx asked, smirking as Ben rolled his eyes, shoving him playfully. "That's a hell of a downgrade, Mumsie and Popsie Hancott will be rather displeased, Andy-pie. You'll be written out of their will, have all your fancy underwear taken away, and will never see your beloved, fluffy Pomeranian again." Nyx grinned deviously as Ben laughed, shaking his head.

"No, you complete toddler, I didn't 'downgrade' and start attending the fine arts school," Ben said, then grinned. "I met a girl."

"Did you now?" Nyx laughed, shaking his head as he turned to walk backwards as his hands went behind his head, his eyes closing halfway. "To whom should I address the chocolates and muscle rub? You know, to ease the bruises that you'll be leaving on the poor girl's ego when she wakes up the next morning, butt-ass naked in your bed, and finds out that the only thing she'll be getting as a 'good morning kiss' from your ass is a swift boot to the door and a fond wave? Unless she'd like a farewell fuck that is. You'll give her that." Nyx cackled as Ben snorted, shoving him slightly as he grinned a bit.

"I am not that bad."

"Oh. Right. You offer coffee as well," Nyx smirked, an eyebrow up as Ben laughed, shaking his head.

"You know, there's nothing wrong with being a bachelor and playing the field. I recall saying 'Good morning.' to quite a few of your early-morning afterthoughts, too." Ben grinned as Nyx rolled his eyes, nodding as they trotted across the campus.

"Yes, Benjamin, but the difference is, I often offer a second date. You offer them a pat on the ass cheek and a thank you note," Nyx said as Ben shoved his free hand into his pocket, snorting. "That tends to cut into a girl's self-esteem a tad."

"If it was that bad, you should have said something," Ben said, grinning slightly as Nyx chuckled.

"You have your reasons for not wanting attachment. I can respect that, but don't sit there and pretend you're some nice boy about it, Ben," Nyx said honestly, his eyes on Ben's as Ben sighed. "If your goal is to get your pole damp and then trot off, then you need to tell these girls that from the get-go."

"Why the hell are you so damn noble?" Ben huffed, grumbling as Nyx shrugged.

"Because. You'll chase the wrong girl off like that, or the right one."

Ben blinked, then got quiet, his head lost in thought. Nyx had a point, he wouldn't find what he was looking for with the attitude he'd had, and that would bite him in the backside in the end. Perhaps Nyx was right, and he needed to slow down, look beyond the bed sheets.

"Anyhow, you said that if I had a date tonight, you'd boot me out of the flat. Why?"

Benjamin smiled, his eyes flitting to Nyx, who was turning to walk properly again as the two neared the primary medical buildings. "Ah, right. Like I said, I met a girl. I want to see if she'd like to come talk this evening, I'll drive her home if she doesn't want to do the drive herself," Ben said, pushing his hair out of his face as Phoenyx nodded, his face mildly surprised.

"Oh. You plan to actually chat then?" Nyx asked as Ben shrugged.

"That was the plan. She's... feisty. I like her," Ben snickered, shaking his head as he looked up, his eyes glittering. "Why're you here, anyhow?"

"Well, I was chatting up a girl at the 'Cat the other night, and we seemed to hit it off, but we got so engrossed in our talk, that we forgot to exchange names!" Nyx laughed, shaking his head as Ben slapped his forehead, rolling his eyes and snorting.

"Very smart!"

"I try," Nyx nodded, his nose up. "Hence why my ass isn't in this hoity-toity university. I'm perfectly happy slinging drinks at the 'Cat while surrounded by beautiful women in corsets."

he said, beaming as Ben laughed. "That girl goes to the fine arts school here though, probably a musician, and said she had a class today if my memory is still decent. I thought I might try and scope her out, see if I could find her, I'd asked her to the pictures this weekend, but if I find her, I'll take her to lunch."

"Well, good luck," Ben snorted, his eyes giddy. "Are you working tonight?"

"I'm working every night." Nyx grinned wickedly as Ben snickered, then gave him a serious look.

"Really though, are you working tonight?"

"No, I'm off. I may go drive my bike and visit Mom, that's why I decided to try and find that girl now instead of just staying at the 'Cat tonight and seeing if she wandered back in," Nyx said, his eyes on Ben as he nodded. "Why?"

"I was just curious, just in case things do go a bit farther." Ben said, his eyes going up as he fidgeted slightly. "That way I could have the flat to myself a bit."

"Say no more. You've got it. I was already planning to be out," Nyx chuckled, a smile on his face.

"You, sir, are the best," Ben beamed, then turned slightly, heading up a set of steps towards a building. "I've got a class starting, You should head back to the fine arts building. Your girlie might come out, well, in about forty-five minutes if she's in an hour-long class. Prop up on a bench and take a nap or something."

"Will do. I'll see you tonight, possibly." Nyx grinned wickedly as Ben laughed, nodding and waving.

"Yeah, yeah. Have fun!"

Nyx snickered, nodding as he turned and headed back in the other direction, back towards the fine arts building.

-PHOENYX-

YOU SEE, NYX WASN'T THE RICH BOY THAT BENJAMIN WAS. No, Phoenyx was a simpler man, and he had enjoyed a simpler life than Ben had.

Where Ben had grown up in Rhode Island, Nyx had grown up in Massachusetts, a smaller town right outside of Salem. His father had passed when he was little, so his mother had raised him the best she could all by herself. While they had struggled, they had done alright for themselves. Nyx's mother had worked various odd jobs, sometimes as a waitress, sometimes as a maid, but she always made sure he was fed and well-cared for, and he'd always wanted to find a woman like that for himself. A nice, strong, reliable woman who was equally as beautiful, kind, and selfless.

So far, he hadn't had much luck.

Ladies, he had noticed, tended to be interested in one thing: money. The value of a man's wallet was what made the man worthwhile and, unfortunately, Phoenyx's wallet wasn't usually worth very much. It was why the women he would ask over would usually not make it past the second date stage, if they made it that far. They simply didn't want to be with someone who didn't have the financial income to treat them to a nice restaurant, wine, flowers, and gifts.

He could kind of understand it, especially coming out of the Cold War era and the Vietnam War. Women needed to know they would have some security, after all. That said, it still stung a tad when he would go to ask a lady for a second or third date, one he'd thought he'd made some kind of connection with, and she would snub her nose at him because his wallet wasn't big enough for her.

Bartending isn't exactly a high-salary job.

Benjamin had the opposite problem, and Phoenyx had to admit that it drove him batty. Women were begging Benjamin for second dates, and he was snubbing them left and right. When he asked why, he got the response of 'Well, I don't want to get committed to someone.' Which Nyx could understand, that was fair.

For a while, that was fair.

But for a little over eight months now, he had watched woman after woman march in and out of that man's room like a fuck parade, and he didn't understand how the hell Benjamin could just snub every inch of companionship like that.

Nyx would kill for one of his dates to accept a second or third date.

Sighing, he chuckled, shaking his head. "Rich boy has no idea how damn lucky he has it," he said, smiling slightly as he got to the fine arts building, his eyes on the sidewalk, and quickly frowning as he heard frustrated muttering.

"Oh! That... that bitch!" Ali hissed, her face furious. "I was all of a minute late! Just a minute! I know more about the dancers and the dance steps we're studying for that fucking class than most of those blue-blooded bitches would any day!" she snarled, going down the staircase of the building with her books under her arms as Nyx looked up at her, then smiled, his eyes widening as he trotted up to her.

"Hey!" Nyx called out, his eyes on her as her frustrated gaze whipped away from the other side of campus and over to him. Her annoyance melted almost instantly and she beamed, her hand coming up and waving as she bit her lip, her eyes widening.

"Oh! Hello! You're the bartender from the nightclub last night!" she said excitedly, coming up to him as he grinned, his eyes taking her full appearance in. "How did you find me?!" she asked with a laugh as he brought a hand up and twined one of her curls as she bit her lip and blushed.

"You said you were a music student at Silverleaf University," Nyx said, chuckling as she nodded, her eyes on his. "I remembered. So, since my friend comes here, roommate actually, but that's beside the point, I know my way around here. I thought I'd take some time on my day off to try and find you. Besides, you look like you could use cheering up, bad day?"

"The worst," Ali muttered, her hands gripping her books, then blinking as he took them from her, frowning slightly as he nodded.

"Go on." Nyx said, shifting the weight of her books as she stretched her arms, the two starting to walk. Ali took a breath, her eyes on the sky, the brightness of the day, and she just shook her head.

"It was just overwhelming. It was my first day, but no one here was very helpful." Ali said, biting at her lip again as she spoke. "I asked a few people, but they snubbed their noses at me. I think it was the clothing, but, I can't afford nicer stuff right now." she muttered, frowning as Nyx nodded, sighing. "It was my parents and I for a while, and it took everything I had to get away from my father in the first place, to go to a university with a fine arts school in Columbia and just get away from him for the first time, and then I transferred here." she muttered, then shook her head as he peered at her, his eyes locked on her as she tucked her curls behind her ears. "Anyhow, my wardrobe from Columbia won't work here."

"Columbia... that's in South Carolina if I'm not mistaken, right?" Nix asked as she nodded.

"Yes."

"No, those clothes won't work up here, not in the fall," Nyx said, blinking a few times at the thought.

"So, my few wintery, cooler-weather clothes? They'll have to do, even if the moths have eaten holes in half of them," Ali said, frowning as he nodded. "But I'll get by. I always get by." Ali grinned, her eyes lighting up again as he chuckled. "It was just a lot to take in at once, and then that utter bitch of an instructor refusing to let me into my class!" Ali growled, her eyes up at the sky again.

Nyx shook his head in confusion before speaking. "Why?!"

"I was a minute late! In her class, apparently you can't be even a minute late, but a girl in a crisp, pressed pink dress came in seconds before me and was fine!"

Nyx grumbled but nodded. Classism was a thing around here, that much he knew. "Will you get in trouble? For being late and missing the class today, I mean."

"Fuck her," Ali spat out, her finger up towards the building they were currently walking away from as Nyx burst into cackles. "I'm so fed up with today, ooh, I could spit nails!"

Nyx grinned deviously, then held up one finger. He handed her books back to her, and she gave him a curious look. She clutched her books to her, watching as he unclasped something from his jacket, then pulled a helmet around.

"How about a ride to calm you down?" Nyx asked, beaming as she stared excitedly.

"You have a motorcycle?!" Ali squeaked, her eyes widening as he grinned.

"I do, yeah. You can stash your books in my leather pouch. Come on, gorgeous, blow this joint with me?"

Ali bit her lip, her eyes glancing around as the other students tossed her awkward, odd glances, then she looked at Nyx, his cocky grin and his helmet offered out to her, waiting for her to just take it and throw caution to the wind, rush out to him, let him take her away for a while.

Fuck it.

She grabbed his helmet, letting him take her books with a laugh. "Let's go!" Ali beamed, nodding as she pulled the helmet over her curls and clasped it, tightening it as he grinned broadly.

"You got it!"

CHAPTER 2

Baby take my hand

-ALI AND NYX-

SHE REACHED OUT AND LET HIM GRASP HER HAND and tug her along, pulling her through the campus as her eyes locked on his, a shiver running down her spine. Whereas the man she had met earlier, Benjamin, his gaze had been cool and collected, almost like a wolf, washing over her like a stream, this man was like a tiger, all fire; passion and impulse and spontaneity. She grinned, smiling for the second time that day, despite the rotten events and how everything seemed to be stacked against her. For whatever reason, this man, and Benjamin, they seemed to make her feel better.

As they ran, Ali's eyes, wide with sheer adrenaline, stayed locked on the man ahead of her. "Hey!"

"Yeah?!" he called back to her, the two weaving past a few students, all of them yelling at them with annoyance as Ali and Nyx laughed.

"W-What's your name?!" Ali asked, her eyes on him as he burst into laughter, glancing back as he tugged her a hair closer.

"See, that's why you go to the fancy university, you're the smart cookie to remember to ask that, I'd forgotten again!" he grinned, then smirked at her. "Phoenyx Coleman, but call me Nyx. It's less of a mouthful."

"Nyx..." Ali smiled, nodding as he weaved them around a few trees on the campus, the two hitting the parking lot, Ali squeaking with excitement. "Oh! Nyx!"

"Fair's fair. Your name?" Nyx smirked, tugging her the final steps to his motorcycle as she skidded to a stop, her eyes wide as she bit her lip, then gave him a smile.

"Alyson Walker, but Ali's less of a mouthful," she said with a laugh as he snickered.

"Ali, huh?" Nyx said, leaning forward, seeming to get nose to nose with her as she held her breath, her eyes widening as she blushed, and his hands came up to tighten the helmet on her head, her breath catching. "Very cute name, Ali."

"T-Thank you...!"

He stashed her books in his leather pouch, nodding as she sucked in a breath, her hands working her curls that had fallen loose back behind her ears. "Any time. Now..." Nyx grinned, hopping on his bike, his eyes going over her, taking in her skirts, her bomber jacket, then beaming. "...Hop on," he said, his eyes impish.

Biting at her lip, Ali nodded, getting on the back of the bike and panting slightly as she peered at him, his eyes on her as she swallowed heavily.

"Nervous?" Nyx asked, tugging on a pair of black, fingerless leather gloves, which he had cut himself, as she nodded slightly, her eyes going to his hands, then back to his eyes.

"I've always wanted to ride on one of these," Ali said, her eyes on him as he snorted and then grabbed her hands, wrapping her arms around his waist as she went pink. "Oh! Nyx, I need to be back before classes end for the day! I have to meet up with a friend!" Her eyes widening as he nodded, grinning at her.

"Sure thing. That's no problem," Nyx said, stretching slightly as she nodded.

"Good, I promised I'd be here later." Ali said, then squeaked as he revved the motor playfully, his eyes going to hers as he grinned deviously.

"Hold on tight, Ali."

He revved the engine, grabbing a pair of goggles from around his neck that she hadn't paid a lick of attention to, and tugging them over his eyes. His face was utterly cocky as he smirked and cracked his neck, looking ahead as he stared at the exit to the parking lot.

His hand released the brake, the tires squealed, and her arms tightened around his waist as she clung to him, her eyes widening from the rush. She could feel him chuckling as he swerved the bike through the parking lot and around some of the other students who were yelling furiously at him, though he paid them no mind. Trees blurred past them; buildings became nothing.

It was liberating.

Her hands splayed out, feeling his stomach muscles, and she sucked in a quiet breath, then let her eyes glance at him as he drove. His intense gaze mixed with the impulsivity in his ash-grey eyes caused her to flush, and she scolded herself again, her eyes widening.

'Ooh, again, Alyson!' she hissed to herself, her eyes widening as she inhaled sharply, then squeaked, her eyes on the road ahead as he ducked a bit and swerved, taking them into traffic. They weaved through the slower moving vehicles, causing her to clutch at him as she peered around his shoulder, her hair flying

around her. His stomach clenched as he let out a small laugh, glancing back at her, then with a grunt Nyx's torso shifted, his arm muscles clenching as he tugged the front of the bike up, the wheels leaving the ground as she clung to his stomach, her eyes huge as she squealed. Her hands clutched at him, one slipping under his loose shirt, causing him to smirk as he set the tires back down with a laugh and revved the engine again, the motorcycle flying down the road once more. *Then again, shit, that was sexy.*

The two flew down the roads, away from the pricey university and its blue-bloods and coming to the less expensive part of town, where the food was affordable, the entertainment casual and fun, and the music exciting, if you were there at night.

As it was, they were there in the daytime.

Bringing his motorcycle to a stop, Nyx glanced back at Ali, who was still letting her fingers tentatively move on his stomach, her eyes giddy. Chuckling, he brought his hands down, clasping them in hers as she panted, looking up at him, his goggles still firmly on his face. He went to remove them, then blinked.

'Phoenyx, silly man, you're riding too fast! You'll be bucked from your horse!'

'Nonsense! There's no such thing, Alyson, my love!'

Phoenyx's head shook, his eyes widening slightly as he peered at Ali, her eyes on him. "Are you alright?" she asked, her face worried as he nodded, a smile coming back on his face.

"Just fine, cutie," Nyx said, his hands on hers as he gently tugged her hands from his torso, her eyes still slightly wide. "Did you have fun?"

"Oh, yeah! It was so much fun!" Ali beamed, nodding fast as he laughed. She glanced around, taking in the buildings on this side of town, and smiled. "Now this side of town I think I like," she said, chuckling as Nyx nodded, grinning.

"This is where I come to grab lunch." Nyx said, chuckling as he helped her off the motorcycle, pocketing the keys and pointing to a small diner. "We have options. If you want pie and enough sugar to give you cavities, there's a diner. My roommate says that the pie there's too sweet, I say that's where the charm is." Nyx smirked as Ali chuckled. "If you want some chili, or a hot dog, even a burger, there's a small place over in that direction. You can smell them if you sniff hard enough. It's my favorite, actually, *Ronnie's Hots on the Go*." Nyx grinned as Ali laughed, her face lighting up. "If that's too greasy for you, then there's another place a street away that has other options."

"I could go for a hot dog and chili." Ali smiled as he nodded, his eyes glancing at his leather pouch to be sure he'd locked her books up, then his hands moving to her head to undo the helmet, clasping it back at his jacket as he smirked. He tugged his gloves off, stuffing them back into his jacket, then tugged his goggles back down to his neck, grinning playfully as he offered his hand to her.

"Great, because I'm starving!" Nyx laughed, his eyes wicked. "I haven't had anything to eat today but some damn poached eggs. My roommate, he's a good guy, but the man still has some very refined tastes." Nyx said, his nose wrinkling up as Ali blinked, her eyes on him as she took his hand, the two beginning to walk to the eatery.

"Oh?"

"He's a little rich boy," Nyx laughed, his eyes mischievous as Ali nodded, smiling slightly. "I love the guy, but he's still learning to live like the common folk. His breakfasts are still in the 'learning' category. He makes fancy eggs, little sausage links, fruit cut into balls." Nyx shook his head as Ali blinked, her eyes widening. "I didn't know you could cut fruit into balls, but he has something called a melon baller, the damn thing is literally for making melon into ball-shapes. Fancy bastard." Nyx snorted, causing Ali to laugh, her head resting on his arm as he blinked, glancing down at her.

Her soft, bouncy curls rested against her back as she moved, his eyes drawn to the bomber jacket that was clinging to her curves. When he had seen her in the 'Cat, she had been wearing a black dress, something simple, a sleeveless number, her curls in an updo, a few corkscrews allowed to go down her neck and ears. But, seeing her now? Her casual attire was gorgeous.

She had been curious about the entertainment, drawn in by the smoke and mystique of the club, but he... he had been drawn to the simplicity that she had worn into the club. Most women came in dressed to the nines, looking to score a man who would fluff their pockets or their bedsheets, but not her. She had come in wearing a simple black dress, black heels, some stockings that may or may not have been held on by a garter, and her hair loosely pulled up. Her makeup had been the same as her everyday attire, minus the smokey eyeshadow that she had added to the look.

She had stood out.

This mystery of a woman had simply sat at the bar, then ordered a rum and coke. He'd slid it over, watched as she'd sipped it, grimaced, then given him a look.

"If I wanted a coke and water, I'd have gone to a diner."

He had utterly swooned. He admitted it.

She hadn't looked like the 'drinking' type, so, yes, he had gone a tad light on her rum. A mistake he did not make again, and when he slid the new drink over, personally staying and giving her an apology, he had watched to see if she actually handled the double shots of rum he'd thrown into the drink.

Nyx had seen men that were seasoned drinkers hold their liquor worse than she had.

So, he had chatted with her. Asked her why she was there, if she liked Salem as a town, so on. Then, he had moved on to flirting.

"You like the town, do you like the people?"

"Yes, they're really nice." She had smiled, sipping her third drink in her two hours there.

"How about its bartenders?" He had leaned forward, his finger tracing her jaw as she had bit at her lip, then smiled.

"So far, they're even better than the rest of the town."

Yep. He had absolutely wanted more.

And then, like a moron, his stupid ass had forgotten to ask her for her name or her address. He had utterly kicked himself silly for it, then remembered details that had led him to the university in their conversation.

This woman, was everything he had ever hunted for in a woman.

She wasn't uptight from what he had seen. She was lively, and she seemed extremely kind. She was spirited, and from what she had said during their conversation previously, she loved to help those in need, and all of those qualities were what he wanted.

Add in the fact that she had to know by now that he wasn't going to be drowning her in gifts and lavishness, he'd brought her to the poor side of the damn town for pity's sake, to see her damn reaction, and instead of snubbing her nose up, she'd grinned and taken the offer of chili and a hot dog.

'For once, someone's actually interested in a goddamn date who isn't interested in my goddamn wallet,' Nyx thought, his eyes glancing down at her as she looked up, then smiled, her head tipping to the side slightly.

"Something wrong?" Ali asked, clutching his arm tighter as he grinned.

"No, no, Nothing's wrong." Nyx smiled, his hand tightening on hers as she inhaled, then sighed softly, a small laugh escaping her lips as he glanced down at her again. "Hm?"

"Nothing. It's just the smell of leather." Ali said, chuckling as she inhaled again, then let out the breath she had taken, moaning slightly. "I love that smell! I don't know why, but I adore the smell of leather."

Phoenyx just grinned, his head nodding as she followed him to the small little hole-in-the-wall eatery, then led her to a seat behind a bar-like set of seating, the place hot and smelling strongly of half-burnt wieners and overcooked chili meat, and the seats a tad sticky. Holding up one finger, Nyx just banged one fist on the bar, causing Ali to jump, her eyes widening as she squeaked slightly. "YO! RONNIE!" Nyx called out, his other hand cupping at his mouth and his eyebrow quirking.

The man cooking turned, throwing a playful scowl at Nyx. With a snort he leaned down, then grabbed a hard-boiled egg from a pile, used for recipes that required a fast-dashed egg, then chucked it at Nyx as he grabbed Ali and tugged her down, both ducking as Nyx laughed, grinning, the egg splatting against the wall behind them. "Shut yer' hole, Coleman!" Ronnie said, pointing with his spatula as the two sat up, Ali's face brimming with amusement. "You gettin' yer' usual?" Ronnie asked, moving around the small cooking area as Nyx nodded, glancing up at the menu as he pointed, gesturing for Ali.

"Yeah, but let me find out what she wants before you start making my food, would you? Alright, Ali, up there's the options." Nyx stated, his eyes going to hers for a moment before he looked back to the menu. "'Hots as they are', those are just hot dogs with the works, and Ronnie here makes them mouth-watering." Nyx grinned, moaning slightly before continuing. "'Pots' are bowls of chili. They come with cheese on top, and they're fucking delicious." he winked as Ali laughed.

"You make the food here sound better than sex!" Ali said, giggling as he blinked, then leaned forward on one hand, his one eyebrow raising.

"I mean, I've had some rotten sex before, the food here definitely tops going into those clam-traps." Nyx winked, causing her to burst into laughter, her arms wrapping around herself as Ronnie snorted.

"That's 'cause you got shit luck with women, Coleman," Ronnie said, pointing at him as Nyx snickered, then flipped him off. "Nah, pretty boy, I don't roll that way."

"Oh, you can go fuck yourself, Ronnie," Nyx laughed, grabbing a napkin and balling it up before chucking at the grease-covered cook. "You aren't my type!"

"What is your type?" Ali asked, biting her lip as Nyx grinned.

"I'll tell you after I feed you." He said, pointing back to the menu. "That there? The 'Wet Patty' is a medium-rare burger with melted cheese, chili, and an egg over-easy on it. It's popular in the early-morning when you're drunk." Nyx said, grinning knowingly. "It's the ONE thing I got my roommate to eat after we'd been out drinking all night one time. Anyhow, there's the 'Bathtub Mixer', which is Ronnie's nice way to say he's going to chuck a bowl of chili together and chop up some extra shit in there with it. You get whatever the fuck he says you're going to get." Nyx laughed as Ali giggled.

"Mmm... Well, what do you usually get?" she asked, her eyes knotting together as she peered at the menu, and he smiled.

"Hots and Pots. Two hot dogs with the works and a bowl of chili. I get a bottle of Coke with it, too," Nyx said, chuckling as she nodded.

"Sounds good to me." Ali said, leaning on the counter as he grinned.

"Is that so?"

"Yep."

"Alright. Ronnie, you heard the girl. Two orders of Hots and Pots, and two Cokes," Nyx called out as Ronnie nodded, waving his spatula as he started rotating food. Nyx leaned forward, his eyes meeting Ali's as she bit her lip, then she grinned.

"I asked you a question," She said, her eyes on him as he smiled.

"Hm. Bad memory here, must be the smoke from the grill clogging up my brain." Nyx said, peering at her as she huffed out a small laugh, shaking her head and chuckling. "Refresh my memory?"

"I asked you, what's your type, Phoenyx Coleman?" Ali asked, her eyes on him as he smiled, then let a hand come up, moving to her curls and twining one, playing with it.

"I happen to find curls very attractive," Nyx said, his eyes on her as she quirked her eyebrow, causing him to smile. "Alright, alright, I... I like women who don't like wallet sizes," he admitted, his face reddening slightly as she blinked, then sighed. "...I don't know if you noticed, Alyson, but, I didn't exactly take you to the Ritz, or come bearing roses. I'm a bartender," his eyes went back to hers as she nodded. "Most women I've met, tend to find that to be a serious turn-off. I often get to the first date, or the bedroom, and then when they find out that their second date's going to be, well, this side of town, they don't take me up on the offer," he sighed once more as she nodded, her arms going around herself.

"I understand that." Ali said, her eyes down. "Can I be honest?" she asked as he nodded, frowning as she sighed. "The friend I'm meeting later? It's some guy who asked to talk with me after classes, but it was before you came around!" she said as he laughed, waving a hand.

"Ali, we're not married or anything exclusive. You're not hurting my feelings," he said, grinning as she nodded.

"Well, he's, he's blue-blood. Very blue-blood," Ali said, her eyes widening as she bit her lip, and Nyx frowned.

'...There's no way in the world...' Nyx thought, his eyes now utterly focused on her.

"I don't see what he wants with me, I really don't. He saw me, confused, on my way to class," Ali said, her face frowning as Nyx nodded, leaning forward and listening intently. "...but where everyone else was ignoring me, he actually stopped and helped me. He listened and got me to my classes," She swallowed and letting a hand go through her hair. "He was kind. So I asked him for his name, and he asked to talk later."

"What's his name?" Nyx asked casually, grabbing the Coke that was slid to him as Ali took hers, sighing.

"He said it was Benjamin... Benjamin Hancott."

Nyx choked slightly, then cleared his throat, quickly recovering. "Hm, you're meeting up with him after classes you said?" he asked as she nodded, her eyes on him as he swigged his drink again. "Alyson, I won't say anything to sway you one way or another. But, I will tell you to keep your guard up," he said carefully as she blinked, then straightened.

"Why?"

"You said he's a blue-blood, right?" Nyx asked as she nodded, frowning.

"Yes..."

"They're all alike." He said, his eyes on the bar in front of them as she sighed, then nodded. His mind wandered as she picked at the table, biting her lip. If Benjamin got to her, then she would never come back around. She would stay away just to stay away from Ben.

Ben would ruin his shot with the damn girl.

Frowning, Nyx ran a hand through his hair. If he purposefully sabotaged Benjamin's date with Ali, he'd be betraying him, but if he let them hit it off...

He might lose his own chance.

"Nyx, are you ok?"

"Hm? Oh, yeah, I'm fine. Honestly, I wish I could take you with me later on," Nyx said, a tinge of regret in his voice. If he wasn't going to visit his mother, knowing how finicky she could be about strangers seeing her living conditions, he'd ask her along.

"Yeah, I really am having a great time." Ali said, sighing.

At that, their food was slid over, along with two spoons, and Ali squealed, her eyes wide. Wriggling in her seat giddily, she gripped her hot dog, covered with coleslaw, onions, chili, mustard, and horseradish with both hands, leaned forward, then took a chomp that would have made a champion hot dog eater proud, a third of the food disappearing in her mouth, her cheeks going out like a chipmunk, and a small trail of chili coming down the side of her chin. She let out a small moan, her eyes widening as she chewed, her hand coming up to her mouth. "Oh!"

Nyx blinked, his eyes widening in surprise at her reaction. He had literally never seen a woman dig into any kind of food like that, and he'd never seen anyone react to Ronnie's hot dogs like, well, he did, to be honest. Clearing his throat, he gave his head a rapid shake for a second, then peered at her. "Ah, Ali..."

"These are amazing!" Ali exclaimed, her eyes wide as she took another bite, not noting or caring about the chili dripping from her chin to the paper on the table. Nyx's jaw dropped, then he laughed, nodding and simply joining in. His mouth opened wide enough to take in half of a hot dog with one bite, moaning and kicking at the bar happily as he chewed.

Once the two had finished the hot dogs, Ali went to move on to the chili, but Nyx chuckled, stopping her. His hand went under her chin, turning her towards him as he smiled, grasping one of the napkins at the table, then deftly dabbing at the chili, clearing it quickly as she blushed, her eyes widening. "I've been eating here for a while now, so I know how to keep from swimming in Ronnie's chili while I eat." Nyx grinned, crumpling the napkin up as she nodded, blushing. "There. All gone, perfection." He said, smiling as she bit her lip, then he chuckled, a thumb coming up to brush at her lips, ghosting over them as she shivered, a tingle going up her spine and making her quake between her legs.

She squirmed slightly, swallowing as he gave her a grin then returned to his food, spooning a bite of chili to his mouth. She bit her lip, then carefully spooned a bite into her mouth, her eyes widening at the taste. "Oh, shit!" Ali muttered, her hand coming up to keep from letting any of the food out of her mouth as Nyx snickered, his eyes going to hers. "This is good!"

"I'm glad you like it!" Nyx laughed, nodding as he spooned another couple of bites into his mouth. "Most girls aren't into this kind of greasy food!"

"I love just about any kind of food!" Ali laughed, spooning

another bite into her mouth as Nyx grinned. "My favorite is pizza, though. A meat pizza, Pepperoni, ham, sausages, hamburger, bacon..." Ali moaned as Nyx stared, his eyes widening as he swallowed, then grinned. "What?"

"I know where we're going on our second date." Nyx said, a smirk on his face as she burst into laughter, then blushed. "As long as you'll accept a second date, that is..." He smirked at her as she smiled, spooning another couple of bites into her mouth.

"I'm not sure. Ask me in a bit, once I'm done eating."

The two finished up, the chili disappearing fast from the bowls, and Nyx tossed a quick wave to Ronnie as he and Ali stood, both pleasantly full. "Hey! Ronnie, the food was great, pal!"

"You always say that, Coleman!" Ronnie snorted, shaking his head as Nyx shrugged.

"The food's always great!" Nyx grinned, then motioned at the door as Ali waved, beaming.

"It was delicious!" Ali smiled, her eyes lit up as Ronnie blinked, glancing over, then pointing at her with the spatula, nodding.

"Her I believe! You? Not a chance, Coleman," Ronnie said as Nyx laughed, shaking his head as he led Ali out of the eatery. As they hit the door, Ronnie called out, "Nyx, feel free to bring her back. I'll remember her order, especially since it's the same one as your dumb ass."

Nyx nodded, chuckling, and the two head out into the streets again, Nyx's arms going up into a pleasant stretch as Ali grinned.

"That was so good!" Ali smiled, her eyes closing slightly, then with a chuckle she darted to a small retaining wall on the sidewalk, some flowers growing over the side, and leapt onto it, her feet easily hitting the ledge as she went onto her toes. Nyx blinked, peering as her arms went out, watching her balance as she walked carefully but casually on the delicate ledge, a grin on her face. "I've had more fun today than I have in so long." Ali said, smiling over at him as he chuckled, nodding and gesturing at her.

"You're nimble." He said, his face curious as she smiled.

"Ballet," Ali said, sighing slightly as he got a surprised look on his face, watching as her hands went up, her legs deftly leaping forward on the ledge, balancing as she landed, her arms going back out. "I study tap dance as well, and I also perform in the drama program, but I'm at the university on a ballet scholarship. It's why I don't really fit in with the blue-bloods, Daddy's not paying my way in," Ali explained, her eyes on him as he nodded, his eyes getting more understanding.

"Ah. You're there based on your hard work, not Daddy's bank account, now I get it. You'd like the 'Cat, we all work hard there, although I really don't think you working there would be a great idea, the clients there can get pushy when they get too drunk." Nyx said, his eyes on her as she chuckled.

"I could handle myself, you know."

"I believe you, but it's them I don't trust," He smiled as she got to the end of the retaining wall, then leapt off, landing on her feet next to him as he smiled. "You're lovely. Maybe I'll be able to draw you at some time." Nyx said as she sucked in a breath, beaming.

"You draw?!"

"I do, yeah. Sketch work, mostly. I didn't bring any of it with me. I tend to keep it all around the flat." Nyx said as she bit her lip, smiling broadly. "Hm? You look like the cat that caught the canary."

"I just enjoy meeting others who enjoy the arts like I do." Ali said, smiling as he chuckled, glancing down at her. Swallowing, he let his hand slip around her waist, and he watched as she stiffened slightly, then leaned closer, relaxing into the unfamiliar movement as they walked, her head resting against his shoulder.

"You're the first dancer I've met from the university who didn't have their pointy toe shoes shoved up their rear. When you said 'fine arts' student, I assumed maybe a musician, not ballerina." Nyx said with a smile as she chuckled, her eyes going up to his as she looked up.

"Are you disappointed?" she asked as he grinned, then took her hand, twirling her out as they walked, smiling the whole time.

"Not one bit."

The two basked in the fall scents, the glow of the lights under the trees, and the way that everything seemed to melt away as they talked. Nothing else seemed to matter, and it was something that both had been hunting to find for a very long time.

As the time grew later, Nyx sighed, his hand clasped with hers as she bit her lip, then nodded. "I should head back," Ali said.

"Yeah, you should. You have a friend to meet up with," Nyx said, his hand caressing her fingers as she bit her lip. "You did make a promise. You should go, one way or the other."

"I know. But I want you to know Nyx, I'm glad you found me," Ali said, beaming up at him as he smiled, nodding. "Thank you for taking me out today."

"Alyson, it was my pleasure. It really was," Nyx said, nodding as the two headed towards the parked bike, both entwined in one another.

The ride back was as exhilarating as the ride there, and

Ali was as wrapped up in him as she had been before. He had carefully helped her from the bike, this time getting her books out, and grabbing her hand, pecking her knuckles as she smiled. "Will you find me again?"

"Or you can find me again. You know where I work." Nyx winked, pulling his goggles back on as he grinned cockily at her, watching her laugh playfully at him. He gave her a wave, then revved up the bike, heading out of the parking lot as she watched wistfully.

Sighing, Ali turned and ran her hands through her hair to get some of the wind-blown effects out of her curls, though she knew that was probably a moot effort. Her eyes glanced into mirrors, sprucing herself up here and there. She wasn't trying to look particularly pretty for the man, but he was one of the blue-bloods, and she knew that the rumors that they could start could make or break you here.

Getting back to the fine-arts building, she panted, her face tired, but a chuckle coming down the walkway made her glance up. "You look like you've run a thousand miles."

Blinking, Ali glanced up and peered at Ben, who was smiling over at her as he walked up, his hands in his pockets, both hands free. "I've had a day," she said honestly, her eyes on him. "And you?"

"Boring. Medical stuff that I learned last term," He rolled his eyes as she nodded. "Everything was easy. Did you know, our brain weighs about three pounds, give or take?" he asked as she shrugged, her eyes on him as he casually tossed an arm around her, her body stiffening and her eyes widening. "It's also about two percent of our body's full weight," he grinned slightly as she nodded again, biting her lip. "Oh, hey, let me grab the books!" he said, tugging her books from her hands as she went to stutter out a protest, her eyes wide. "It's fine! You look tired! Now, there's a coffee shop I want to take you to, my treat," he smiled as she bit her lip harder, nodding and frowning slightly as they walked, her eyes knotting up.

From the sidewalk, where he'd come to take a peek in on the meeting...

"I don't have to say a damn thing. He's treating her like a fucking blue-blood princess and fucking it up all on his own, not letting her say a goddamn word," Nyx said, shaking his head and turning to head back to the parking lot, his footsteps echoing behind him.

CHAPTER 3

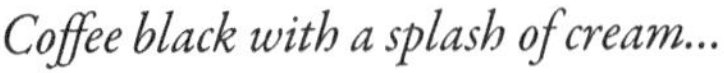

Coffee black with a splash of cream...

-ALI AND BEN-

ALI GLANCED UP AT BEN, WHO HADN'T STOPPED talking since he'd started up at the university. She honestly hadn't realized someone could chatter so much, and all about themselves, at that. He simply hadn't shut up. His hands had animatedly moved about, his eyes had glanced all over, and his arm had stayed thrown over her shoulder, despite her wriggling and trying to subtly hint that she'd much rather walk out from under his grasp. At one point, he had gotten so worked up that his hand had almost swatted her nose from moving so fast. Now, as they headed towards the coffee shop, he blathered on and on about a situation in class where he simply couldn't have been in the wrong.

"And so, I told the professor, I swear, Alyson, the man's so boring..." Ben said, rolling his eyes as Ali bit her lip, frowning.

You'd know a thing or two about that, wouldn't you...', she thought, trying her best not to look as disinterested as she felt.

"...I told him that his facts on the cardiovascular system were wrong. He actually argued with me. Can you believe that?!" Ben asked his eyes surprised as Ali looked at him, her eyebrow quirked.

"...Isn't it his job to teach you?" she asked as he shrugged, the hand on her shoulder waving dismissively.

"Yes, but I have peer-reviewed evidence that proves he's wrong!" Ben said, his voice annoyed as she snorted, rolling her eyes heavily. "I collect medical journals for a reason! I have up-dated evidence that he isn't up-to-date on the latest trials and research! He should have listened!"

"And you thought that the middle of his lecture was the best time to correct him on his information?" Ali asked, her face skeptical as he blinked, then straightened, his cheeks reddening as she continued. "Seems to me that you dug your own grave there, Benjamin."

He looked down at her, his eyes wide as she stared forward, refusing to back down, and a small grin grew on his face. "...I didn't think of it like that," Ben said, his eyes on her as she shrugged, her eyes forward as he peered down at her, watching as she tucked her curls behind her ears. "I've been coming to this university for years now. How do you like it?" he asked as she glanced at him, waiting to see if she was going to get to speak, then nodding as he kept his mouth shut, waiting for an actual reply.

"Well, today's my first day." Ali said, her eyes down as he nodded. "So far..."

"You'll love it here," Ben said, nodding firmly as she bit her lip firmly, her eyes knotting together. "People say that everyone's snobby, but I swear, it's simply a crap reputation. Everyone here's great from what I've seen, I've yet to meet someone completely rude. Actually, if you want to know the best places on campus, I can point those out-"

"Enough!" Ali yelped, wrenching herself out from his grip as he blinked, his eyes widening as she shook her head. Her face screamed that she was just done, and her body was utterly tense. "I can't take another second! Look, the little princesses here might enjoy you going on about your classes, not letting them speak, and telling them where to go and what to do, but I don't!" She pointed at him as he stared, his eyes getting huge. "If you had shut your mouth for one second, you'd have found out that my classes were utter shit!" Ali said frantically, her eyes wide as he let his mouth snap closed, his body straightening. "I didn't even get to attend!" Her eyes welled up as she leaned forward, yanking her books from him, her bottom lip quivering. "Now, if you'll excuse me!"

Ali turned on her heel, about to stomp off, but his hand went to hers, gently grasping her as he sucked in a breath. "Hey..." Benjamin murmured quietly, his eyes on her as she whipped her head to him, her eyes narrowing. "...I'm sorry..." he said, his face concerned. He watched as she melted slightly, her body losing some tenseness as he sighed. "Come here... I know I've got no right asking, but what happened...?" Ben asked, frowning as she wiped at her face.

"...I was late," Alyson said, her face falling as he nodded understandingly.

"It happens, I've been late a lot, but the professors here are usually pretty understanding."

"She wasn't," Ali said wryly, her eyes dark as she wrapped her arms around her books, the two walking again. "I was only a minute late at the most, and a girl in a beautiful dress came in seconds before me, but she wouldn't let me in." Her eyes stayed on the ground as Ben straightened, his face getting slightly angry. "She was nasty. 'We are a prudent class, Miss Walker, and if you cannot be on time here, perhaps this is not the school for you. You may be better off back wherever it was you were before, Our art demands timeliness.', that's what she said." she sniffled slightly, her eyes brimming up as Ben frowned.

"Alyson, your major, what do you study?" Ben asked as she bit her lip, then sighed.

"...Ballet." She said as he nodded, then she clutched the books tighter. "...scholarship," she muttered as he frowned, leaning down, unable to hear her.

"Sorry, I didn't catch the last bit..."

"...On a scholarship..." Ali said quietly, her eyes on the ground as he stared. She was protective of the books she carried, but he noted why now. The scuffs on them, the shears on the edges and the marks, the signs of a used book. She was hiding her social class from him, and every other blue-blood on campus, knowing damn good and well what they could do to her reputation.

"If you're here on a scholarship, Alyson, then that means that you're that much better than the other girls in that class, doesn't your professor see that?" Ben asked, frowning as she snorted, shaking her head.

"Oh my God, better than the princesses? Benjamin, be careful! They'll burn you at the stake!" Ali said, her head shaking as she stared forward.

"No! No! Let me go! It hurts! It burns! Phoenyx! Benjamin! Help me, please! Please! Make them stop!"

Ali's eyes unfocused as the thought crossed her mind, her skin paling as she stumbled, and Ben caught her, frowning as he peered at her. "Are you alright?"

"Y-Yes..." Ali said, her hand at her forehead, rubbing her temple. "...I'm fine."

"Alyson, your professor. What's her name?" Ben asked, his eyes firm as Ali shook her head, her eyes going to his.

"Don't worry about it. I can handle it," Ali said, her eyes going up. "I didn't get to where I am by having someone else handle my problems," she said as Ben nodded, then sighed, running a hand through his hair.

"I suppose I screwed this all up, didn't I?" he said, his eyes on her as she tilted her head sideways, then shook her head, looking down.

"...No. You didn't. I'm sorry I snapped." Ali said, biting her lip as he put his hands in his pockets. "I'm just... I was on my guard. The other people have been... nasty. I don't like it here so far." Ali said, sighing as he frowned. "I honestly just want to go home. I hate the city, at least, this side of it. I prefer where I live when I'm not in class..."

"Where's that?" Ben asked as they reached the little coffee shop, the two moving to a set of seats, Ben holding two fingers up at the passing waitress as Ali nodded.

"...Salem," she said as he coughed, his eyes wide. "...What?"

"I live in Salem, too!" Ben said, leaning forward in his seat as she got a surprised look on her face.

"Oh!"

Ali bit her lip, her eyes widening as Ben got an odd look on his face, his face dumbstruck. She hadn't expected him to be, well, slumming it in Salem, to be honest. Boston was where the rich people lived, not Salem. As the waitress brought the coffees over, Ali nodded, smiling up at the woman and tugging out a couple of dollar bills from her jacket pocket and placing them in the waitress's hand as Ben frowned.

"Hey, I had it." Ben said as she shook her head, chuckling as the waitress smiled and took the money. Ali started fixing up her coffee, adding cream and sugar to her liking before sipping the drink, then speaking.

"No, I appreciate it, but it's ok," Ali said, her eyes glancing up as Ben peered at her, frowning. "I don't want you to pay for me. Not yet," Her eyes stayed on his as he straightened, then snorted, nodding.

"Alright then," he said, chuckling. Fixing up his coffee, he took a sip and sighed, leaning back heavily as he closed his eyes. He turned and glanced out the window, then began drumming his fingers on the windowsill, peering out at the students going by one by one, his eyes concentrating, slightly unfocused.

"Alyson... my God, you're beautiful... I love watching you dance... and I love when you do that more... that right there, my beautiful goddess..."

"This? What about when I sink down on you... just like this..."

"Ah... Come here..."

"...Benjamin?" Ali asked, leaning forward as he glanced over, then smiled, shaking his head.

"Yes, Alyson?"

"It looked like you were daydreaming..." she said as he nodded, his eyes on her as he smiled.

"And if I was?" Ben grinned, his hand coming to hers as she shivered, biting her lip. "Perhaps you're my muse. Perhaps you give me ideas to write, stories to put to paper..." Ben smiled as she straightened, her eyes widening.

"D-Do you write?" she asked as he shook his head, patting her hand.

"No, I leave that to those who have a far better imagination than I do." Ben sipped his coffee again as she sighed, nodding. "No, I sing," he nodded as she got a surprised look on her face.

"Not professionally, but it is a hobby. I enjoy it." Ben smiled as she grinned, nodding.

"Singing is nice, it puts a tune to my dance. Well, it's one way to put tune to my dance. I can't play an instrument to save my skin, but I can hold a tune in a bucket at least." Ali smiled as he beamed.

"So, we do have something in common!" Ben laughed, his eyes brightening. "Thank God! I was starting to think I didn't have a chance!" he grinned, leaning forward as she burst into giggles, taking a sip of her coffee. She bit her lip, then nodded, her eyes bright as he grinned. "What are you doing later?"

Ali coughed into her cup, then blinked fast, her eyes widening as he snorted. "I-I...I wasn't planning to do anything, Benjamin... that is, I planned to get the train home, then study on what I probably missed today. I might do some stretches, train for my physical classes." Ali said, trailing off as he nodded, smiling at her. "Why?"

"Well, I drove here, let me drive you to Salem, home if you want, but, I was hoping you'd come to my place." Ben said, smiling at her as she bit her lip, her eyes on his. "I live over a small bar, a former speakeasy. I thought you might like it."

Ali sipped her coffee, her eyes curious, then bit her lip. She actually was curious, to be honest. She was interested in learning more about Benjamin, though she had thought for sure that he would be like the other blue-bloods of the area.

Something in his eyes was alluring her, drawing her in, like falling into a lake of water...

Cool and comforting.

"Alright." Ali said quietly, her hands going to her lap as he smiled, nodding. Finishing his drink, Ben set a few coins on the table, then stood, a hand coming down and offering her assistance in standing. *'He's a gentleman, too...'* Ali thought, her eyes going to his again as she let her hand slip into his, blinking a few times timidly. He tugged her up, nodding as she swallowed slightly, her breath catching as she shivered.

"Are you cold, Alyson?" Ben asked, concern on his features as she shook her head.

"N-No..."

"Alyson, get out of the lake! You'll catch a chill!"

"Benjamin, hush! I enjoy my morning swim in the lake before the sun has had a chance to spoil the day!"

"I'll make you get out, I swear to the deities, woman!"

"Oh! Benjamin! You stop that! Make your waters release me and put me back in the lake!"

"No! Look at you, you're shivering! You've caught a chill! Come here, so I can warm you!"

Ali blinked, her eyes hazing over as voices seemed to flutter through her head, and Ben's eyes seemed to almost glow at her, his face seeming to get worried. "Alyson?" he asked, a hand coming down to cup her chin, stroking her face. She shook her head as the voices faded, and she focused on his bright sapphire eyes, noting that whatever glow she had imagined, it was gone...

'Of course it is, you imagined that... silly girl.' Ali thought, sucking in a breath as Benjamin stroked her cheek. "I'm sorry, I got a bit lightheaded." she said, shaking her head.

"Not at all, you're absolutely fine." Ben said, a hand moving to go around her shoulders, then stopping, his eyes going to hers as she peered at him. "Uh, may I?" he asked sheepishly as she chuckled, then nodded.

"Yes, you may. Thank you for asking this time!" Ali smiled as he grinned, nodding as he let his arm rest around her shoulders, the two leaving the diner and chatting pleasantly.

From the opposing sidewalk, in the shaded area near the trees, a figure stood. Slender and tall, she wore a long white dress, the hood of the shimmering fabric pulled over her blonde hair, and her bright blue eyes glowed faintly, a frown on her face as she watched the two leave the diner.

"They've found one another, though they do not realize it yet," she murmured, her eyes narrowing.

The dark necromancer, she was the High Priestess of the Order of the Necrotic Flame, longest lived of their order. She had been gifted by their Dark Lord centuries ago the blessing of longevity, prolonging her lifespan and beauty by consuming the life force of others.

Over the years, the belief in the arcane had come and gone, sometimes even carrying a stigma of pure evil with it, no matter how it was wielded, Abaddon had particularly enjoyed that era in time, It had made dispatching the three nuisances more fun than usual when she had sent the stupid Puritans to break down their door, and she had gleefully watched as they had ripped the woman from the house they had built, dragging her by her arms and hair, vowing to burn her alive, a promise they had kept at sunrise. It had made her job so much easier when the men had come later the next night.

They had never managed to come as a triad, and that, it was foretold, was when things would truly be dangerous for her.

The spell work and charms they could cast, their blood magic and enchantments to lock the portals down, they did not last. However, if the three managed to combine their arcane abilities, use the three of them together, it was foretold that her world would forever be locked away, the demonic realm and the black arcane magic that she and the other necromancers of the Order used inaccessible to them.

Luckily for them, they still had time...

The three never did realize when they had found one another, not right away...

It always took them time to forge the bonds that they had made so many centuries ago. They never trusted one another right away.

She had time to put a stop to it, and since she had found Benjamin before he had awoken, she had kept an eye on him. Staying near him would ensure that when the others came around, she would have access to them as well.

Phoenyx had wandered into Benjamin's life almost a year ago, and they were swiftly becoming close friends, and they had more feelings for one another than the two would care to admit without their memories. She had been waiting on Alyson, the kinetic sorceress.

Now, she had her too.

"I can intervene this time," Abaddon hissed, her eyes on the two as they headed towards the campus. "I can keep them from even awakening, and allow my rituals to have the time they need to take root. I have the resources I need this time, the souls I need to experiment on, to awaken them." she said, her eyes dark as they let out a deep, sapphire glow. "I just need to keep those three out of my plans..."

Meanwhile, the two got to Benjamin's car, Ben casually pulling his keys out of his pocket and taking Ali's books from her as she sputtered, her face paling. "T-This is your car?!"

Ben glanced at her, then looked at his car, then back at her. "Yes?"

"A-And you let it leave your garage?!" Ali asked, her eyes wide as he snorted, setting her books in the rear floorboard, then opening the driver's side door and pointing at the passenger side door. "I'm scared I'll scratch it," she said honestly, biting her lip as he laughed, shaking his head.

"No, no! Get in!" Ben grinned, his eyes lit up as she opened the door and slipped into the comfortable seat, sinking into the cushion with a small groan. "Comfy?" he asked with a laugh as she bit her lip, then stuck her tongue out slightly, her nose scrunching up. "Oh, very cute!" he chuckled, turning the key to start the car, then shifting gears, glancing behind him as she peeked around the red seats.

"...don't know why I was surprised..." Ali muttered as she peered around the seats, watching him casually back out of the parking space, then pull forward, her eyes wide as she curled up slightly. "...fancy-pants..." she said, a grin on her face as he laughed, his eyes widening.

"Excuse me?!" Ben grinned, his eyes flitting over to her as she squeaked, then glanced over at him, her fingers going to her mouth as she bit down on them, biting back openly laughing.

"I said, I don't know why I was so surprised by the fancy car," Ali said, her eyes glittering mischievously as he grinned, glancing over at her again for a second. "...your perfectly-pressed pants, crisp white shirt and fancy jacket. You just screamed 'fancy-pants' when I first saw you," she bit down on her finger as she giggled, her eyes wide as he started laughing, his eyes widening.

"I don't look like a 'fancy-pants'!" Ben said, grinning as she nodded, her eyes bright.

"You do. It might not be your intention, but you do," Ali chuckled, her eyes on him as he shook his head, grinning.

"My roommate says the same damn thing!" Ben snickered as the wind blew through their hair. "He says I look like a 'rich boy' with how I dress, I've let him buy me new clothes, but apparently the way I put them together makes me look like a 'rich boy', or maybe I just look like a 'rich boy' in general," He grinned as she laughed, shaking her head.

"You do have this air of intelligence about you, but that's not a bad thing." Ali said, leaning back as she peered up at the sky, the clouds going by. "Mmm, it's a nice day."

"It is. I'll take us to Salem. You tell me the directions to your home when we get close, alright?"

"Thank you, Ben."

CHAPTER 4

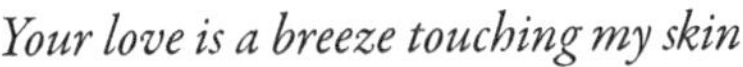

Your love is a breeze touching my skin

-ALI AND BEN-

THE TWO HAD QUICKLY MADE IT TO ALI'S APARTment. Ali let him know that she would be back down as soon as she had changed into nicer clothing, as it was growing late and they were, after all, going to a nightclub. Up in her flat, she had swiftly changed, tugging on a lovely deep wine-colored satin dress that hugged her curves and went to the floor, a set of lace undergarments to hold up her stockings, and a pair of black heels. She was lucky enough to be able to be very good at thrift shopping, so when she found dresses that were beautiful, she brought them home, tailored them to fit her measurements, then hung them up.

It was a hobby.

A few hair combs in her hair to tug her curls back completed her look, as well as some quickly redone makeup, some smoky shadow at the edges of her eyes and a deep plum-toned lipstick.

Grasping a shawl, she pulled it over her shoulders, then grabbed her black purse, grasping it in her hands. She checked for her keys and other necessities, nodding as she closed her door and locked it up, then went to go down the staircase. Ben was waiting four flights down at the bottom for her, as he had insisted that it would be rude to go into her apartment with her at this point.

He really was a gentleman.

Her heels clicked on the stairs as she came down, and Ben peered up from the bottom, his eyes on her as she nodded down. "I'm sorry it took so long!" Ali called to him as he shook his head, chuckling. She glanced up, noting the pipes that were leaning on the wall, sighing. The construction people must have picked the empty apartment above hers to store all of their tools, and they had put their bigger concrete pipes against the wall up there, tying them in a bundle. Fantastic. Shaking her head, she smiled back down at Ben, who was grinning up at her.

"Not a problem! It only took fifteen minutes!" Ben said, leaning on the rail and watching as she hit the third floor's stairs, her heels steadily clicking.

On the floor above Alyson's apartment, cloaked and unseen to the two, Abaddon glared down, then began muttering. In the darkness, her eyes began glowing a deep sapphire hue, her hand extending towards the heavy piping leaning against the wall. The concrete pipes began to wobble and shake slightly, shifting in place, sliding...

Then, as Abaddon let out a small laugh, one fell with a loud crash, the shockwave reverberating through the ground. Chuckling, she gave it one last push, and it went hurtling down the stairs, thundering down towards Alyson like a beast on the rampage.

"...Goodbye, Alyson..."

A sudden clattering behind Alyson caused her caused her to jump, and both of them narrowed their eyes, trying to see in the dark staircase. Her eyes grew huge, staring as a pipe from the construction equipment being stored few floors up rolled down the staircases, now one set of stairs above her.

"Shit! Alyson! Run down!" Ben yelled, his eyes wide as he stared at the large piece of cement pipe, rolling awkwardly down the stairs, gaining speed and force as it moved, causing Alyson to pale. It would flatten her if it hit her, there was no doubt in her mind about that. She wouldn't survive...

Her feet moved deftly down each stair, her eyes wide and a whimper leaving her throat, clutching at her purse. She passed the third floor and hit the second, almost there...

Her foot slipped.

Crying out, her body turned as she stared at the pipe as it awkwardly rounded the corner, nearing her as she raised her hand, yelling. Her eyes, widening, went a bright white as she closed them, her body tensing with pure terror. A shudder went through Ali's body as she let out a scream.

"No!"

"Alyson!"

Suddenly, the pipe wobbled and jerked to the side, toppling off the stairs as Ben let out a yell, pressing himself against the staircase wall as the pipe came crashing to the floor, cracking the wooden floor as it landed.

Benjamin darted up the stairs, his eyes huge as he went up to Alyson, who was shaking like a leaf clinging to a tree on an extraordinarily windy day. His hands came to her waist, then her hand, which was still up, lacing in hers carefully as she whimpered. "Alyson, you're safe..." he said quietly, his eyes on her as she opened her eyes carefully, her eyes going wide as her brown eyes met his blue ones. "Fuck. That was..." Ben tried to speak but had nothing he could truly say that really encompassed the situation.

"...I-I..." Ali murmured, then swallowed, peering over the edge of the stairs, her face paling at the cement pipe as she bit her lip. "Thank God it rolled over the edge." she said, her legs shaking as he nodded.

"Absolutely. Tomorrow, you need to call your building manager." Ben said, his eyes wide. "I can't believe they left construction materials loose like that."

"It looked secure when I glanced up, I thought it was tied up." Ali said, her face confused.

"Do you want to stay home?" Ben asked, sighing and giving her a worried look. "Your night just got really shitty, nerve-wracking..."

"No! Absolutely not!" Ali said, her eyes huge as he blinked. "This is the last place I want to be! D-Do you mind if we still go?"

Ben nodded, his hand coming up to cup her face as he kept her hand grasped in his. "Of course. Come on. I'll get you a few drinks, maybe I can find you somewhere else to stay tonight." he said quietly as she nodded, her eyes damp.

"T-Thank you." Ali muttered, a hand going to her forehead as she let him lead her out, his arm carefully going around her waist as she looked up, glancing at the pipe on their way towards the doors, then up towards the other equipment that was leaning on the railings or bound together in the hall in utter confusion.

Up with the construction tools and the other concrete pipes, Abaddon let out a hiss of anger, her eyes widening. Her hands clenched on the rail, her body leaning over to allow her to glare at the pipe that was upright in the wood floor, the floor cracked around it.

"Damn that witch!"

The pair had decided to continue with their evening despite the fright they'd both gotten, so they had gotten into Ben's car and, after a bit of time, began to talk and learn more about one another. Soon enough they were pulling up at The Black Cat, the time having flown by. Alyson's eyes widened as she stared at the former speakeasy-turned-nightclub, her hands clenching on her purse as Benjamin grinned broadly, pulling around to the side of the club, stretching as he cut his car off.

"T-This is where you live?" Ali asked as he nodded, smiling.

"Yes, actually. It's gone through some improvements over the last year, I found this place a little over a year ago you see, and I loved it here. It was cozy and comforting, the alcohol was fantastic, the women that were working here were lovely... but the décor was outdated, like it was set in the 70s," Ben explained, getting out and moving to her side as she nodded, letting him help her from the car. "I wanted to fix the place up, and they had an open room, so I asked them if I could rent the room that's above the bar. I also offered to be a patron, giving them monetary loans to improve the interior, hire new waitresses and performers, and so on," Ben said, leading her to the other side of the car, then jogging down a flight of stairs to the basement of the nightclub. He hauled out the top of his car with a grunt as Ali gasped and came over, helping get the hard top up the stairs as he shook his head, panting. "I got it!"

"No! Let me help!"

"It's heavy!"

"Which is why I'm helping!" Ali said, her eyes on him as she helped him heft it over the car. Ben was quick to get in and secure the top, then lock the doors, closing the vehicle up to keep anyone from stealing it.

Taking her by the waist, Benjamin led her in through the side doors, a wave of smoky air hitting Ali in the face as she bit back the urge to cough. She bit her lip, her eyes widening as she stared ahead, her eyes adjusting to the sudden lighting change. Blue lighting flared into her eyes, and a pretty redheaded woman clad in nothing but a bra and lace pair of panties came up, a cigarette in her hands and a grin on her face as she leaned forward and cupped Ben's face, his eyebrow quirking playfully.

"Ben!" she squeaked, her eyes lighting up as he snorted, then smiled broadly down at her, his eyes going to Ali, then back to the woman.

"Hey, Olivia. Busy tonight?" he asked casually as she shrugged, then pointed at the stage.

"You'd have to go out and ask Paddy, but it's seemed pretty steady," she said, smiling fondly, then looking over at Ali, her eyes glittering. "Who's this?"

"My date. Alyson, this is Olivia, she's one of the dancers here." Benjamin chuckled as Ali smiled, nodding and offering her hand as Olivia blinked in surprise, then grinned, taking her hand and giving it a small shake, then letting go.

"It's a pleasure, Olivia." Ali said, her eyes lit up as Olivia smirked, shaking her head.

"Not yet it's not, but give me a few hours, sweetheart." Olivia purred, her hands coming up to cup at her breasts in her bra, winking slightly as Ben snorted, shaking his head and pointing at the dressing area.

"What's your next act?" he asked as Olivia licked her lips and grinned wickedly.

"'*What's Love Got to Do With It*', in about 30 minutes."

"Oh, that'll be fun." Ben laughed, then wriggled his fingers. "Off you go."

"Bye, Alyson! Don't let Benjamin here sneak you up to the flat, we'll all be hearing you then." Olivia said deviously as Ben let out a small laugh, shaking his head again and pointing at the dressing area once more as Ali flushed slightly, biting her lip.

'*She says that like it'd be a negative...*' Ali thought quietly, then glanced around as Ben led her through the back, around stages and other dancers, watching as women danced in private booths and gave personal shows.

It was alluring, to say the least...

Benjamin tugged her back to a quieter area, a small booth in the back where they could see the main stage, but where they could talk and have some privacy as well. People were dancing around the stages, allowing the girls to perform but still giving those who wanted to dance a space to move freely. Blinking, Ali glanced up, watching as a lovely girl in a black corset came up and asked what they wanted to drink, and Ben quickly ordered 'his usual', then glanced at her.

"What about you, Alyson?"

She wasn't sure, to be honest...

She wanted something a hair stronger, since she'd had such a rough afternoon, but she also knew she did not want to lose her inhibitions. With how Olivia had said that 'going to Ben's flat' would make it so that they would all hear her, Ali was sure that he was notorious for bringing ladies here.

"A rum and coke," she said, her finger coming up to go between her teeth as the waitress nodded, smiling brightly at her. One rum and coke wouldn't take away her ability to think straight. Biting back mild nerves, she glanced at the bar, noting that Nyx seemed to be off tonight. Well, at least she wouldn't look like some kind of tramp to him, not yet. A mild bit of relief went through her at that, she liked Phoenyx.

The thing was, though, she was really getting to like Benjamin too...

"The girls here are fantastic performers," Benjamin said, his eyes flitting to the main stage as a girl came out, white furs covering half of her body. "They entice without being pornographic."

Alyson simply nodded, peering at the woman as she swayed and began to sing, her hand coming out and her eyes on the crowd of men and women watching her. The power to tantalize and entice a crowd like that was utterly intoxicating.

"Who is that?" Ali asked, her eyes curious as Ben nodded, smiling.

"Evie. She actually has two little ones at home, twins. There's a sitter with them on her nights that she works. Their father, the prat, he took off on her when she told him she was pregnant," he explained as Ali's head turned fast, her eyes darting to his as he chuckled. "She's had to bring them here once or twice, when I was free and not busy with a date or studying. I offered to babysit for her, since her usual sitter had backed out. They're four, and Lucy's a handful." Ben laughed, his head shaking as Ali laughed, her eyes widening. "When you meet my roommate, ask him about that, Lucy drove him batty once, he got off his shift here and found her running rampant upstairs. He told me I needed to call in a priest, that he thought she might be possessed." Ben laughed as Ali, who had just taken her drink from the waitress that had come by and sipped it, coughed, her eyes widening in shock.

'Oh.' She thought in utter disbelief, staring at Ben as he relayed the tale to her. *'Oh, there is no way...'*

"Davy's a good boy, though," Ben said, sipping his whiskey and leaning back. "I told Evie that the next time I babysit, I demand that Lucy not be given sugar for a good twelve hours prior.

She laughed and agreed," he snickered as Ali grinned, her face softening.

"You help the girls here a lot it seems." Ali said as he blinked, then shrugged.

"I help when I'm needed," Ben said, his eyes neutral as she nodded. "I don't like leaving people in a tough spot, not when I can do something about it. It's why I went into medicine."

Ali smiled, sipping her drink as he watched Evie perform onstage with mild interest, his eyebrow quirking as she let the fur stole she carried drop from her silken gloved hands, a white and blue corset pushing her breasts up pleasingly. As she walked, her backside was accentuated in the white satin panties she wore, and white heels finished the look. She looked almost angelic, her deep blonde hair flowing down her back as she turned and danced, gaining the attention of every male in the audience.

"She's lovely." Ali murmured, her eyes on Evie as Ben nodded.

"She is, she's also very kind," he said, smiling as he sipped his drink and sat back. His hand carefully moved to her waist, his head tipping sideways as she sucked in a breath, her lower regions getting warm. "What about you?"

"What about me?" Ali asked, her eyes going to his as he smiled.

"You're a ballerina, an easily lost ballerina. What else are you?" Ben asked quietly as she shuddered, his fingers splaying on her lower back as his eyes seemed to inspect her very soul.

"I'm not from here," she said as he nodded, chuckling. "I'm from South Carolina, warmer areas," He was watching her intently, listening to her every word. "I... My mother was... is... kind. My father was... less than. I left when I was younger, around sixteen... didn't look back. I don't know if she's alive, but I think he is." Ali murmured as his eyes went to her mouth as it moved, a shiver going through her as he brought his splayed hand up her back. "I donated... everything I could... to local c-charities every year, not that it really matters right now." Ben grinned, nodding at her and stroking down her spine, causing goosebumps to flare along her arm. "I-I... I love children, but something keeps me from wanting some of my own. I'm scared to have my own children." She admitted as he glanced up at her, his stroking stopping for a moment as she sighed slightly. *'And you've scared him off...'* her mind scolded herself for a moment, but he nodded, his face understanding.

"I'm the same, to be blunt. My parents are furious," Benjamin said, stroking her spine again as she bit her lip, then relaxed more into his strokes, whimpering slightly as a rush of heat flooded her upper body. "You pegged me right. You're very observant." he chuckled as she watched him. "I'm not from here either. I'm also not from Boston. I'm actually from Newport, Rhode Island," He kept his eyes on hers as she got very quiet, her eyes wide.

"B-But, that's not even what most people would call blue-blood, that's downright..."

"Rich." Ben confirmed, his eyes on her as she stared in disbelief. "The car, the clothing, it all comes with a large home back in Newport as well, but my parents want me to marry, and I'm not at that point in my life," He grabbed his drink with his free hand and gulped it. "I haven't found anyone..."

"Anyone?" Ali asked, her eyes on him as he chuckled. "You've met no women that suited your fancy? No polite damsels?"

"Sure, I had many nice ladies pushed at me, all of them shoved into etiquette classes from the tender young age of one and taught how to properly serve tea before they could walk and talk. I was taught that I would find a wife to extend the Hancott line before anything else..." Ben said, his face growing annoyed as he looked up, his hand resting on her back. "I hate that the only true use that my dear old Mother and Father seem to have for me is for my goddamn sperm, if you want me to be blunt." He tipped the last of his drink back as she sighed, her eyes on him as she turned and brought a hand up to stroke his face, his eyes widening in surprise. "Alyson?"

"No one should have the control of their body stolen from them," Ali said quietly as he stared, then shifted slightly, turning to look fully at her as his hand pressed firmly on her back.

"You speak like someone who has had that control taken from you," Ben said, his eyes on her as she swallowed, then nodded, her eyes firm as she bit her lip, then took a breath, swigging her drink heavily and avoiding eye contact. "I'm sorry. Men can be dicks." he spat out as she snorted.

"Yes, they can, and your guard goes down when they're the ones who create you and are supposed to be the one protecting you from all the dangers in the world," she muttered, her eyes going down as he got a confused look, then clarity. His color drained from his face, then he blinked, his eyes wide.

"Christ."

"My mother stopped it. Hence why I said I don't know if she's still alive, but it's why I left home," she muttered, then glanced over at him, nodding. "...and no, it never fully got to that point, but it got very close. I ran that night, during their fight, with what I had on my back. And my choice in the matter was non-existent, from the time all of it began until the night I left. So yes, Benjamin, I understand losing that control, and I'm so sorry your parents have been pushing you into making offspring you simply are not ready for."

His eyes locked on hers and his hand went back to stroking her spine, but his body inched closer, cutting the space between them in half as she shivered again. She had stopped paying attention to the stage, not noticing the change in dancers, and was now focusing on him and his movements.

"You're very caring," he said quietly, his eyes soft as he brought his hand up to the center of her back, between her shoulder blades. "You care so much about people you barely know... why?"

"Perhaps if the world had more people who cared about those they barely knew, there would be less darkness and more light in it," Ali said, her breath catching as his hand moved to her neck, cradling it in his cool grasp. With a small tug, she felt herself melt forward, her body pulled against his tightly. His hand moved from her neck to her cheek, stroking it as she stared up at him. "B-Benjamin?"

"Am I moving too fast?" he asked quietly, his thumb coming up to stroke her lower lip as she moaned quietly, then shook her head, her hand coming up to rest on his chest.

"N-No..."

"Good." Ben murmured, letting his lips dip down to ghost over hers as she gasped quietly. Careful, gentle kisses went across her lips as she panted, her body pressing heavily on his in the quiet little corner booth, and with a small groan, he pulled them apart, his eyebrow quirking. "I do have a flat upstairs." He said quietly as she nodded. "Shall we?"

"Alright."

With a small grunt he was separating them, helping her up carefully and subtly moving them past the stages as she glanced around, her hand grasping at her purse. "Come on." he muttered, his eyes on the stairs up to the flat as she bit her lip, her hands trying to scrabble at her purse for change to pay for her drink.

"B-But, I didn't... pay for my drink..."

"I never pay for my drinks, neither do my dates. I have a running tab that I pay once a month. Lewis keeps up with it," Ben said, his eyes on the stairs as she nodded, trotting to keep up and noting that his stance in his walking had shifted. Climbing the stairs, he reached back and took her hand, his other hand going into his pocket and digging for his keys. Unlocking the door, he let it open, then let her enter first as he tugged his jacket off, his eyes locked on her figure.

She turned, glancing around the flat. The styles were so mixed. Chaotic. An art easel and sketch work materials lined the one wall, as well as some tools, causing her to pale as she bit her lip, her eyes widening as she prayed she was wrong. *'Nyx... can't be his roommate. He'd have told me. I gave him Ben's name earlier.'* Ali thought, her eyes knotting in thought as she looked around. A small piano was in one corner, near the window, causing her to focus on Benjamin as he nodded.

"That's mine. I admit it, I do play a bit. To be honest, I liked finding out how much you enjoy music," he said as she nodded, setting her purse on a coffee table in the center of the living area. The kitchen was small but well-kept, as was the living area. A nice, large burgundy-red couch with a few fluffy black pillows sat in the middle of the room, as well as two black, cushioned chairs and a television that sat in the left corner, opposite of the easel. A fireplace in the room brought it all together, and Ben went straight to it, throwing a fresh piece of wood into it and beginning to light the coals, working to get a flame going as she looked around. She slipped her heels off and let the shawl she'd worn go over a black chair, exposing her arms and the curves of her breasts to the room as she walked about, looking for more clues.

"Your roommate draws?" Ali asked curiously as he nodded, glancing over at her.

"Yeah, he's really good at it. I've told him to sell his work instead of hiding it away." Ben said, shaking his head as Ali nodded. Moving to the window, she stared outside at the hustle of nightlife, hearing the music from downstairs still thudding and bumping against the wooden floors.

He came up behind her as the fire began crackling in the fireplace, his arms going around her as she swallowed heavily. His hands splayed on her stomach, his mouth going to her neck as he moaned quietly, and she turned, her eyes going to his. "I don't know what's come over me. I'm not normally so quick to move to this," she said carefully as he nodded, letting his hands move to her hips and begin scrunching her dress up, his eyes hungry and staring at her.

"I don't think you're easy, Alyson," Ben said carefully as she nodded, her eyes locked to his. "Quite the opposite."

"I just have this feeling that you bring a lot women up here," Ali murmured as he cringed, then nodded, his hands slowing as he stroked her thighs.

"You're not wrong. I have and I'm not usually interested in more than purely sex." Ben said as she looked down, biting her lip and nodding. "I said usually. Would you mind going out tomorrow morning with me for breakfast if you stay?" he asked quietly as she glanced up at him, her eyes widening. "I can drive you home before classes to change, get your books and things that you would need." Ben muttered as she swallowed heavily, her eyes locked on his.

"That sounds nice" Ali murmured, nodding at him as he let out a small groan, then gripped her tightly, tugging her towards the couch. She followed as though she were in a dream, unable stop her feet from moving with him, not that she wanted to. The heat between her legs and the dull throb was intense now, and she was aching for him to make it stop.

As if he had heard her thoughts, he gently nudged her atop the couch's pillows and cushions, his hands back at her thighs as she let out a loud moan. His eyes got a hair darker, like an animal on the hunt. His lips moved back up to hers, ghosting over hers again as she whimpered, her back arching up to meet him as his hands slid further up her dress.

"P-Please, Benjamin." Ali moaned, her legs sliding open slightly, and with a small growl he shoved his mouth on hers hard, his tongue sliding into her mouth and his one hand moving the last bit of the way from her thigh to her core, sliding over her mound as she let out a whine and ground against his hand. He pulled back and glanced at her, his hand at her undergarments, tracing over them, and she nodded, biting her lip as he tugged them to the side and let his hand dip into her slit, right into her dampness, causing her to bring a hand to her mouth and bite down, crying out.

"You sound gorgeous." Ben muttered, his hand moving to find her bud, his fingers teasing and tantalizing. As his fingers hit their mark, her back came up, pushing her flush against him as he got a look of pure, unadulterated arousal on his face. "Good, good girl." he murmured, letting his fingers swirl on the bead he'd found hidden in her dampness, watching as she whimpered and brought the hand that had been at her mouth up to clasp around his neck, holding herself upright.

Her other hand, however, had snaked down, between them, and was pushing against his pants, causing him to groan and buck against her, his hand moving faster on her. She let her legs open further as he growled, his mouth moving to nip at her throat.

"B-Benjamin..." Ali whimpered, her hips rocking with him as he nodded, peering at her and sucking at one spot on her throat, the heat between her legs growing from a dull ache into a roaring flame, and she desperately needed someone to ease the heat...

The hand that had stayed on her thigh moved, his own body beginning to grow more frantic with need, more chaotic, less controlled. He let his hand slip between hers and his trousers, undoing his belt, then the button and zipper of his pants as hastily as he could. Her hand moved down to work with his as he let out a breathless chuckle against her throat, his hair falling into her face. "Don't normally do 'petting'..." he murmured against her throat breathlessly, grasping for her again once his trousers were open and she could let her hand ghost over his own underwear, which were firmly being tented out at the moment. "I haven't done 'petting' since I was a teenager." he snorted as she laughed slightly, moaning as his fingers moved on her.

"A-Are you complaining?" she asked, her hand moving to the slit in his briefs to finally graze at him, getting a loud groan out of him in response.

"Not in the slightest, it's actually kind of fun." he said, smirking as he tugged his pants down slightly, getting a small squeak out of her, her eyes widening as he grinned. "Just being helpful! I have easier access. I don't want you to sprain your lovely wrist getting to my parts." he quipped as Ali burst into giggles, then tipped her head back, his fingers pressing down on her harder.

Her hand moved up his belly, slipping under the waistband of his briefs to grip him as he let out a moan, thrusting forward into her hand at a steady pace.

"P-Please don't stop that." she moaned loudly, her hips thrusting on him as he nodded. "Just a little more, Ben."

"You come for me." Ben nodded, his eyes focusing on her as she whimpered, biting at her lip as a flush crept up on her neck. His fingers, skilled at their task, went from swirling to firmly flicking, and his teeth dug into her neck. He dripped into her hand, groaning, biting back pleasure, and in that moment she saw white.

Moisture crept up her slit as she arched up and moaned, whining and clutching him to her roughly. Ben's own eyes rolled back as his orgasm began creeping up on him, his hips roughly moving and his hardness sliding in her hand. Slickness coated her palm and gave him the delicious texture he needed to lose himself, her hand clenching on him and tightening, squeezing teasingly.

Ali's hand went to come up as she panted, and he brought his hand down, wrapping over hers and stopping her as he moaned, shaking his head quickly.

"Just a little more, please?" he begged, his eyes desperate as she flushed further, then nodded, swallowing heavily. His hand squeezed around hers, giving her hand guidance on cadence, timing, causing him to moan and gasp, shuddering as he tugged the tip of himself from his briefs and covered himself with both their palms, catching most of the mess within their hands.

Panting, he leaned back, his eyes rolling back slightly as he caught his breath, hips still jerking slightly as she went to nip at her lip, her eyes locked on him. Moving atop her moments later, he tugged her mouth back to his, moaning as he kept their hands free from the couch or one another, to keep from making an utter mess.

That was the exact moment that keys jingled in the door.

CHAPTER 5

Hot like a flame, then cold as ice...

-PHOENYX-

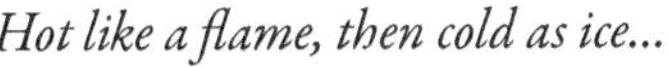

THE DOOR OPENED AND BOTH SAT UP, ONE LOOK-ing curiously at the door, his eyebrow quirking at the curly brown-haired man and his motorcycle helmet, the other paling to an almost ghostly white. Ali held her breath, her eyes getting huge as Ben let his head tip back, his face pleasantly flushed and not noticing that she was utterly uncomfortable.

"Nyx, you're home already?" Ben asked as Phoenyx nodded, then peered over at Ali, his eyes hardening slightly before moving to get a drink, his face going neutral.

"Yeah. Mom's not feeling well. I did a few chores for her, then came back." Nyx said, leaning against the counter.

"Alyson, this is Phoenyx Coleman, he's the roommate I was telling you about." Ben said, chuckling slightly as Ali's eyes got damp, staring at the darkening look on Nyx's face.

"So, you actually did end up here," Nyx said casually, shrugging as he moved around the counter as she frowned, her hands tugging her dress back into the proper places, her eyes growing hurt.

"N-Nyx…"

"Wait, you two know one another?" Benjamin said, his eyes widening in surprise as he sat up, staring between the two as Ali nodded quietly, biting her lip hard. Nyx just shrugged, moving to the window with his drink. He was smirking slightly, but the hurt on his face was obvious to anyone who knew him, he was just doing a very good job of hiding it.

"Not as well as I thought we were getting to know one another," Nyx said, then looked at Ali, who was turning red. "It's alright," he said, setting his drink down as his arms crossed as she shook her head, her eyes getting damp.

"But, I-I told you his name when I said I was meeting up with a friend." Ali said, her voice almost pleading as she stared at him, her face completely confused. "Why didn't you tell me he was your roommate when I said something?!" she asked, standing up and shaking her head, watching as he snorted.

"I honestly hadn't pegged you for the usual gold-diggers that he ends up with," Nyx said as she stepped back, looking slapped, and Ben's eyes widened, his head whipping to Nyx in shock. "I guess I was wrong." Nyx's voice was cold as he looked back out the window.

"I…I'm going to go," Ali said quietly, her voice quavering as Ben stood, adjusting his clothes and shaking his head.

"No, wait." Ben said, his eyes soft and on her as she gathered her things, her eyes spilling over. He hadn't watched someone go from shocked to utterly hurt in seconds like that in a long time, and it had been when his mother had said something disgusting to him before he'd left home. He had looked just like Alyson looked.

She picked up her purse, her face half-hidden in her curls,

which had slipped from their combs in their time on the couch, and shook her head as he sighed, his hand reaching for hers.

"Goodnight, Benjamin."

As she walked past him, about to close the door, Nyx spoke up.

"Alyson?" he said, causing her to stop, glancing up at him. He walked over to her, then grasped her one hand, where the evidence of the last half an hour was still in her palm and fingers, and held it up as she reddened, her eyes dripping further. "You might want to find a sink on your way out." he said casually, letting her wrist go as she rushed for the door, her hand tucking into her shawl and a huffed sob coming from her chest, the door closing quietly behind her.

Benjamin, his eyes getting huge, let his head whip from the door, then back to Nyx, who was walking back to the counter with the mask of neutrality dropping, allowing some mild hurt to hit his features. "Phoenyx, what the hell was that about?" Ben asked, his eyes locking on the other man as Nyx sighed, then glanced over at him shaking his head.

"I'm sorry to ruin your night, Ben." Nyx said, grasping for a bottle of whiskey in the upper cabinet, pouring a healthy glass before swigging it.

"How in the hell do you two know one another?!" Ben asked, shock still on his face as Nyx snorted, peering over at Ben over his glass, shaking his head.

"I told you earlier today that I was meeting up with the girl that I had flirted with at the 'Cat this last weekend." Nyx said, frowning as Ben nodded, shrugging and coming over to him, his face concerned.

"Yes, and?"

"Are you really that stupid?" Nyx hissed, his eyes growing annoyed as Ben stared, then coughed, his eyes getting huge.

"...was that her?!" Benjamin asked, spluttering as Nyx glared, nodding with annoyance.

"Yes. Finally, your thick mind puts it together." Nyx snapped, turning away as Ben gaped at him, then blinked, his eyes widening in confusion.

"But, wait, she said she mentioned my name when she said she had someone to meet up with later. You didn't tell her we were roommates?" Ben asked, his eyes knotting up, perplexed. "I don't understand."

"When I met her earlier, she didn't strike me as the usual gold-digger, like I said. You can have her," Nyx said, gulping another swig of his drink as Benjamin frowned, his eyes narrowing. "My wallet'll appreciate the fact that I found out early about that." Nyx chuckled wryly, shaking his head as Ben shook his head, scoffing.

"Phoenyx! Stop that! She's not a damn gold-digger!" Ben said, his face annoyed as Phoenyx snarled.

"So, she got up here based on..."

"We have a lot in common, probably the same as you two do. Terrible parents, for example." Ben said, his face softening as Nyx's eyes got a hair gentler. "I invited her out for drinks this evening after she was in an accident at her apartment, the poor girl was scared out of her mind." he explained, his head shaking as Nyx stared, his face getting concerned.

"Wait, what?" Nyx asked, straightening as Ben nodded, his eyes on Nyx.

"Some construction equipment being stored came down the staircase. Concrete pipes, one almost tumbled over her." Ben explained, his hand going through his hair as Nyx went pale.

"She'd have been killed. She got very lucky that it went over the rail rather than hitting her." Ben said, his head shaking quietly as Nyx sighed, his eyes getting wide as he leaned against the windowsill.

"Oh, shit..." Phoenyx breathed, almost choking on the air in his lungs as Ben nodded.

"She didn't want to stay home, so I brought her here." Ben explained, his eyes going out to the street. "I had already asked her for a drink and to chat, but honestly, just to chat," Ben said, his face honest. "Besides that, she had already put me in my place earlier, she's very spunky," Benjamin chuckled, shaking his head slightly as he watched people entering and exiting The Black Cat. Next to him, Phoenyx swallowed heavily, then ran a hand through his hair, shaking his head.

"Goddamn it," Nyx whispered, looking down as Ben continued.

"She's amazing. I've met some of the ballerinas in the fine arts programs, they're usually snobby, but she's... she's a kind soul," Ben said, his eyes outside still. "I was telling her about Mother and Father and their garbage about wanting me to provide a stupid heir to the Hancott name, and instead of offering to help with that, and believe me, that was the pickup line a lot of girls tried, Nyx, she apologized for the fact that they've been trying to steal my body's control from me, because she's had her own body's control taken, and if you're wondering if that means what you're thinking, yes, but let her tell you that at her own pace," Nyx paled, his head whipping to Benjamin as he nodded, leaning on the window, his face soft. "She's comforting, gentle. I felt better having her around, Phoenyx. I don't know why. I had asked her for breakfast tomorrow," He shook his head, then hit the edge of the window, his eyes on the people still walking to and from the building. "I hope she doesn't try walking home dressed like that, in that gown and shawl, it's not safe. Someone could attack her." Ben muttered, moving to the sink to clean up, then fixing his shirt and pants. Nyx nodded, moving to the window to watch where Ben had been. "I'm going to try and catch her, give her a ride."

"Go. She probably doesn't want anything to do with me." Nyx murmured, his eyes growing wet.

"I'll be back later." Ben said as he grabbed his keys, then stopped at the door, sighing. "Look. I didn't know you were interested in her, but..."

"I am, but you are too. We'll figure it out," Nyx said quietly, staring out the window as Ben nodded. "Go."

-ALYSON-

Downstairs, Alyson had swiftly found a restroom, washing her hands quickly, her face covered in dampness. She felt like utter garbage, like she had been filthy.

Moving around backstage, she went back to the staircase, moving to knock quietly, to ask for a ride, as she didn't feel safe walking home, and then stopping to listen as the two went back and forth, her eyes wide as they brimmed over once more.

"Are you truly that dense?"

"...was that her?!"

"Yes. Finally, your thick mind puts it together..."

"But, wait, she said she mentioned my name when she said she had someone to meet up with later. You didn't tell her we were roommates? I don't understand."

"When I met her earlier, she didn't strike me as the usual gold-digger, like I said, You can have her." Nyx's words stung, causing Ali to let out a quiet sob, wrapping her arms around herself.

She hadn't meant to hurt anyone, she had even asked him earlier if he was sure that he'd be alright if she went out with someone this evening. He had seemed to be fine with it. *"My wallet'll appreciate the fact that I found out early about that."* Nyx spat out, and she turned, moving down the stairs without knocking and finding a spot under them to curl up, her face broken as she sobbed. *'You act like a tramp, and they will think you're a tramp.'* she scolded herself, her arms going around herself tighter as she rocked, her hand coming to her mouth to quiet her tears, to keep others from hearing her. *'And I... I liked both of them. I know I shouldn't... but I did.'*

"Sweetheart, are you alright?"

Her head whipped up to meet greenish-hazel eyes and long black hair, and she sniffled, wiping at her face as she nodded, her eyes widening. "I-I'm fine." she said, taking a shuddering breath as the woman stared, a long black robe covering her body. She knelt in front of Ali, then placed a hand on her shoulder, her face worried, and Ali's eyes brimmed over again. "I'm fine." she lied, her lips quivering as the woman sighed, shaking her head and leading her from the steps, an arm going around her waist.

"I don't know what happened, but I've seen many a woman come down from there in tears." she sighed, leading her from the stairs of the flat as Ali shook her head, clutching her things.

"No. This is my fault." Ali muttered, biting at her lip as the woman stared at her, then tugged her back to the dressing area, her eyes going to Ali's things.

"How in the world could it be your fault?" she asked, watching as Ali sniffled, her eyes down. "That's not my business... I'm sorry." she said, then she reached over, grabbing a handkerchief, dabbing it in some water, then bringing it to Ali's face, rubbing at the lines going down her cheeks as Ali sniffled. "But whatever it is, it is not worth you being like this."

Ali's lip quivered, then she nodded, her eyes still wet. "Thank you."

"You're welcome, miss." She smiled. "I'm Delilah, but you can call me Lila." Lila smiled, her eyes on Ali as she smiled, patting her cheek. "Did Benjamin pull his usual?"

"Oh, no. Like I said, this is my fault." Ali said, sighing. "It's... It really is a long story. It has been a long day, and this was the straw that broke my back." Her hand went up to her hair, releasing it from the hair combs completely as Delilah nodded. "It feels like the world is trying to swallow me whole and cause me to drown," Ali admitted as Lila sighed, then knelt in front of her, patting her knees.

"I don't think you'll be swallowed, and you look like you can swim well," Lila said, her eyes glittering as Ali smiled slightly. "I think you'll land on your float just fine."

"Not if things don't come around," Ali muttered, looking at the side as Lila frowned, straightening.

"How do you mean?"

"I... I need work." Ali admitted, sighing. "Everywhere I've gone isn't hiring, they've hired their help for the season." she said, her head going into her hands. "I've used all of my savings, and my rent is almost due, I'm drowning. I won't be able to stay in school." she admitted as Lila got a thoughtful look on her face, then chuckled.

"I heard Lewis is hiring." Lila smiled, shrugging slightly as Ali whipped her head to her, her eyes widening. "Couldn't hurt to ask."

Ali was about to speak, but heavier footsteps behind her made her pause, and Delilah frowned at the figure behind her, pointing. "What-" Ali went to ask, but Lila cut her off.

"Benjamin Hancott! What in the hell did you and Coleman say to this girl?" Delilah asked, glaring as Ali paled, cringing as the figure behind her sighed. "She was sobbing under the stairs of your flat..."

"Yeah, I'll bet she was. I'll take care of her." Benjamin's eyes were gentle as Lila gave him an untrustworthy look, frowning. "I swear, Delilah. I'm not going to let any more harm come to her tonight." Ben said quietly as Lila huffed, then nodded, kneeling as she looked Ali in her eyes.

"If you need me..."

"I'll find you..." Ali said, sniffling, then she clasped her hand, smiling slightly as she swallowed heavily. "Alyson, since you told me your name, but I wasn't in much of a state to tell you mine."

"Alyson. I'll be here a few more hours, but Lewis'll let me off early if need be." Delilah said, glaring over at Ben as he sighed, then nodded. She moved for the front of the nightclub, and he moved around to Ali's front, kneeling in front of her and staring into her eyes. Without warning, her eyes welled up again, and he shook his head, grabbing the same handkerchief that Delilah had been using on her face and offering it to her, his eyes gentle.

-BENJAMIN-

"Don't cry," he said softly, his hands going to her knees as her lips quivered, her eyes on him.

"I'm sorry, I didn't know." she said as he nodded, watching her intently.

"I could tell, he knew, and he should have told you. You were blindsided." Ben muttered, stroking her kneecaps as she took the handkerchief and wiped at her eyes.

"Why would he keep that from me?" Ali asked, confusion on her face as Ben sighed, his own eyes confused. "I swear, I told him your name while we were out having lunch! He asked me your name, for goodness sakes!"

"I think he suspected we'd taken an interest in the same girl." Benjamin said quietly, his eyes down. "...but he'd gotten to know you while out with you and thought you and I wouldn't be compatible at all, so he'd let us play out. No one gets hurt. It would all just be a funny coincidence." Ben said as she sniffled. "...but we did have compatibility, and he wasn't counting on that."

"If he wasn't alright with it, why would he send me with you..." Ali murmured, her eyes still wet as Ben sighed, then cupped her face.

"Because I believe he actually likes you, he's just very piss-poor at showing it," Ben said, his head shaking as she sighed.

"He probably thinks I'm a whore now." Ali moaned, her eyes spilling over as Ben's eyes widened, his hands coming up to wipe at the tears as they fell.

"No! He doesn't think that! He never said that at all!" Ben said quickly as she sniffled, letting him swipe at the lines of moisture falling from her eyes. "Alyson... Phoenyx, had he mentioned going on more dates out?"

"Yes."

"And you said?"

"I said I would." Ali said quietly as he chuckled, nodding.

"That is why he got like he did. Most women don't accept when he asks, because of his socioeconomic status." Ben said quietly as she frowned. "Women want monetary security, and Nyx has more issues with that than some women would be alright with. It's not that he's incapable, but he's taking care of his mother, and his spare money goes to her now." he explained as Ali nodded, sniffling as Ben stroked her cheek. "Nyx was talking about us figuring something out," His eyes were locked on her as she blinked, her eyes widening.

"F-Figuring something out?"

"We both have an attraction to you." Ben said, his eyes on her as she bit her lip. "I've never been a conventional man, Alyson, and I don't believe Nyx is, either. We'll figure it out after we've had time to think." He watched as she bit her lip, glancing around. "Now, what was it that I heard about you needing a job?" Ben frowned, watching as she blushed, then groaned.

"You were there for that?" Ali asked as he nodded, smiling.

"I've been told I'm very stealthy when I need to be."

"I... I need work." Ali admitted, toeing the ground as he nodded. "I've applied all over Boston and Salem, it's like I'm cursed," she moaned, shaking her head as he sighed, running a hand through her hair. "Nowhere will hire me, I have no idea why." Ali said, shaking her head. "Waitressing, secretarial work... I... I don't know what to do."

"Do you need a loan?" Ben asked as she shook her head, frowning.

"What I need is a job." Ali insisted, then glanced at the corsets on the hanging rack near them, her eyes slightly nervous. "I know it's a lot to ask, but..."

"...You want to work here?" Benjamin asked, surprise in his voice as she nodded, her eyes nervous as he blinked fast. "...Alyson, you are aware of what you'd be asked to..."

"I know. It's performance. Nothing more, nothing less."

"No, you don't understand. Sometimes the women do get nude." Ben said carefully as she bit her lip, her eyes going down. "We keep it very tasteful, hide them behind props, but we see them backstage. They're completely nude, Alyson. We help them dress sometimes, but otherwise... Are you comfortable with that?"

Ali frowned thoughtfully, then stood. Reaching behind her, she undid the clasp of her gown, then slid the zipper down, her eyes on him as he flushed, staring at her outright. "Well, let's see how comfortable I am," she said firmly, her hands slipping the dress off, then stepping out of it as she kicked it to the side, then nudging her heels with it. Her hands went behind her back to her bra, unclasping it to free her breasts, slipping her arms free of the contraption before tossing it with the dress, her hands moving down to her panties, slipping them down with the rest of the clothing, kicking them to the side as he coughed, standing up. Peering down at her, he swallowed heavily, his arm coming up to trace her side, then he grabbed a deep black and violet corset and panties outfit, spinning his finger.

"Turn around." he said huskily, his eyes on her as she obediently turned. He helped her step into the bottoms, sliding them up her legs, then her hips, his fingers grazing her hipbones as she bit back a small moan. "Hold your hair up. Above your head, your arms up..." His eye were focused on the task at hand as she nodded. Her hands laced into her curls, pulling them above her head and holding them up and out of the way. His hands began to tightly lace the corset, glancing at her as she grunted, almost as though he were trying to discourage her from the task, which he was. As he got to the top, his hands tied it expertly, then stroked her shoulders as she sucked in a breath. "Let go of your hair, then look in the mirror. Adjust your breasts on your own, you know how best to do that," Ben murmured, his eyes on her as she dropped the handful of hair, watching her curls drop down her back in tousled waves. He had to bite back a groan as she moved to the mirror, her hands going into the corset to grip at her breasts and move them about, pushing them up, where they should be, and she turned.

His mouth dried.

Her curls fell into her face, the deep plum lipstick she wore giving her the look of a seductress. Even with her tear-streaked face, her eyes had enough makeup that she looked sexy, alluring. The corset caused her frame to be accentuated beautifully, her hips gorgeous, and every speck of pale skin...

He was hard again, damn it.

Clearing his throat, he nodded. "Are you sure you want this job?"

"Yes."

"It's yours." Ben said, his eyes on Ali as she bit her lip. "Come in tomorrow evening, your first shift will start at seven, but you need to get here at five to go over routines. I'll talk to Lewis later." he said, watching as she nodded.

"Alright."

He quickly undid the lacing, then pecked her cheek, his eyes closing as he swallowed heavily, resting his head against hers as he pressed himself against her gently. "I am so sorry for what happened up there." He breathed, his one hand coming around her waist as she clutched the loose corset to her. "I had every intention of keeping you here tonight, then us going out tomorrow." he said quietly as she nodded, then glanced up at him.

"We can still do that. Just, not tomorrow. I need a day or so..." Ali said quietly as he gave her a small nod.

"Understandable. I definitely think we all should have a talk. You, myself, and Phoenyx. We should discuss things," Ben said, stroking her face as she bit her lip. "Your apartment isn't far from here. Can you catch the bus or a taxi? I'll leave you money for it. What time are your classes the day after tomorrow?"

"I have my first class at one, then another at three." Ali said as he nodded, smiling.

"Good. We can all get up and talk, then I can drive you to the university if you'd like. Get here at seven." he said. "I'll haul him out of bed kicking and screaming if I have to."

"Not a morning person?"

"Not in the slightest."

Ali snorted, then sighed as he leaned down, picking up her clothing. "Here. Get dressed." Benjamin said, stroking her cheek as she nodded.

"Thank you."

Ben quickly drove her home, his arm around her the whole time as she curled into his side, her body absolutely exhausted. He guided her up to her apartment, then simply cupped her cheek as she opened the door. He smiled at her as she tiredly stepped inside, letting him kiss her knuckles as she stepped inside.

"Goodnight, Alyson. Sleep well," Ben said softly, his face gentle. "We'll see you tomorrow."

"Goodnight, Benjamin, and..." Ali trailed off, then got a nervous look on her face. "W-Will you tell Phoenyx I said goodnight as well?"

Ben chuckled, nodding as she smiled gently, then went into the apartment, waving as he headed down the stairs. With a click, she had shut and locked her door.

Getting back to the flat, Benjamin unlocked the door, his face tired, but not as upset as he had been when he had left. Phoenyx glanced over, his eyes still upset as he leaned forward in one of the black chairs, worry on his face. "Benjamin?"

Ben frowned, trying to bite back the snark that he knew was bubbling to the surface, but it boiled over anyhow. "I hope you're pleased with yourself." he said wryly, his eyes on Nyx as his eyes got more troubled.

"What?" Nyx asked, the worry deepening as Benjamin sighed.

"Alyson was a wreck." Ben muttered, a hand going through his hair tiredly as Nyx groaned. "Apparently Delilah found her under the staircase to the flat crying and brought her to the dressing area, cleaned her up. She thinks that you think she's some kind of a skank now," Ben said sternly as Nyx sat bolt upright, his eyes widening.

"But that's not true! She's not attached to anyone! She can see whoever the hell she wants!" Nyx said quickly as Ben stared at him, shaking his head.

"Firstly, that isn't how you sounded earlier when you found us on the couch. Phoenyx, you should have never reacted like that." Benjamin scolded, his eyes hardening as Nyx groaned, leaning back with his hands going to his hair.

"I know, alright?! I lost my temper, but I saw you on her... and it's what I had wanted all fucking day. Ben, I got..."

"Jealous?" Ben asked with a curious quirk of his eyebrow as Nyx sighed, nodding. "Mmhmm. Second, we don't have the same views as many men do when it comes to a woman's sexuality. Most men would think that any woman who was growing even remotely attached to two men in any kind of romantic way is a tramp." Ben said as Phoenyx nodded, then sighed.

"True enough. Men are idiots. Sensual women are... fuck, they're amazing in the bedroom." Nyx groaned as Ben snorted, shaking his head. "What?! It's true!"

"I'm not disagreeing with you. We can talk about it more

with her the day after tomorrow, though, over breakfast," Benjamin said casually as Nyx sputtered, his eyes widening.

"Breakfast?! Day after tomorrow?!"

"Yes. About seven, so you'll have to be up at six," Ben said as Nyx groaned loudly.

"Fuck me."

"You're not my type," Ben snickered, moving to the refrigerator as Nyx snorted.

"Fuck you."

"I'm not your type." Benjamin said as he bent over and grabbed a bottle of soda, straightened, then opened the bottle and took a gulp, clearing his throat as Nyx stretched. "Nyx, one more thing..."

"Ben?"

"She'll have her first shift that night." Ben said carefully as Nyx sputtered, his eyes widening. "I want you to look out for her."

"Her what?!"

"She asked for a job," Benjamin said, his eyes down. "It... it was ALL she asked for. She didn't want comforting or a ride home, though I did offer those as well. She wanted a job." he said, sighing as he took another drink of the soda. "She's been penny-pinching since she got to Salem, and her reserves are dry. She was close to taking out a loan from the bank to get by. She needs work..." Ben said, watching as Nyx's eyes got huge as he leaned against the chair, staring aghast at him. "She got into one of our spare corsets, our spare outfits, to see if she could pull off the look, and I won't lie, she'll attract attention, Nyx. She'll get business in. My damn mouth went bone dry." he admitted as Nyx gave him a glare, then pointed at him, his voice rising.

"The drunks won't keep their goddamn hands off of her!" Nyx yelled, staring as Ben shook his head.

"And we have Nicholas and Frank for that, that's their job. They're good at keeping the drunks off of the girls." Ben nodded, finishing his soda. "They'll keep her safe. She enjoys performance. She wants this job," he said as Nyx stared at him. Ben got closer to him, and Nyx looked up into his eyes, a glint in the corner of his eye.

"I don't like it," Nyx scowled, watching as Ben shrugged.

"I don't care." Ben said, shaking his head. "Go to sleep, Phoenyx, clear your head, start out fresh in the morning," He headed for his bedroom, then stopped at the door. "And Nyx?"

Nyx looked over at him, his eyes narrowing. "What now?"

"She told me to tell you 'Goodnight.'. I just wanted to let you know."

Ben went into his room, and Nyx stared as the door shut, his eyes widening in surprise.

CHAPTER 6

Take my heart and fuck me tonight

-ALYSON AND BENJAMIN-
GLASTONBURY, ENGLAND
457 A.D.

CHIRPING BIRDS ECHOED AROUND THEM AND sunlight streamed through the trees in the clearing, the sounds of the rushing waterfalls streaming down the beautiful crystalline rocks and geodes that made up the cavernous walls of the lake's side. The skies were bright blue, a pleasant change from the dull grey that they had been dealing with as of late. The water, crystal-clear, flowed from the top of the ridges of the crystalline edge of the rock face all the way down into the lake, pooling into the deep, blue waters and glittering amethyst lakebed. River plants grew all along the edge, including grasses, lily pads, and various shades of water lilies.

Laughter erupted from the center of the lake, two people seeming to walk on the water like they themselves were enchanted, not a speck of clothing on them as they moved. His black hair gleamed in the light, the water from where they had been swimming clinging to him as he twirled her on the surface of the lake, her eyes glistening giddily.

"Benjamin! I'm going to fall through!" Alyson squeaked, her wet curls clinging to her as he clutched her to him, grinning playfully.

"You won't! I've been practicing! This is one of the things I've been working on, my control over the water," Benjamin beamed, his eyes lit a bright white as the water below them stayed a firm surface for them to move along, her feet flitting across the surface as he moved her carefully.

"You say that, but I'll be the one paying the price should you fail!" Alyson laughed, her arms going around his neck as he shook his head, his arms around her waist. Her hand reached down and gently stroked at his elemental marking on his chest, an upside-down triangle, hearing him chuckle slightly as he grasped at her hand.

"Never, my love."

His eyes let out a brighter glow and his hand came up, causing the water to bubble around them, making stairs for them to dance up as she squealed, her eyes widening. "Oh! You have been practicing!" Alyson laughed as he beamed, nodding. "You do realize that Phoenyx will be back soon, right?"

"Phoenyx can join us if he wishes," Ben said wickedly as they went all the way up the spiral staircase, the water flowing to make another floor for them to dance along, their skin still gleaming with moisture.

"Phoenyx dislikes the water," Alyson chuckled, giving Benjamin a look as he smirked deviously. "And you know that."

"So, I want you to myself for a small time," Benjamin said quietly, spinning her out, then tugging her back to him, his hand going to her chin to cup it, then draw her lips to his as she moaned, their mouths moving on one another gently. "I do not mind that we share, that we are equal in our love for you, and that you love us equally as well, but sometimes I want some time with you where I know I won't be interrupted by him." Benjamin admitted, his blue eyes on hers as Alyson nodded, nipping her lip and lacing her hands through his hair. "If we weren't on our hunt, and we did not have to do our duty..."

Alyson peered at him, her eyes widening slightly as he sighed, his arms going around her, clutching her to him. "Yes?"

"If I had found you, and only I..." Benjamin sighed, stroking her damp hair, then pecking her cheek, his eyes on hers as she frowned. He lifted her hand, his eyes still bright white, then brought his other hand up, a drop of water coming up to swirl around her ring finger as she whipped her head up to stare at him. "I think our lives would have been quite different."

"...but we cannot change destiny," Alyson said, her face gentle as he sighed, letting the water melt off of her hand. "That does not mean that I would not be your wife and his. If you asked, that is. I have heard of that in some places. Triad marriages," Alyson smiled as Benjamin chuckled, then brought her knuckles to his mouth again, his head shaking.

"Always the problem solver..." he said, continuing their dance as she shrugged. His hand came to her ribcage, tracing at her side and carefully touching the triangle and line marking there as she shivered.

"Of course, I have to be." Alyson said, her eyes on him as she let her eyes glow, a hand coming up to coax a water lily from the water's edge to flow up to her, a vine creeping it up her body as she plucked it free, the glow leaving her brown eyes as she let the vines creep back away, then pushing the flower into his hair as he grinned. "Phoenyx is impetuous. Hot-headed, like his flames. He is swift to temper and swift to say things he does not mean." Her hands braided the roots of the water lily into his hair, focusing as she spoke. "You are focused, calm like the lake, rational, but like a waterfall, when your emotions are pushed over, you spill uncontrollably, you lash, and together, you and Phoenyx can be dangerous," Alyson chuckled, her eyes on him as she brought her hand down, the flower firmly in his hair as he caught her hand, kissing her palm and smiling.

"...and you are?"

"...I am balance, or so I like to think," Alyson smiled, her hand coming up to touch his shoulder as he smiled softly. "Where you two are fire and water..." Her hand moved from him to her own shoulder, "I am winter. I need you both to live, to be me." she said as she smiled once more. The marks seemed to be scarred into their skin, the same as their elemental marks, marks they were born with, with Phoenyx bearing a matching one as well. "Your water makes my ice... his heat keeps my heart warm." Alyson's eyes were on him as he brought his lips closer, his eyes on her mouth. "We need one another, all three of us. You both need each other, just as I need you both."

"Because without you..."

"You are the light and the dark, without any balance between you to temper you, to keep you where you should be," Alyson said gently, her lips swiftly captured as he moaned, his hands wrapping around her carefully.

"I love you, you are aware of this, right, Alyson?" Benjamin murmured as she nodded.

"I am, yes..."

His eyes flickered, and the floor below them grew less stable, causing her to squeak and wrap her arms around him as she gave him a look. "We won't fall through!" Benjamin chuckled as she swatted at his chest, glancing down at the height that they had climbed up to.

"I certainly hope not, Benjamin, that would be a long fall." Alyson said worriedly as he smirked, then grasped her hips, nudging her to the watery floor as her eyes widened. "You are not serious!"

Gesturing down at his growing hardness, Benjamin simply smirked. "Do I appear to be serious?"

"Benjamin!"

"We won't fall!"

Crawling over her, he nipped at her breasts, his eyes on her as she arched up, her body writhing slightly as she laced her hands in his hair. "Benjamin…" she moaned, her legs opening up as his hand slid between them, one of them causing a stream of water to flow carefully along her slit, putting pressure along her bud as she whimpered. "I love when you do that…"

"I'm well aware," Benjamyn grinned, leaning over her deviously as he brought a taut nipple to his mouth, nibbling gently as she cried out. Her hand went to her mouth to stifle her yells, but he brought his water up to tug her hand back, his eyes glowing brighter as he exuded more control. "I want to hear you, beloved…"

"The whole forest will hear." Alyson moaned, her eyes glancing down as he changed the pattern of his water, the stream between her slit now moving along the bead hidden in her depths in a figure-eight pattern, swirling and pulsing and causing her to kick her legs out. "Ah!"

"I love when I get to hear you…" Benjamin groaned, his hand darting down to grip at himself roughly, stroking himself to relieve some of the pressure. "You sound so damn delicious, Alyson..."

"T-The last time... you or Phoenyx m-made me yell... we couldn't hunt p-properly for days!" Alyson hissed as he chuckled, then moved down where his water was swirling, coaxing it from her entrance as he knelt lower and licked at her folds, her back arching up as her breath caught, his tongue plunging into her and his water still moving on her.

"It was worth going hungry for a few days." Benjamin said, grinning wickedly as he lapped at her, his hands gripping at her thighs as she panted, her hips grinding against him. "Besides, I have all that I need to eat right here." He murmured, his tongue flitting out to trace at her opening as she whimpered, her head falling back as he plunged back in, dragging his tongue along her upper walls, causing her to arch up.

"Ah! Y-You'll make me..." Alyson gasped, her hand darting down as he snorted, nodding.

"I know. I'm rather good at it..." Benjamin smirked, his hand coming up to push into her, two fingers curling upwards as she cried out. "It likely has something to do with my connection to the water, and Phoenyx hates that I can make you do it, and he cannot," Benjamin said cockily as Alyson moaned, leaning back into the water that cushioned them. His fingers pushed into her upper walls as he let the water at her slit drain away, his other hand replacing it and swirling on her gently, putting careful pressure on her.

With a whine, Alyson looked around to glance up at him, watching as he leaned over her, both hands working carefully, with purpose. "I enjoy watching you do this." Benjamin grinned, leaning down to kiss her thigh as she kicked one leg out, her eyes locked on him. His crooked fingers pressed upwards, her eyes growing completely desperate.

"Benjamin…" Alyson whined, watching as he leaned down to bite her nipple hard, his hands moving harder, rougher. "I-I'm almost…"

"Yes, I can tell, my love." he smirked, his teeth grasping her nipple once more before he straightened, pushing his fingers into the swollen mound of flesh along her upper walls. Fluid began leaking from her, causing her to let out cries of pleasure, his fingers on her bud swirling faster. "…good… come on…" Benjamin groaned, his eyes focusing on the fluid beginning to drip from her, his fingers hitting the swollen spot harder, with a frenzied purpose.

"Ah! Beloved!"

Benjamin's eyes locked on her as she arched her back, a stream of clear fluid leaving her folds the moment he pulled his hand out of her. He groaned loudly, his hand moving back down to stroke himself roughly once more, his other hand staying on the bead of flesh he was carefully moving on. Every touch caused her to whimper and shiver, another shudder and jolt of pleasure running through her, another spurt of fluid coming from her.

He brought his hand off of her, causing her to moan from the lack of touch, but a quick wave of his hand made a small flow of water go over her mound, rinsing any of the fluids from her gently as she wriggled, his movements careful. As soon as the water flowed off of her, he was leaning over her, pressing his body onto her hungrily, his eyes all passion.

"Every time I make love to you…" Benjamin murmured, his white, glowing eyes on hers and his face gentle. "I love you even more, if it were possible." he said, nuzzling her neck as she wrapped a leg around his waist, nodding.

"And I you, beloved." Alyson groaned, panting as he reached between them, losing focus for a moment as he aligned himself with her core, and causing the floor they were on to turn into more of a blob. They sank into it somewhat, causing his other arm to wrap around her firmly as she locked her arms around his neck, her eyes getting huge. "Benjamin!"

"Faith, Alyson." he chuckled, his eyes regaining their focus as the staircase they had climbed fully melted away, flowing towards them to prop under them as a base. He gripped her waist, then pushed into her as he let his forehead dip down to hers, her eyes staying on his as she moaned. "Yes, I have you."

His hips pushed into her gently, his pace like a stream that had been flowing for decades, smooth and easy, but with insistence, power.

He filled her to the brim, causing her to gasp and cry out, her arms going around his neck and latching to him, clutching him to her desperately, her insides still sensitive from his ministrations before. Her mouth dropped open, cries leaving her throat as he clung her to him, thrusting forward harder. Gentle kisses brought his mouth to her shoulder blades to nip and bite at her, his eyes closing as he fought to control his pleasure and his focus.

Her head moved to his neck, dropping to the crook of it as he clung her to him, a deep groan leaving his throat. "B-Benjamin." Alyson whined, pressed flush against him as he moved. "I won't last, not after..."

"I don't want you to." Benjamin moaned, nipping at her skin as she panted, feeling him thrust harder, rolling her to be atop him as he held her tightly. "I need you to let go, beloved. Please." he gripped her to him, his skin damp as her wet hair clung to her, her curls defined and corkscrewing against her.

As she whimpered, his hips thrusting harder and faster into her core, she balled her fists against his chest and cried out, her head curling into him. Her body tightened, Benjamin clinging to her desperately, his hips roughly moving as he lost his control, his eyes widening and his mouth opening in a yell of pleasure as he spasmed into her, his back arching and his body curling up into her.

His body tensed and he lost himself, his eyes going from glowing white to sapphire blue, and the solidity of the water they rested on wavered, then lost itself. Both began to drop with the water that they were on without preamble, the both of them letting out shouts of shock as Alyson yelled in surprise. Her eyes widened as the two separated during their freefall. Benjamin's arms went out, one wrapping around Alyson, the other going to steady them and try to regain some control as they fell, but failing miserably, and the two plunged into the center of the lake with a loud, echoing splash, water flying everywhere.

Sudden laughter burst from the shore of the lake, and as the two emerged, all they could hear was the uproarious laughs of, well...

-PHOENYX AND ALYSON-

PHOENYX, WHO HAD COME BACK ABOUT TEN MINUTES prior, and had just chuckled as he had watched the two with amusement, waiting for a moment to join in.

Both whipped their heads around, trying to spot Phoenyx, finally spotting him at the water's edge, kneeling and shaking his head as they pushed their hair out of their faces, sputtering. "Oh, that was fantastic! Well done!" Phoenyx laughed, his eyes mirthful as the two swam over, peering at him as he crossed his arms and grinned at them.

"Phoenyx! When did you get back?!" Alyson asked, her eyes on him as he snorted, one eyebrow quirking.

"About ten minutes ago." Phoenyx smiled, then grinned at Benjamin, who was smirking slightly, his eyes glittering. "You still need to learn proper elemental control, Benjamin," he snickered, pointing at the other male as Benjamin snorted.

"I'd like to see you retain your full control when you're in the midst of orgasm, Phoenyx," Benjamin grinned, leaning forward onto the lake's edge as Phoenyx laughed, shaking his head, then looked over at Alyson, who was blushing slightly. "It's rather difficult."

"Ask Alyson, I do," Phoenyx said, his eyes glittering as Alyson bit her lip slightly. "Instead of playing with your water all the time, making funny shapes with the children in the villages as you do, you should train with it," Phoenyx said pointedly, scolding Benjamin slightly, then winking as he leaned forward, his eyes utterly devious. "Do you feel better, though? I know we've all been a hair high-strung lately, not a moment to ourselves, always on the go." he asked as the two laughed, their faces and upper bodies pleasingly flushed.

"Yes. Much better, actually, it's been over a week since any of us have had time to be with one another." Alyson laughed, stretching and leaning back in the lake, her breasts coming to the surface as Phoenyx smirked, then nodded. "However, if you wish to join us, we always have time for you to come in with us."

Chuckling, Phoenyx just tugged his shirt off as Benjamin dove under the lake, peering at Alyson as her hair spread around her. "Fine, then, but you tell the water sprite there that he's to keep his fountains to himself. I've no interest in flying while fucking." Phoenyx said pointedly, pointing at Benjamin's form as he rose slightly, a grin on his face.

"I heard that," Benjamin said wickedly, his head poking from the water as he peered at Phoenyx, who nodded.

"Good. We're clear then. Last thing I need is a free fall into the lake. Poor Alyson looked terrified." Phoenyx said, tossing his shirt to the side as Alyson nodded, her eyes widening.

"You're no fun," Benjamin pouted, ducking back into the lake as Phoenyx dropped his trousers, diving in with them, then grabbed Alyson, who squeaked, curling into him.

"No. I'm plenty fun, but water is your thing, Benjamin, not mine." Phoenyx said, then bent forward, pecking Alyson on the lips as she smiled, her arms going around his neck. "How are you today, my angel?" he asked as Alyson smiled softly, her hands cupping his face.

"I'm wonderful, how was your trip?" Alyson asked as he grinned, nibbling her neck, then pulling her flush against him before speaking.

"I was able to acquire the alchemy ingredients I was missing, so I can make what the sprite over there was asking me to make," Phoenyx smirked as Benjamin pulled water into his mouth and sprayed it like a jet over at Phoenyx, watching as Phoenyx brought his hand up, his eyes going white and a flame appearing in the center, the jet evaporating in a puff. "Excellent try."

"Hot-head," Benjamin snorted, then went back to swimming, rolling onto his back as Phoenyx rolled his eyes and put his hand up.

"Benjamin, if you don't mind, we're not all interested in seeing your water serpent right now." Phoenyx teased as Benjamin grinned, his eyes glittering deviously.

"Aw, afraid it will bite you?" Benjamin snickered as Phoenyx quirked an eyebrow, then grinned wickedly, leaning forward slightly and wrapping his arms around Alyson as she squeaked.

"No, you water-devil. Afraid it will spit at me instead," Phoenyx said with a grin as Benjamin let out a bark of a laugh.

"Ha!" his voice echoed as he dove under the waters, his body vanishing for a moment as Phoenyx grinned at Alyson, watching as she chuckled at him.

"Child," she said playfully as he nodded, beaming at her.

"And you *adore* me for my childish nature. I make your life fun." Phoenyx grinned, his hands going to her waist and his fingers wriggling as she squealed, her eyes getting huge.

"Phoenyx! No! Oh, you vile man!" Alyson yelped, her feet kicking as they churned the waters, his ashy eyes on her. "Wicked!"

"Well, if that's how you feel about me, maybe I shall keep the meal I've brought along with me," Phoenyx said innocently as Alyson blinked, her eyes widening.

"Meal?"

"Yes. I managed to get a deer on the way home, I brought it for us all to have for supper. But if I'm so wicked, maybe I should keep it." Phoenyx said, his hands wrapping around her waist as she bit her lip, pouting.

"You wouldn't allow me any of your deer?"

"That depends. Am I wicked?"

"Yes," Alyson said pointedly, then smiled, pecking his lips. "But in all the best ways."

"Now, that I can live with," Phoenyx grinned, his hands snaking up her back as Benjamin stretched, popping up from the water again.

"Are you ready to go in yet?" Benjamin asked pointedly as Alyson blinked.

"Hm?"

"I know him, he can't tolerate the water for long, and he's as hard as a damn tree," Benjamin said pointedly as Phoenyx pointed at him.

"You were stealing glances under the water again, Benjamin!"

"I cannot help that my vision under the water is better than yours, hot-head!" Benjamin said, then continued. "We should go in. He won't do anything to remedy that while in the lake," Phoenyx gave him a pointed glare at those words, then blinked as Alyson chuckled.

"It's fine, you know. Let us go inside, get warm by the fire."

"Now that I can agree to."

With a grunt, Phoenyx hauled her into his arms as Alyson let out a squeal, her arms going around his neck. One of Nyx's hands firmly held her to him, his other hand tugging them out of the lake, balancing them as he climbed out. He watched as Benjamin dove under the water, his eyes bright white as he used his elemental abilities to move faster than he should, getting to the edge in seconds and popping out like a sea creature, his eyes glittering mirthfully. Phoenyx simply snorted, shooting him a smirk as he headed for their large hut, leaving their clothes as Alyson clung to him, Benjamin climbing out of the lake after them.

"You could wait for me," Benjamin huffed, his eyes annoyed as Phoenyx grinned.

"I could," he said, shrugging as Alyson bit back a chuckle. "I'm not."

Carting her across the grass and towards the path that led to their hut, they were quickly inside, Phoenyx letting his ashen eyes flare white as he brought his palm up, a blast of flame going from his hand straight into the fireplace. The fireplace roared to life, crackling and popping, and Phoenyx let his ash-grey eyes go back to normal as Alyson smiled, one eyebrow quirking.

"You cannot stand to be damp, can you?" she asked playfully as he blinked, then grinned wickedly, moving her to the furs they had at the base of the fireplace. At the door, Benjamin was finally coming in behind them, closing up and grabbing a few things as Phoenyx, his eyes devious, leaned atop her, watching as she wriggled into the bear fur.

"I cannot stand to have my skin damp from swimming, no," Phoenyx said, his eyes latched onto hers as she panted. "I enjoy getting wet…" he purred at her, bringing his mouth to her breast as she whimpered, writhing on the fur. "…but only when I am in you," he smirked, glancing up at her as she rocked her hips slightly, swallowing heavily. Her eyes locked on his marking for a moment, a triangle pointing upwards on his right shoulder, and she let out a small groan.

"Phoenyx…"

"He had time with you…" Phoenyx said, growling slightly as Benjamin snorted, coming over and kneeling beside them, his eyes latched to her. "He can have you again when I've had my fill, satiate his needs then," Phoenyx hissed, glancing over at the blue-eyed man, his own ashen-eyes glinting. "…take care of yourself until then."

"You do not tell me what to do, hot-head," Benjamin snapped, moving close enough so that Alyson could get her hand to his hardness, which she quickly did, wrapping her hand around it and stroking him as the two stared one another down. "I do not stand in your way, but you do not tell me what I am allowed to do."

"Do not bicker," Alyson muttered, her eyes on them as they glanced down at her. "I enjoy our time so much more when we're all in harmony, not when you're fighting one another." she murmured, her one hand dipping between them to slip into her folds as she moaned. "Play nicely, both of you," she panted, her fingers moving into her entrance as her hips rocked, the two men exchanging glances, then nodding, coming to an agreement.

"As you wish," Phoenyx said, his hand coming down to grasp at the hand at her entrance, tugging it up as she whined, her eyes widening. "Oh, we plan to play nice, but that does not mean we plan to let you do whatever you want." He grinned as he tugged one of her fingers to his mouth, sucking it clean as she panted, getting a groan out of him. "Mmm, Benjamin, care for a taste? She left us with some dessert." Phoenyx smirked as Benjamin nodded, letting him bring her other finger to his mouth so that he could pull it into his mouth, sucking it clean and moaning quietly.

"That she did. I had a taste earlier. If you'd like to make a meal out of her, she's rather sensitive today," Benjamin said casually, his hands snaking down her sides as she moaned, her back arching as Phoenyx nodded, his hands spreading her thighs.

"I think I would, but you should keep her occupied as well." Phoenyx muttered, his hands sliding up to her stomach, then down over her mound as she cried out.

"You are teasing me!" Alyson moaned, thrashing slightly as the two exchanged a knowing smirk, then got innocent looks on their faces.

"Us? Never!" Phoenyx said, his eyes widening as Benjamin's hands came down to her wrists, pinning her down. He leaned over, his mouth biting at her breasts carefully as he glanced up at Phoenyx, watching as the other male finally scooted down, nipping at her thighs before letting his mouth go to her bud. Her back arched up completely as her eyes widened. Dragging his teeth along the bead of flesh, he growled slightly, his eyes narrowing slightly as she wriggled her hips. "You *are* sensitive today," Phoenyx said, his voice huskier as Alyson moaned, her head hidden under Benjamin's frame. Benjamin's hands released her wrists, moving along her torso to stroke her stomach and the undersides of her breasts as she let out a loud cry.

"She is," Benjamin groaned, feeling as Alyson began moving around below him. "What are you up to down there?" he muttered, glancing down as her hand grasped his hardness, stroking him once or twice, then, her head tipping back, slipping him into her mouth as he bit back a loud moan, his eyes going white. Time slowed around him for a moment, his hand stroking her breasts, his hips thrusting into the softness of her mouth, and both causing her to whine, because when he caused his time to slow, those around him felt as though he was moving faster, as though he was in more places at once. His hand felt like multiple hands, grasping and stroking her breast, all at once, for a mere moment, and his hardness, in her mouth, moved roughly and fast, so fast that she could barely comprehend it. It was a delicious sensory overload, causing her to dampen further, a rush of juices flowing from her around Phoenyx's mouth as he snorted.

"Did you lose control of your chronal ability again, water sprite?" Phoenyx asked, glancing at Benjamin as the man moaned, his eyes a bright white. "You did. Alyson, beloved... You cannot simply pull him into your mouth without warning like that, you know that the emotional one here cannot handle it." he teased, his mouth moving back to sucking at her as she moaned, feeling Benjamin thrusting into her mouth, her back arching once more.

Phoenyx, shaking his head, nudged himself up and positioned himself at her entrance, his eyes locked on the two moving in front of him as he pushed into her. Alyson, her body already beyond primed, kicked a leg out and moaned around the hardness in her throat, feeling hands latch into her hair as Benjamin's eyes grew wide with need, his thrusts increasing, then stopping as she gasped out. He backed up, his eyes wide as he cupped her face, his mouth moving to hers as he glanced up at Phoenyx, his hands moving to hers to pin her hands, a grin on his face.

"Let him take you away, beloved." Benjamin grinned, his eyes glittering as she moaned loudly, Phoenyx thrusting roughly into her core, his body straight above her as he watched her. "Allow him to make you lose yourself." he said, kissing her neck. Phoenyx, his hands gripping her hips, thrust forward roughly, his eyes hungry.

"Tell me that you are mine," Phoenyx growled, his hands moving down to grip at her hardened nipples, his thrusts coming rougher and faster as her head tipped back, her eyes wide. His one hand moved up and grasped her chin, forcing her eyes to his as she moaned. "Tell me, Alyson!"

"I am yours..." she moaned, her muscles tightening on her body as Phoenyx grasped her lower half tightly, curling around her and using the closeness to increase the speed of his thrusts, his eyes going white as he allowed his body's temperature to rise slightly, her eyes getting huge as she thrashed in their grasps. His hardness, warming with the rest of him, caused her core to get deliciously hot, not a burning heat, no, her Phoenyx could control his heat, his inner flame, he could keep her from being burned.

Phoenyx gave her a groan, then pulled her hips to his fast, his mouth seeking hers as Benjamin moved out of his way, still pinning her wrists. His mouth pushed insistently on hers, his hips roughly slamming into her as he brought his head down to her neck, panting. "Come for me, my love." Phoenyx moaned, his body sweat-soaked as she arched up, her lower half tense and tight. She felt him reach between them, his fingers warm, and he brushed against her bud.

Jerking upwards, her body lost control as she spasmed, her eyes wide. Benjamin's hands held her tightly as Phoenyx moaned, his mouth moving to swallow her cries, his hips pumping in her harder, his face losing the control he had been keeping, his breathing growing rapid. Her core was filled with heat, intense heat, as it always did when Phoenix filled her and spilled himself in her, his seed always hot like his flames.

Without missing a beat, Phoenyx's mouth stayed on her, but he slid out of her, moaning from the lack of sensation, and his warm hands took the spot of Benjamin's. The coolness of Benjamin's hardness, a distinct difference over Phoenyx, pushed into her, causing her to gasp out and buck from the sensory change, her eyes wide as Benjamin moaned, kissing her neck and panting, his hips thrusting at a steady but strong pace.

Phoenyx, his head resting next to hers, simply nuzzled her quietly, his eyes darting up to Benjamin before speaking. "Come on, my love, we know how you are, and once is never enough for you." Phoenyx said with a smirk, his eyes on her as she writhed, her body's senses on overdrive. Benjamin's eyes glowed as he brought a small orb of water to her slit, causing it to pulse over her bud and making her cry out loudly, her hands pulling at Phoenyx as he grinned, his eyes wide. "You're driving her insane, Benjamin."

"P-Please!" Alyson moaned, her hips wriggling as Benjamin moved, his hips thrusting at their firm pace. "D-Do not stop!"

"That's our beautiful angel." Phoenyx moaned, his mouth dipping around her to nip at her nipple as she arched up once more before returning to his spot. "More, Benjamin, make her come again."

Benjamin simply groaned, then grasped her hips, the orb of liquid at her hips steadily pulsing as his hips thrust forward hard. "You may be his, but you are also mine," Benjamin said quietly, his hand coming down beside her head as he pushed his mouth to hers. "I want to hear that come from your lips, Alyson. You are mine."

"I... I am yours, Benjamin." Alyson moaned, her eyes closing as he moved, his eyes rolling back slightly as she spoke.

"You're ours. We love you." Phoenyx said carefully, his hands carefully stroking her wrists as Benjamin nodded, his forehead coming to hers.

"He is right. You are not only mine, you are his. You are ours," Benjamin moaned, his thrusts growing more rapid as Phoenyx pushed his head onto the side of Alyson's head, hearing the two pant. "We are yours."

"Forever yours," Phoenyx said, his eyes on her as she moaned, watching as Benjamin let out a deep groan, then stiffened, his body thrusting into her roughly as the orb that rested between her folds added more pressure, and that, combined with Benjamin's movements, their words, their actions... Alyson saw white, her body exploding as her eyes began glowing. Her body rose, beginning to levitate, the two chuckling as the reasoning for their pinning her became clear, because once she truly lost control of herself, she would not be able to control herself.

Her insides pulsed, her body merged down to the soul to her two lovers, and she left the ground completely.

Alyson's eyes squeezed shut as she screamed out, the intensity of the climax causing her to send a few things in the hut flying, the two bursting into laughter.

"Alyson! Again!"

"There goes your glass bottles, Phoenyx. I suppose you need a new set."

"That set was new…"

Her whole body quaked, and so did the earth itself, the two simply stroking her skin as she floated in the air, letting her ride out the orgasm, Benjamin having risen to his knees to accommodate her. Things began to shake from their shelves, tumbling to the floor.

"Alyson."

"Beloved."

She opened her eyes…

And flumped to the bed, the brightness of the apartment overwhelming her senses.

CHAPTER 7

Surrender all your dreams to me...

-ALYSON-

ALYSON'S EYES, GLOWING A VIBRANT WHITE, opened wide as she fell hard onto her bed, her arms going up and her body going limp. The icy chill in the air had her breath coming out in a puff of steam, a faint sheen of frost on the walls. She flung herself about on the bed, tangling up in the sheets and comforter as she yelped, a few trinkets hitting the ground with a clattering noise, including one that made the sound of bells. "Oh!" she cried out, kicking the sheets off of her as she sat up, her curls all around her and her body pleasantly relaxed. "Oh... fuck."

She let a hand go through her hair, the purple tunic shirt of her pajama set bunched up on her, and the bottoms... She blinked, then glanced down, between her legs, and realized that she had literally dampened through her clothing and sheets. Her pajama shorts and panties were soaked through, and her sheets... those weren't much better.

Pulling her pillow over her face, she let out a small, frustrated scream and flopped back down, kicking at the mattress in annoyance, then huffily pulled the pillow away, her eyes knotted together as she groaned up at the ceiling. "I have to do laundry now." she whined, kicking her legs on the bed in frustration, her hands coming up to her forehead to ball up into her hair. "I don't want to do laundry."

Staring up at the ceiling of the bedroom with a resigned frown on her face, she allowed herself a moment of reflection. The dream had been utterly mind-blowing, to say the least. Benjamin and Phoenyx... Both of them, treating her like she was a temple to be cherished. She could still feel the orgasms from the dream, and small shudders went through her with each memory. The lake, the water... Thinking about that, though... caused her to gasp, wriggling around as she touched the sheets. "Oh! That's... that's not all... Did I actually do that in my sleep?!" Ali squeaked, touching at the cooling dampness as she bit her lip, remembering the sensation of fingers in her, coaxing the liquid that had pooled in her to jettison out.

She flushed again, then growled at herself. "Stop that," she admonished herself, then huffed a bit, allowing herself another moment, Nyx... no, Benjamin was still technically Benjamin, but he seemed to pronounce it differently, Benjamin, but Nyx, he was Phoenyx. He had joined them, and once he had, things had gone... Mmm. "They seemed to fight, but then got along, and then... Oh God, my legs shook." Ali moaned, biting her lip as she brought a hand down and grazed at her soaked mound, then sighed. "Ugh. All this over two men I didn't even know a couple of days ago." she groused, then turned, looking around for her alarm clock to check the time, noting it wasn't on her table. Her eyes searched through she scattered items, coming to rest on the clock across the room. She let out a yell of shock, sitting bolt upright as she saw the time on it. "Oh! Fuck! 6:25?! Crap, I'll never make it over in time! I'll be so late!" Ali moaned, her eyes widening as she whipped out of the bed, glancing at the soaked sheets. "I have to throw these in the wash before I leave and throw on clean sheets. I'll never get there in time!"

Her head whipped around, then she bolted to the phone, still in the wet clothes, then rushed into the kitchen and went into the counter, digging around and hauling out a phone book. Flipping through the pages, she begged to the deities, then let out a yelp of glee. "There! Hancott!" Ali squealed, her eyes widening as she grasped the phone and dialed, praying...

On the other side of the line, Benjamin was simply having a cup of coffee, ready to leave, and listening to Phoenyx whine about having to be up so early when their phone rang. His eyebrow quirking, he moved to the kitchen and picked it up, frowning slightly. "Hello?"

"B-Benjamin?!" Ali's voice on the other end was relieved as he blinked, then chuckled, leaning onto the counter.

"Alyson, what a lovely early morning surprise! But I thought I said to come over, not call." Ben smiled, his eyes glittering as Nyx leaned around the corner, a towel around his waist and his eyes wide.

"Is that Alyson?! Tell her I said good morning!"

"Phoenyx said to tell you good morning," Benjamin snorted, his head shaking as Ali's voice got louder.

"G-Good morning to him too, but... I-I'm running extremely late!" Ali squeaked. "I woke up after the strangest dream, a complete mess, and my alarm clock was clean across the room! I must have hit it in my sleep! I set it to go off at 5:30, but I just woke up!" Ali moaned as he chuckled. "Benjamin, I'm sorry!"

"It's fine. Would you like us to come over?"

She got quiet, then took a breath. "Y-Yes! I can make a kettle of tea, or coffee! And then we can get breakfast! I have enough time to tidy up. It's presentable but not the nicest."

"We're unexpected company, it's perfectly alright for it to not be perfect," Ben laughed, then pointed to Nyx. "Phoenyx! Get dressed! We're heading to Alyson's! She's running late, so instead of her meeting us, we're meeting her!" Ben said as Nyx nodded, his eyes widening. With a small salute, he threw his towel over his shoulder and headed around the corner from the shared bathroom, causing Benjamin to groan and block his eyes. "Well, that was something I didn't need to see."

"Hm?" Ali asked, causing Ben to chuckle.

"Just Nyx's trouser devil hanging in the breeze while he walks from the bathroom to his room," Ben snickered as Nyx whipped his head around the corner, his eyes wide.

"Hey!"

"She asked."

Ali's voice broke into giggles, and she just let out a small, giddy sigh. "I'll see you soon. Just come up. Fourth floor, apartment B."

"I remember. We'll watch out for the pipe." Ben said, then smiled. "See you soon." He grinned, hanging up as Nyx blinked at him. "Don't just stare at me, you naked fool, go dress!"

Ali, in her apartment, was now bolting towards her own bathroom, kicking off her wet clothes and squeaking as she skidded towards her shower, starting the water to get it going. As soon as she had that started, she picked up the laundry, tugging her shirt off with it and chucking it all into the hamper, then pulled off her sheets and comforter with it, shoving it all into the hamper and growling as she pushed it all to the laundry area to do later.

Back to the bathroom, she rushed for the shower, quickly getting into the warm spray and grasping for her shampoo, her head going under the water. Lathering and rinsing took no time, but conditioning her wavy curls took longer. Wrapping them around the top of her head, she grabbed her scrub brush and began lathering herself, her eyes up as she bit her lip, firmly scrubbing off the areas that had gotten damp in her sleep. "Last thing I need is a rash. That'll make dancing in class today just that much more fun," she muttered, rolling her eyes. Setting the lathered brush down, she grasped her safety razor and some shave cream, then set to work, one leg and thigh, then the other, then both armpits. A dancer needed to stay sleek. A bit of foam over her mound while performing the five basic ballet positions without falling or cutting herself, and what little growth had appeared over the last few days was gone, leaving her completely smooth again. She had to wear her tights and leotard today, and she couldn't get away with peach fuzz while wearing that.

She let her eyes drift closed, one hand trailing through her now-smooth folds as the memories of the dream overtook her once more. She could feel their hands going down over her skin, smell their scent over the scent of her own flowery shampoo. Her mouth opened slightly as she panted, her fingers finding her pearl and carefully swirling on it. Their hands had pinned her, causing her to give in to their movements and motions. She had thought she'd hate someone holding her down, but this had been explosive.

Her hand moved faster, her mind drifting. It was like the scene she'd seen was moving past what she had watched earlier, into territory that was untested but familiar in some way. She could see them in front of her, both watching her while they moved in front of her. One tugging her face closer, her nose brushing against the rough hair below his navel, and the other stroking himself firmly as he watched, smooth black hair falling in front of ocean blue eyes. She could almost taste him, pushing needily into her mouth and dribbling pre-cum onto her tongue. Her fingers were moving faster, slipping down further to push greedily into herself a few times before moving back to swirl on the sensitive bead of flesh. She whined quietly, seeing one grasp her hair firmly as he moved, his curls covering his ashy eyes as he focused on her mouth, her heat, praising her and telling her how good of a fuck she was being for him.

She let out another whimper before roughly sliding her fingers onto her wet skin. Her hips jerked forward with each thought that went through her mind, causing her to let out little cries of pleasure as the heat from the shower combined with the heat in her inner core.

'Good job, my angel. I wanna cum down your throat, can you make me do that? That's my good girl...'

Phoenyx's voice was in the back of her head, purring sweet nothings and praise into her head as she let out a hoarse cry. White flashed behind her eyes, her fingers roughly moving to shove back into herself as she let her hips move with each orgasmic contraction. On the windowsill, ice curled and made beautiful patterns on the glass of the window, as though a faerie were skating along the surface. As her pleasure had grown, so had the frost, culminating in an explosion of snowy beauty that left the window looking like winter had come early, which was quickly melted by the heat of the shower before she had noticed.

She opened her eyes as the water began to cool, looking at the ceiling and bringing her hand up gently from between her thighs. Streaks of creamy white were going down her fingers, and she bit back a moan as she heard Nyx's voice in the back of her head.

'You left me a treat, it's only right that I share. Lick them clean, my angel.'

Her fingers went up to her mouth, touching it tentatively. Her lips parted, and with a small groan she slipped the digits between them and sucked them clean, getting another aftershock of pleasure as a reward for her good behavior. With a moan, she pulled her fingers from between her lips before leaning back and rinsing her curls, sighing as the heat went through her scalp. Her hands ran through her hair, working the conditioner out of her hair, loosening the hair product and getting her head clean before washing her face. Turning off the water, she grasped a towel and dried off, beginning to move to the bedroom again. Her hands grabbed a second towel and wrapped her curls up as she moved towards her dresser to get fresh clothes.

Rifling through her drawer, she found tights and a black leotard, tugging them both carefully on, as well as a pair of cloth black ballet slippers that she wore when around the house in her leotards. She rolled her hair up around her head into a loose bun, pulling it up in the back of her head with a hair comb, a small moon dangling off the back of the silver comb. Moving to her spare linens, she grabbed sheets and an extra comforter, the sheets a light purple and the comforter white with a pattern of lavender growing along the hemline, and made her bed quickly, then rushed to make some coffee.

As soon as she set about getting the coffeepot going, there was a knock at the door.

Biting her lip, she moved to the door and cracked it open, then smiled. "Ben. Nyx."

The two both waved, then one blinked at her, his eyes widening as he took in her appearance. "You look gorgeous," Nyx muttered, his eyes wide as she tilted her head to the side, then stepped back and let them in through the apartment doors as Ben chuckled, taking off his hat and tan coat.

"It's just a leotard and a pair of tights," Ben snorted, shaking his head as Nyx glanced over at him, removing his black leather coat, then swallowed, his eyes on her figure. Both men were dashing in their own way, Ben in his khaki slacks and pressed button-down shirt, and Nyx in his blue jeans and his black t-shirt. "Normal ballet wear. I assume your classes today are physical?"

"Yes." Ali smiled, shutting the door as both men hung up their coats. "The table is right there, ignore the hamper over there, I have laundry I have to do later." She frowned as they nodded. "I was just getting coffee going," she said as Ben smiled, moving to sit. Nyx, however, was staring her up and down.

"Phoenyx, sit." Ben laughed, shaking his head as Nyx stared outright.

"You... do you shave? You know, down there?" Nyx mumbled, his eyes on her lower regions as she blinked, then flushed, nodding.

"Nyx!" Ben spluttered, his eyes widening. "Sit down!"

"I just noticed!"

"Idiot!"

"It's ok! At least he asked up front!" Ali chuckled, shaking her head slightly as she grabbed some coffee mugs, Phoenyx moving to take a seat next to Benjamin at the table. "I do. A lot of dancers do. Otherwise, our pubic hair would poke through our leotards and tights, which would not only be annoying, but male dancers that work with us would be annoyed with it, and could snag them, which would be an 'ow' moment," Ali said as Nyx winced, a hand going down to rub slightly as Ben laughed outright.

"Ouch." Nyx said, his eyes wide. "You say that as though you've had it happen."

"I have." Ali said, her eyes neutral. "You think that hurts? Try eating a balance beam." she shrugged as Phoenyx's eyes widened. "Balance is important in ballet, so I took some gymnast classes. I can do flips now, but I slipped and caught myself between the legs numerous times," Her words had Nyx's hands grasping between his legs, his eyes wide.

"Screw that." Nyx muttered, staring aghast as Ben laughed, his hand over his eyes.

"Oh, that's fantastic," Benjamin cackled, grinning as Nyx whipped his head over to him. "That said, before she even gives you a cup... Don't you have something to say?" Ben asked, giving him a pointed look as Nyx sighed, then nodded.

"I'm sorry, Alyson," Nyx said quietly, his eyes going to hers as she blinked, then looked over at him, setting down the coffee mugs. "I let myself get jealous the other night when I knew that you had a date with Ben, and I didn't mean a word of what I said." he sighed. "I just came home, and saw what I had been fucking craving since our lunch together."

Ali, her eyes knotting together, brought the mugs to the table, then handed them out as she looked down. "Phoenyx..." she muttered, her hands grasping one mug, her fingers tapping the rim of it. "I'm sorry if you think l-less of me... now." she said quietly as he sat bolt upright, his eyes wide. Benjamin pointed at him, giving him a look that screamed 'I told you so'.

"Hell no! Of course not! You aren't engaged, and you're not in a committed relationship with myself or anyone else! You're free to explore your options, Alyson!" Nyx said, his eyes wide as she bit her lip and gave him a skeptical look.

"You're sure?"

"Yes." Nyx said, his eyes firm. "Look, sit." he glanced at Ben, then gestured to the kitchen. "Ben, would you..."

"Coffee, right." Ben said, moving to get the coffee as Ali sat, her eyes getting wide. "Let him talk. We talked on the way over, and I think this idea of his might work."

Nyx nodded, his ashen eyes glittering. "Look. Benjamin and I both want you in every way that we can have you, and if we're reading you right, you have the same desire for us, right?" Nyx asked as she went red, her eyes going slightly wide as he smiled. "It's alright to be attracted to and interested in us both!" he chuckled.

Benjamin grasped the coffeepot, bringing it over carefully and setting it down, then moved to the refrigerator and grabbed some cream and a bowl of sugar cubes, bringing those over as well before sitting back down.

"You'll think I'm a tramp." Ali muttered quietly, picking at her nails as Nyx shook his head, grabbing her hand and making her look at him.

"We won't. We want to know you better, and this is how we both can." Nyx said, grinning.

"He's right. I want to know more about you, just as he does. I want to take you places, spoil you as much as you'll allow me to, and he wants to spoil you as much as he can. We want you to come to the flat, spend time with us alone and time with us together." Ben said as she went reddish, her eyes widening as thoughts of last night's dream hit her mind.

'He did not mean like that!' she scolded herself, her eyes widening as she peered between the two.

"On the outside, we'll appear as your close friends... maybe the people at the 'Cat will figure out there's more going on, maybe we choose to tell them about our arrangement," Nyx said, shrugging as she nodded carefully. "...but to everyone else, when all three of us are together, we limit our public displays of affection, unless we go somewhere that one person has taken the other often, like Ronnie's." Nyx said with a wink as she beamed. Ben gagged as soon as Nyx gave the name of the restaurant, his eyes wide.

"You took her to that grease pit?!" Ben asked, his face going green as Nyx burst into laughter, nodding and grinning at Ben, who shuddered in disgust. "She's a ballerina! She can't eat all that crap!"

"Hey! I'll have you know the chili and hot dogs were good!" Ali said indignantly, her arms crossing as Nyx smirked, grinning wickedly at Benjamin, who stared in shock. "I also love pizza, ribs, and pie! Ice cream is amazing, and Chinese takeout is to die for!" She stuck her tongue out as Benjamin's eyes widened, and Phoenyx snickered deviously.

"Not all ballerinas eat salad and drink water, Benjamin," Nyx grinned as Ben stared.

"Apparently not," Ben said, his eyes wide. "I guess we'll be doing a lot of ordering in then," he shook his head slightly as Ali smiled, then moved forward, pouring coffee for them all. "Anyhow, that's our idea. Date us both. Get to know us both," Benjamin watched her as she finished pouring, then looked up at him, her face worried.

"What if I fall for you both?" she asked as the two exchanged a look, then shrugged slightly.

"We cross that bridge later," Phoenyx kept his eyes on hers, drawing her in. "You don't have to choose now. We won't put any pressure on you. You don't choose until you're ready, whenever that may be," Nyx said as she glanced into her cup. Ben, smiling, leaned forward and began plopping a few sugar cubes into the cup as she blinked, then he grinned.

"I remember from yesterday," he smiled. "We won't pressure you, Alyson. You can make your own decisions at your own pace," Ben said, nodding as Ali sighed. "If this situation isn't what you want, then we can forget the whole thing, but I really think it's a way for us all to get what we would like from one another."

Ali bit her lip, then glanced between them. "I'm not a nun," she said, her face firm as they both snorted, each one having fixed their coffees to their liking and in the process of taking a sip. "If the same situation happens as last night, or more?"

"I won't be blindsided." Nyx nodded and smiled. "I really, honestly thought you and this rich bastard..." he glanced affectionately over at Ben as the other man chuckled. "...had nothing in common." he said, smiling again. "I thought you would tell him off and go home, not go home with this stupid shit."

"Screw you," Ben snorted, glancing over at Nyx as he smirked over at Ben.

"You aren't my type, rich boy."

Ali laughed, her eyes lighting up as she watched the two, then she nodded as Ben spoke. "If I walk in on you and Phoenyx, I swear that I won't have that reaction." Benjamin said, his eyes glittering as Ali sighed, looking over at her windows. "Honestly, we want that kind of relationship with you." Ben said, his eyes on her as she bit her lip, then let out a huff of a laugh.

"I'm sure you do," she glanced over at Ben as he snorted. "If last night was any indicator." Ali said, grinning slightly, then looking up. "Alright. We can try this. I'll date you both, and see where it goes," She took a deep breath as they nodded.

"Fantastic," Ben grinned, sipping his coffee as Nyx smirked, then glanced around the apartment. He noted the hamper full of sheets and things, the scattered things on the floor, then glanced at Ali.

"Alyson, why were you so late in getting up, if you don't mind me asking?" Nyx asked curiously, and Ali groaned, her head tipping back as she sighed.

"Ugh! I'm so sorry about that! My alarm clock didn't go off, I found it halfway across the damn room, and I woke up a mess." Ali groaned, then pointed to the hamper and its overflowing laundry. "Well, I had to do laundry, which I still haven't done, that was next on my list of things to rush to do. I had this dream, you see, and it, well, it completely ruined my sheets, to be blunt, and my pajamas!" she said, groaning as the two men blinked, then flushed slightly at the implied visual. "So, I had to run around like mad just to get ready, and I didn't have the time I needed to make it to your place on time." Ali explained, sipping her coffee carefully as she sighed, a small smile creeping onto her face.

"Was it a dream about us?" Nyx asked, his eyes devious as he grinned at her. Benjamin, shaking his head, just snorted and shoved his arm.

"Nyx, that's not nice!"

"I'm only teasing, Ben! A dream where she ruined her sheets? I'd be honored if it were about us." Nyx chuckled, then glanced over at Ali, who had stiffened and was scarlet now behind her coffee cup, her eyes wide as she blew small bubbles into her coffee. "Alyson?"

"Nyx, I think you may have embarrassed the poor girl," Ben's eyes widened as she tugged the mug closer to her lips, squeaking loudly. "He was only teasing!" He leaned forward to try and look into her eyes as she went redder, her eyes huge. "Phoenyx, look what you did!"

"I didn't do anything!"

"...how the fuck..." she muttered, her eyes wide as she peered between them, then shook her head. "...lucky guess..."

Nyx's eyes widened, then he stared at Ali, who was groaning and squirming, her mind gone. "...I think it was about us," Nyx flushed slightly as Ben straightened, then glanced at Ali, who was blowing more bubbles into her coffee, her face a healthy shade of burgundy. "And I think I sent her into dreamland," Nyx said, bringing his hand down and snapping his fingers a few times as she jumped, a loud squeal coming from her as she peeked over her cup. "Alyson! Hello! We're still here! You can go back to sleep-fucking us later," Nyx grinned wickedly as she nearly dropped the mug in shock, her eyes wide. Benjamin, chuckling, smacked the back of his head, his hands going out to steady her cup.

"Ignore him," Ben snorted, shaking his head. "Dreams are dreams." Ben grinned, his eyes glinting as she bit her lip. "...and no, I won't ask you to share. Your dreams are your own. Though it must have been rather pleasant, to cause you to need new sheets, a new comforter, and to drift off mid-conversation like that," he chuckled as she bit her lip, then nodded.

"...it was," she said quietly, then frowned. "...and it was a bit frightening. Parts were, anyhow. I held... immense power... that I didn't know I had. I don't know." Ali admitted, her eyes wide as they gave her thoughtful looks. "Is that odd?"

"I don't think so," Nyx said, shrugging. "I dreamt I was a dog once."

"That's because you roll in shit daily," Ben snorted, then smiled at Ali, ignoring Nyx's finger going up into his face.

"Alyson, dreams do have meaning, but that's to the person that dreams them. Maybe yours are telling you that you have power that you aren't aware of, that you need to take the reins of your life and not allow those who have hindered you to continue to do so." he said as she got a thoughtful look on her face, her mug coming up to her lips to sip at her drink.

"...and maybe the rest is telling you that you're really horny and want to go have a good fuck with one or both of us," Phoenyx smirked wickedly, leaning forward and grinning at her as she coughed, Ben's hands coming out to grasp the mug as he whipped his head over to Nyx.

"Phoenyx!"

"Dreams have meaning. You're telling me that a dream about getting fucked doesn't mean she wouldn't like to be fucked?" Nyx grinned as Ali let Benjamin take the mug away, her hand fanning her face as she peered over at them. "Well?"

"So, what if you're right?" Ali asked, her eyes on him as Nyx blinked, then straightened. She narrowed her eyes, then leaned forward across the table, her arms in her leotard pushing her breasts up, and he noted that she wore nothing under the thing. Just the leotard and tights. He gulped, his eyes widening. "If I offered right now, what would you do?"

"Now?" Nyx asked, glancing around as Ben snorted and leaned back, setting her cup aside and observing the two interestedly as Ali nodded.

"Yes. Right now. Let's fuck right now, on this table, or on the bed. Benjamin could watch." she said, her eyes on Nyx as he stared with his jaw dropped, then stuttered, stumbling through words for a moment. "You could give me a good, hard going over, since you seem to think that's what I'd like so much, tug my leotard to the side, I'm nude under here after all, with the exception of these tights, and to be honest, screw the tights, rip them for all I care, drop your jeans, and fuck me, right here." she said, her finger going between her teeth to gnaw on it slightly as he flushed, his eyes wide, and after a moment of his silence, she nodded, her face unsurprised. "Just what I thought. You don't have the balls. So don't offer what you do not plan to give." Ali huffed as she straightened. "Now, if I'm not getting laid, can I get fed? I'm hungry. I would really like pancakes, would that be alright?" she asked as Ben burst into laughter, his eyes wide as he nodded.

"Absolutely! Get your school things!" he said, grinning as she moved about her apartment and watching as Nyx stared, flabbergasted, his trousers tenting out firmly. Ben, snickering, pointed down, and Nyx's eyes widened as he began adjusting himself, shock on his face.

"I've never had a girl talk to me like that..." Phoenyx murmured, peering at Ali as she grabbed actual shoes and a skirt, tugging them on to make her ballet clothing look like real clothing.

"You see why we ended up in the flat now?" Ben grinned, shaking his head as Nyx nodded.

"Yeah."

Benjamin grinned, his eyes on Ali as she grabbed a bag and began putting other things in it for later, throwing a shawl over her shoulders. "Oh, and Nyx?"

"Yes?"

"I'd have taken her up on the offer and fucked her stupid right here on this table in front of you," Ben said casually as Nyx's head whipped over, his eyes getting wide.

"What?!"

"Next time, don't look a gift horse in the mouth."

After the three finish up around Ali's apartment, which took a hair longer than expected with the two men making mild jokes here and there about her laundry and her making them start it since they thought it was so amusing, they headed around the corner to a local eatery to get a late breakfast, all three curling around a round table in a corner so that they all had equal access to one another, the boys each quietly bringing their hands down to stroke hers as she bit her lip and blushed, chuckling.

"Do you really think this idea will work?" she asked as Phoenyx grinned, nodding and tucking a curl behind her ear.

"I hope so. You're too pretty to let slip through my fingers just because you want to know him too." Nyx said, his eyes on her as she chuckled, her fingertips grazing his carefully as the waitress came up.

"Hey, folks! What can I get'cha?" she asked as Ben peered at the small menu, his eyes curious.

"Do you have any poached eggs? Eggs benedict?" he asked hopefully as she gave him a curious look.

"Sorry, handsome, our cook's only got the time to do the basics, fried or scrambled, pancakes and waffles." she said as he sighed and sat back, thinking for a moment while Nyx snickered.

"Two fried eggs, over easy. I like them runny." Nyx grinned as the woman beamed and nodded. "Two sausage links with them, a cup of coffee, and some toast to soak up the yolks." Nyx said as Ben wrinkled up his nose.

"You're revolting sometimes," he said as Nyx snickered.

"You do it!"

"With a biscuit, not toast. Toast is disgusting. Who the hell wants to eat burnt bread." Benjamin muttered as Ali chuckled, then looked over at her.

"Do you have any fruit?" she asked as the woman nodded.

"Strawberries and cantaloupe."

"Can I have a bowl of those, lightly sugared, two pancakes, syrup on the side, butter, and three bacon strips?" she asked as the woman grinned and nodded. "...and a cup of Earl Grey breakfast tea?"

"Oh, I don't know if we have anything that specific, honey. Would you settle for whatever black tea we have?" she asked as Ali nodded, smiling.

"Yes. I'm sorry, I'm used to picking my teas when I order," she said sheepishly as Ben beamed at her.

"I love tea!" he grinned as Ali blinked, then smiled.

"Lavender and hibiscus tea is delicious, have you tried it?" she asked as Ben stared, then shook his head, his eyes widening.

"No, but if you have some, can I borrow a bit to try?" Ben asked, his eyes hopeful.

"Oh, of course!"

"Ahem!" Nyx interrupted, shaking his head as the waitress chuckled. "Benjamin! As adorable as this is... you need to order!" he chuckled, watching as Ben went reddish and nodded, his eyes widening.

"Right! My apologies! Er, I suppose... Do you serve biscuits?" he asked hopefully as the woman shook her head apologetically again.

"Toast only, honey."

"Scrambled." Ben said, sighing as he nodded. "Two scrambled, three strips of bacon, and a bowl of fruit please, with a cup of tea?" he placed his order as the woman nodded, quickly writing the requested items down.

"You got it! It'll be out in a jiffy!" she said, leaving them be as the three went back to their hand stroking, their eyes on one another. Nyx smiled, watching as Ali's fingers against his hand tapped to the music playing, and he chuckled.

"I've got a question for you, Ali," he smiled, glancing over to Ben with a small wink. "...what's your opinion on rock music?"

Ali blinked, looking at him thoughtfully. "That's a random question."

"I promise it's not." Nyx smirked.

"Well, I enjoy it. I actually happen to be a big fan of Heart, Fleetwood Mac, Metallica, and AC/DC, among other groups," she said, her eyebrow quirking as Nyx's smile grew. "What?"

"So, in about two weeks or so, there's going to be a concert at the Black Cat. Ben and I, we play in a small band. Nothing really serious, a lot of covers of popular songs, you know? But we like doing it. Would you want to come?" Nyx asked, watching as what he was doing dawned on Ben.

"Hey, that's right! I'd forgotten we were doing that!"

"That's ok, you're allowed to have moments where the rocks outside think more than you."

"Screw you!" Ben laughed, then looked over to Ali, who was starting to nibble at her finger interestedly. "He's right though. I know we said we'd play it safer, but I think us going to this would be fun. It's on Halloween night, so we're going to dress up for the concert."

"What's your band's name?" Ali asked curiously.

"Strange Magic." Nyx nodded, leaning forward as her smile grew.

"I like that. Yeah, I'd love to go! Do you two want to coordinate our costumes?"

"Absolutely. We're still figuring out our costumes, but I think we can all come up with something for the night!" Ben said with a broad grin. "It's a date."

Ali nodded, then blinked before shrinking in her seat slightly. "I wish I'd get paid before then, though." she sighed quietly as Nyx nodded.

"I will be, actually. Today is payday. We get paid weekly on Thursdays. Maybe Lewis will give you what you make for this pay period a day or two early?" Nyx suggested, watching as Ali nodded.

"I hope so, so that I'll actually have some money to spend of my own," Ali smiled as Nyx stuttered.

"B-But you'll be out with us, so we'll be paying for you!" he said as Ali shook her head.

"For some of it, yes! But if I want my own things, band merch and the like, I'll buy my own!" Ali said fiercely as Nyx pointed over at her, his ashen eyes focusing on her, then Ben snickered, shaking his head.

"Not worth it, Nyx," Ben said, his eyes focusing on his nails as he inspected them.

"But...!"

"She paid for herself yesterday while out with me as well. She won't accept our charity unless it is on her terms." Benjamin smiled over at Ali, who nodded, a faint smile crossing her features. "We need to remember that.

"Alright."

CHAPTER 8

You should be scared of...

-ALYSON-

BREAKFAST FLEW BY, AS IT WAS A LATER ONE, AND after the meal they drove to the university. All three piled into Benjamin's car, Phoenix sprawling himself happily across the backseats, yawning as Ali curled and refused to touch the paint still.

"It's going to chip, knowing my luck!" she said firmly as Ben laughed, shaking his head.

"It's not that fancy!" Ben had said, his eyes on the road.

"What kind of car is it?!" Alyson asked, her eyes on him as he simply chuckled, refusing to answer, but in the backseat, in a sing-song voice...

"It's a 1986 Ford Mustang GT, with a modified convertible top!" Phoenyx beamed, his arms behind his head as he leaned across both backseats, his feet up. Ali, her eyes wide as she stared above them at the clouds, since Ben had insisted again on riding around with his top down, sputtered in shock.

"A-A Mustang GT?!"

"Thank you, Phoenyx. You're such a huge help," Benjamin

said, glancing in the rearview mirror as Nyx threw him a salute, then a finger with a grin attached to it. "...Classy."

"I try."

"And you leave it with the top off at the university?!" Ali asked, her eyes huge as Ben sighed.

"Yes, because I have the keys." Ben chuckled, glancing over at her as she stared. "Alyson, did you notice I have literally nothing of value in the main part of the vehicle?" he asked as she blinked, then nodded slowly. "I am well aware that my car might be nabbed while I'm in class. It is a risk I take." Ben said, grinning over at her as her jaw dropped.

"Just keep the top on!" Ali said loudly as Nyx laughed, bursting into claps as he sat up and grinned.

"I told him that!" Nyx snickered as Ben grinned. "You're not telling him anything I didn't say!"

"The vehicle is rare, even around here! It's not worth being extraordinarily cautious about!" Ben laughed, his eyes on them as Ali's eyes got bigger. "Honestly! The police would find it fast! I would get it repaired, the thieves would likely be found! All better!"

"And you and Nyx were teasing me about living in a dreamland." Ali said, her eyes wide as Nyx laughed loudly.

"I told you, Alyson, rich boy! This thing is like pennies to him!" Nyx snorted as Ben rolled his eyes. "You have to be careful not to wrinkle his fancy gold-lined underwear when you stay over, that truly offends him, and be careful how you speak of his Pomeranian back home. Fluffy deserves love, damn it," Nyx grinned wickedly as Benjamin broke out into laughter, shaking his head.

"Shut up! At least my underwear doesn't have holes!"

"That's just because I'm too big for them. I just wear through them too fast." Nyx growled deviously, his eyes on Ali and watching as she giggled. Ben snorted, rolling his eyes and laughing as he drove.

"Just sit back and take your nap, moron!"

The three quickly got to the campus and rushed to Ali's side of the campus, as she had her class first and was nearing being late again. Worry etched across her features, her eyes wide and her skin paling as she clutched her bag to her, all of them moving swiftly down the halls.

"There. There she is. Ms. Kincaid," Ali said, pointing as the woman patted a student wearing a pink leotard and pink tights on her shoulder, welcoming her into the classroom as Ben grinned.

"Well, she seems to be in a better mood at least!" Ben said, his eyes forward, but Nyx watched as Ali swiftly redid her bun, sleeking it as best as she could, trying to smooth her skirt, making herself look like she came from more money than she did.

"Alyson, you look lovely," Nyx said gently as she looked over at him, giving him a soft smile.

"Thank you,but I have this feeling that she won't care." Ali muttered, glancing over as they got close. "I'll see you both in a bit." She said, trotting forward.

Ben and Nyx watched her near the teacher, her face paling. "She's so frightened, I don't understand." Ben said, shaking his head. "The woman seems perfectly nic-" he started, then stopped, his eyes widening as the woman leaned forward and hissed in her face, grabbing her arm tightly, her nails digging into Alyson's arm. "What in the hell!"

"I had a feeling," Nyx hissed, then nodded as they trotted forward, catching up to her as they caught the tail end of the conversation.

"...late again, you little wretch!" Ms. Kincaid hissed into Ali's face, watching as Ali's lip quivered. "I have ballerinas here who pay good money to be here, you little rat, not floating in here on tin cans of donor money!"

-BENJAMIN-

BEN, BITING BACK HIS ANGER, AND KEEPING PHOENYX from stepping in, cleared his throat. "Ahem!" he said, his eyes on the woman as she turned, trying to size him up, then smiling brightly. He knew damn good and well that he looked like he bled money if you cut him, that's one way Nyx put it. No matter how he dirtied himself up, it was how he held himself, according to Nyx, his mannerisms. "Ms. Kincaid?"

"Yes?" she asked, her hand locked on Ali as she bit her lip and shook her head at Benjamin, who nodded at her, his eyes soft. "Can I help you, Mister..."

"...Hancott." Ben smiled, watching as she paled. *'There we go.'* His name always got their attention. The bastards always seemed to recognize that if nothing else.

"H-Hancott!" Ms. Kincaid squeaked out, then blinked at Ali, who was peering at Ben and Nyx. "Did you do something to annoy Mr. Hancott or his friend on the way over here, rat?!" Ms. Kincaid hissed to Alyson as Nyx went red with anger, the hand going to his chest the only thing stopping him from moving to rip Ali from her.

"Actually, Ms. Kincaid, is it? Miss Walker is our friend." Ben smiled serenely, standing straight-backed as Ms. Kincaid went white, her eyes going wide. "We were walking her to class when we noticed the rather animated conversation you two were having." He said, his voice getting syrupy-sweet, dangerously so. "Now, that could only mean one of two things. As you had just brightly welcomed in another student, either you were doing the same to our lovely Alyson here..." Ben's eyes went up to her hand, which was firmly attached to Ali's arm still. Ms. Kincaid, fear flitting through her eyes, released Ali's arm in an instant at the hard look in Benjamin's eyes, watching as he tilted his head to the side. "The other option..." Benjamin began, nodding as Nyx grabbed Alyson and tugged her to him, inspecting her arm carefully, noting nail-marks that had been dug into her arm. "...is that you're being classist and plan not to judge my friend fairly in this class at all. You plan to shunt her to the side, if you even plan to teach her at all, maybe even force her to drop out." Ben said, his eyes locked on the instructor as she blinked, then shook her head.

"Oh, o-of course I wasn't planning to do that!" Ms. Kincaid said, glancing at Ali, who was biting at her lip. "I was simply complimenting her on her ability to put together an outfit around her leotard." She panicked, her eyes glancing in at the other girls. "M-Miss Walker, please come in once you're done out here. We're choosing music for individual performances, I want to see what each of you are c-capable of," She glanced at Ben before moving into the auditorium, her eyes wide as she shut the door.

Ali, looking at Nyx and Ben, bit her lip hard, then glanced at the closed door. "What was that?!" she asked as Ben snorted.

"My name carries weight," Ben admitted, sighing as Nyx grinned.

"He's a Hancott. Around here, that makes him nearly royal!" Phoenyx smirked. "She probably shit herself."

"Why though?!"

"My family is more than rich," Benjamin said, his eyes staying on hers. "We're very influential, powerful, and we invest in a lot of businesses, including the university. Well, I do, I should say. My parents haven't actually done the investing since I was a teenager, I have. But officially, it's them they fear, not me." Ben nodded as Nyx smirked. "Alyson, your arm…"

She grasped at it, shaking her head. "I've had worse than a few nail-mark bruises," she said, her eyes gentle as they frowned. "I swear. Don't worry. Thank you for getting her to let me into the class, though. She was about to kick me out permanently," Ali smiled, her eyes on them as Ben nodded.

"Of course. Go, get to work!" he said, chuckling as she nodded, darting into the class, slipping off her skirt, shawl, and day shoes, then slipping on her ballet slippers, and Ben glanced in, making eye-contact with Ms. Kincaid, who told the girls to stay on their stretching, including Alyson, who had now thrown her bag with her things into a spot and darted to a ballet bar with the others.

"Yes?" Ms. Kincaid asked, her eyes on them as Ben smiled.

"My friend and I will be in the audience. We'd like to watch, I have nothing more to do until my next class." Ben said as she took a breath, then nodded, gesturing to a set of doors around the corner as the two began walking, the classical music that the girls were practicing to echoing in the halls.

"Do you think that she'll be treated alright?" Phoenyx asked as Ben nodded.

"That's why we're staying," Ben said, opening the auditorium doors and going up, climbing into the middle rows as the women went through a stretching routine, pulling a leg upwards near each of their heads. "They're limber." He chuckled as Nyx snickered.

"I couldn't do that. I'd pull a muscle near my balls." Nyx grinned as Ben brought a fist to his mouth, stifling his snorts.

"Stop that!"

"I would!"

"Imagine, though... Alyson is that limber..." Ben said, his eyes widening as Nyx blinked, then grinned wickedly. "Oh, the things she can probably do..."

"Have you been with a ballerina, Benjamin?" Nyx quietly asked as Benjamin shook his head, his eyes glancing down as the girls went into another set of stretches. "Me either, closest I've been with was with this girl who could do lots of jig dancing. She could get a leg behind her head." Nyx shrugged as Ben sniggered. "The sex wasn't terrible, but fuck, she looked like a briar patch down there." Nyx said, his nose wrinkling up as Ben brought his fist back to his mouth, his face reddening to stifle his laughter again, his eyes tearing up as he curled in his seat. "...and I mean that in the fact that things got stuck in it, too..." Nyx shuddered as Ben shook his head, his hands covering his face as he snickered. "Can you imagine trying to actually get a woman off and finding random lint tidbits? Because I did. I had to pluck those little balls of fluff out like a cat trying to go after goldfish in a gross pond," Nix gagged as Ben bit his lips, tears flowing from his eyes and a moan of laughter creeping from him, and with that, Benjamin had to step outside and into the corridor.

Ben stood, his eyes red and streaming with tears as he bit his lip and quickly trotted back out the way they came, let the doors shut, and burst into laughter as the women all jumped in surprise. Ali, her eyes wide, glanced up in the audience, not knowing they were up there. She made eye contact with Phoenyx, who gave her an innocent look, shrugging and mouthing at her.

"I have no idea, Alyson! I swear!"

"Pay no mind, ladies! Back to your stretching! We must pick your music soon so that you can each perform today! I want to see what you can do so that I can pick roles for the winter performance!" Ms. Kincaid said, glancing over them all as Nyx leaned forward interestedly.

Ben, panting, his eyes wet, came back in, running back up and sitting as he glanced over at Nyx. He pointed one finger at him as the other man began to open his mouth, shaking his head. "Not a word, Phoenyx!"

"But, Benjamin!"

"No!" Ben said, focusing on the women and their dancing as he steadied his breathing. "Goddamn child."

"You enjoy it."

Ben took a few deep breaths, focusing on Alyson and her movements, her arms going over her head and her straight legs, her pointed toes. He didn't know much about the fine arts, but he could tell that her posture was beautiful. She had worked hard to get here, especially if she had been mostly on her own from a young age. Even if she let herself slack in her off-hours, her ballet posture was lovely.

"Alright, ladies! Pick your music and take it over to the assistant! I will pick an order for you to perform in while you choose!" Ms. Kincaid called out, her eyes sharp as she pointed to a shelf off to the back of the stage Each of the women headed towards the shelf, glancing through the music and trying to pick something to dance to. The sounds of chatter could be heard, including some giggling, and some curious looks around the side curtains up at him and Nyx, then more chatter and giggling.

"I believe Alyson's being questioned about us," Ben chuckled, his eyebrow quirking up as Nyx smirked.

"We're not available."

"Oh, look at you," Ben grinned, glancing over at him playfully. "You must really enjoy Alyson's company."

"I do. I really enjoyed my time with her yesterday, like you did," Nyx said with a small smile. "Otherwise, I wouldn't be remotely interested in sharing her in any way with you."

"I know."

The women came out, smiling broadly at them and the instructor, and Ms. Kincaid clapped her hands. "Alright, ladies! Miss Walker, since you seem to have an audience, why don't you announce your music to us and give us your improvisational ballet," she said as Ali nodded, her eyes a bit on the timid side.

"Oh, don't be nervous." Ben chuckled, sitting forward and smiling softly as she started speaking on the stage.

"Yes, ma'am. I chose *Pyotr Ilyich Tchaikovsky's 'Dance of the Sugar Plum Fairy' in E minor, from the Nutcracker Suite.*" She said carefully as the woman nodded, moving to a spot down on the first row in the audience to watch. As the music began to play, Ali's body began to sway, her arms going around herself as the balanced on the toe-shoes she'd slipped on while backstage. Her arms extended, her eyes soft and gentle, and she beamed as she began to fully move

In the audience, Nyx and Ben straightened, their eyes widening as she moved across the stage, leaping and rolling, raising her arms dramatically to the tune, her face emotional. "Fuck, Benjamin." Nyx said, his eyes widening as Ben nodded, staring intently.

"I see it." Ben muttered, his eyes watching as her feet moved swiftly in place, then flowed like water across the stage, her mind putting movement to music like instinct. "I'd have continued to defend her even if she were as graceful as a rock being dropped into a swamp, but..."

"...she dances like a swan," Nyx said, his eyes locked on Ali's frame. "I don't know anything about dance, but she's beautiful."

"Yes, she is." Ben nodded, smiling slightly as she bolted across the stage and leapt upwards, her legs spreading and her arms going upwards. Her eyes closed and her face never lost composure, even as the other girls muttered at the height of her jump. Behind those closed eyes, though no one could see it, bright white flared for a moment. Twirling on her toes, her arms out, she let her eyes open once more, focusing only on the music and the sounds of twinkling ice.

"If she doesn't get a role in this winter program, if she's shunted down the line..." Ben said quietly, taking a deep breath as she moved and took another leap, her legs extending as she jumped in the air.

"...then it'll be for the same reasons that they give me shitty looks when I come onto the campus, and the same reasons that they chase off almost anyone who comes on a scholarship here." Nyx muttered, his eyes on her as her body arched. "The classism here needs to stop, Ben," Nyx said, frowning as she curled around herself once more, her arms out. "People with raw talent in any field shouldn't be chased out by those with money and power."

"I agree, believe me, and there are plenty of people on campus who agree with me. But then there are people like that professor, and it makes change difficult." Benjamin said, his eyes on Ali as she moved into a flurry of movement, going from her toes to her heels again as he leaned forward. "But it needs to happen, for people like her."

"People like myself..." Nyx started, leaning forward as Ben looked over, his eyes surprised. "We will never try for a better education..." Nyx said, his eyes locked on Alyson as she darted forward, then leapt, her arms extending. "...as long as we're told we aren't worth that education."

Sighing, Ben nodded, then clapped Nyx's shoulder. "You are worth it, if it means anything to hear."

"It does, but I'm also not smart enough to do this shit," Nyx chuckled, shaking his head.

"You are, though you always say that you aren't." Ben nodded. "You are more than smart enough for whatever you'd want to do here."

"No, Benjamin. I'm a bartender. Nothing more. Nothing less. I've accepted that. But, you and Alyson, you two could truly do something with yourselves. You'll be magnificent one day, I know it, even if I'm just along for the ride for now," Nyx said, grinning over at him as Benjamin frowned, about to speak, but the music slowed and Ali went into a low bow, and the other girls began tittering and clapping, their eyes bright and their faces lit up. Ms. Kincaid, shocked, blinked as she stood up and clapped a bit, then spoke.

"M-Miss Walker, where was your formal training before this?"

"I was attending college at Columbia. Columbia College with their fine arts program." Ali said as Ms. Kincaid blinked.

"You were on scholarship there as well?"

"Yes, and I worked to make the difference." Ali nodded, her face firm. "I also made enough to attend dance training at *En Pointe' Dance Academy* in Columbia three days a week in between my classes and my work."

Ben got a shocked look on his face, but Nyx's the one who

spoke up. "She had to have been exhausted with that kind of schedule!"

"Yes, no wonder a job like the one at The Black Cat would be better to her, honestly, it hones her dance skill, she makes some money to fund her college and rent, and she has more free time than she would usually have."

"Miss Walker, before that?"

"I was in dance academies in Myrtle Beach from the age of two until I was sixteen. I... I moved then." Ali explained, her face hardening as she let out a small breath. "I moved out on my own, to another town, and finished schooling by myself to be able to attend school, to get this far," Ali said fiercely, her voice growing as she looked over at the instructor, her eyes wide. "So, I am not a rat, on a tin can." she said, her eyes strong. "I have fought for every step I have taken to get here. I have bought every leotard I own, every pair of tights, every pair of toe-shoes, everything is my own, my parents have not been in my life to fund me since I was a teenager. I am independent. I have endured, I am strong, and you won't break me like you have tried for multiple days," She shook slightly before turning and heading back behind the stage, her face hard and emotionless.

In the audience, Benjamin and Phoenyx were grinning from ear to ear.

"That was fantastic!" Nyx hissed, his eyes on the area she had disappeared off to. "That is what needs to happen more around here!"

"Agreed, though I hope it has the effect that we're aiming to see and not a negative one," Ben said, his eyes watching for Ali at the side wings of the stage as Ms. Kincaid took a few breaths, then sat and made some notes in her book, having the class continue on.

Near the end of the class, the woman called the women together again, all of them sitting at the edge of the stage as she moved forward.

"I've reviewed all of you, and you are all rather talented. Some of you make beautiful leaps, some of you have a better frame. Some need to work on those, but we will get there. I have your positions for the winter performance. This year, we're doing Tchaikovsky's full *Nutcracker Suite*, but it is up to the lead in how we do it. I've yet to see much diversity in this piece and how it is performed, so I am curious this year to see if there will be much difference," Ms. Kincaid said, moving forward and handing out slips of paper as each girl began looking them over, then chattering. "You will work after classes beginning in November, make sure any jobs you have will be willing to accommodate your schedules. We have a few male dancers who will be at rehearsals, and the lead in here gets the task of choreographing and planning the performance." She said, glancing at Ali as she handed out the paper. Ali, glancing at her paper, went white as a sheet, clasping it to her tightly as she stared in shock.

"I think she got a bad score." Ben said, frowning as Nyx growled.

"I'll go down there and let that woman have it."

"You're dismissed for today. Miss Walker, stay behind. I need to discuss that outburst," she said curtly as Ali nodded, her eyes huge. The other women darted to their things, swapping toeshoes for regular shoes, throwing on skirts and shawls, picking up bags, and leaving, leaving her and Ms. Kincaid alone, with only the two men in the audience listening.

"I apologize." Ali muttered quietly, her eyes on her as Ms. Kincaid put her hand up. "No, honestly, I was just... Both days, I had tried coming in, and you had berated me, but been so nice to them, I blew up..." she said, her eyes ashamed. "I'm sorry..."

"No, I'm the one who owes you an apology," Ms. Kincaid said quietly, her eyes on Ali as her head whipped up. "I have not had a ballerina move as you do in over 10 years of teaching. I get spoiled little girls that come in here all the time, and I forget that sometimes, the shiniest gems can come in a dirty package. So to speak." She chuckled, then got a stern look on her face. "Do not get comfortable with your role. You have a lot of planning to do. Be prompt, be studious, and be generous and kind to others," Ms. Kincaid said as Ali nodded.

"I'll be fair to everyone." Ali said as Ms. Kincaid smiled, then glanced at Ben and Nyx, who were giving Ali a worried look, but then softened at her smile.

"Gentlemen. Miss Walker, I'll see you next week. Be sure to come in with some ideas prepared."

"Yes, ma'am."

Ben blinked, coming up and taking the paper from Ali's hands as Ms. Kincaid left the room, then laughed with glee as she smiled. "Lead role?!"

"I guess she was impressed with my dancing." Ali said with a small smile as Nyx grinned.

"I don't blame her. You were gorgeous."

Ali just smiled slightly, letting her hair out of its bun as she sat and undid her toe-shoes. "Thanks. I love dance, but not just for the music or the movement itself. I don't know. Something about it always connected to, well, nature, for me," she said, smiling. "We bend and sway like snowflakes drifting down from the sky, extend our arms like tendrils of ice..." She slipped on her regular shoes and grabbing her skirt, tugging it on, "...leap like fire going from one ember to the next. We're like nature itself, working our magic, but onstage," She chuckled as she ran her hands through her hair and pulled the front back, fastening the front pieces with her hair comb.

"That's a beautiful way to think of dance," Ben said, his eyes genuine as she smiled. "I'd never thought of it like that."

"Most don't. It's just silly girls dancing for them, but, for me, it's so much more."

Phoenyx smiled, watching as she stood up and stretched, and Ali's eyes went to both of them. "I have one more class. It's a few buildings down." she said as Benjamin nodded.

"Unfortunately, it's time for my class of the day as well. Phoenyx, would you take her to her class? I can give you some extra money to go to the cafeteria for a bite if you want food. I know we had a later breakfast, but if you're peckish..." Ben said as Nyx shook his head, a hand going up.

"I'm not hungry. I'll be glad to take Ali to class, then I'll take a nap on a bench or something," Nyx said, chuckling as Ben nodded. "Do you need to go get your books out of your trunk, then?"

"I do. Alyson, I'm afraid I have to leave you with this trickster," Ben smirked, glancing over to Nyx as he rolled his eyes and raised his finger to Benjamin, who smiled wickedly. "Again, Phoenyx. You're not my type." Ben grinned, then grasped Ali's hand as she laughed, shaking her head. "Alyson, have a good time in class."

"You too, Ben."

He nodded, pecking her hand, then grinning at Nyx, and flipping him off in return as Nyx smirked. "Ha! So, the rich boy does come off his high horse every so often!"

"Sometimes, you have to speak a language that the other person understands!" Ben called, waving cheerfully as he left the stage area, the door closing behind him as Ali chuckled.

-PHOENYX-

"You're aware that he plays up the rich boy act to annoy you, right?" Ali asked as Nyx snickered.

"Yeah. He slips and behaves like any other person would when he's not trying to tick me off, and it's why we became best friends." Nyx said, smiling as he offered his arm to Ali, who cheerfully accepted it, the two heading out of the stage area and down the hall.

"I could tell you were more than roommates. You had to be very close, to be willing to have this arrangement." Ali smiled broadly as Nyx chuckled.

"Yeah. He took a chance on me when we met, got me the job at the 'Cat, and asked me to move in with him. I'd told him that I didn't have anywhere to live in Salem and he didn't want me on the streets. So, he took me in, even though I could have found a run-down hotel to take me just as easily," Nyx smiled.

"Benjamin isn't like the other, really wealthy people, that I've met," Ali said, smiling broadly as Nyx nodded, grinning.

"He isn't. He's a fantastic person. I've helped that man go down to the homeless areas downtown in Salem and bring food and drink to those who had nothing. Dressed down, of course. I knew that if he wore his usual things, he'd be pick-pocketed." Phoenyx smiled, feeling her clutch him. "Together, we've tried to do various things around the town, fix wrongs that we find. I'll admit though, it's more my finding the charity cases, and his wallet that does the fixing," Nyx sighed as Ali beamed, her free hand coming up to turn his head to make her look at him, her eyes glittering.

"Even what you do is wonderful," Ali smiled, stroking his cheek. "Money isn't everything and though he funds your projects, you put heart behind them." Ali beamed as he chuckled, grabbing her hand and turning it so that her palm opened to him, giving him access to kiss it and causing a shiver to run through her body.

"I appreciate that," Nyx said gratefully, his eyes going to hers as they went down a few stairs, then headed to the next set of buildings. "Your next classes, will you be okay?"

"I believe so," Ali said, smiling gently. "My papers for starting were late as it was, but the only reason Ms. Kincaid was being so nasty was, well..."

"She found out about your scholarship?"

"Before I even stepped foot in here, and some people don't like those who don't come from money around here," Ali said, shrugging slightly. "But my next class, I asked, and the other women told me that the instructor is very nice. I should be fine." Ali nodded as Nyx smiled.

"Good. Go on then. I'll wait out here. I do this when I wait for Benjamin all the time," Nyx grinned, moving to the bench as she nodded, about to trot into the building, then stopping. She turned, then moved back to him, leaning over and pecking his lips gently as he blinked, then grinned cockily at her.

"See you in about an hour and a half." Ali grinned as he nodded.

"See you then."

She ran in. He leaned back, and he dozed for a while.

Laughter in his head made him wake up...

His eyes opened in a startled daze as he stared about, glancing around, but no one was around. He glanced up at the large clock on one of the buildings. "...4:05. Alyson's been in class a while now," Nyx said, stretching and grimacing as he looked about. "So has Ben. They need to hurry, though. We need to get to the *Cat* soon, otherwise her and I will be late and that'll look shitty on her first day. He should never have told Lewis to have her come in at five if she had a later class," Nyx mumbled, shaking his head.

His mind wandered as he sat back, thinking back to Ali dancing, a smile on his face. "She was lovely, a gem on the stage." he said, thinking about her flitting around. Then his mind went elsewhere, thinking about what she had said this morning.

"Let's fuck right now, on this table, or on the bed. Benjamin could watch. You could give me a good, hard going over, since you seem to think that's what I'd like so much, tug my leotard to the side, I'm nude under here after all, with the exception of these tights, and to be honest, screw the tights, rip them, for all I care, drop your trousers, and fuck me, right here." she had purred at him, and he had gotten hard in seconds. If Benjamin hadn't been there, he would have taken her, but...

He really wasn't sure where he stood on audiences.

Though, thinking on it,the fact that his cock had jumped when she had flat out said that Ben could watch led him to believe that maybe having someone watch wouldn't be so unappealing after all.

Sighing, he snapped his fingers absentmindedly, looking up at the dimming sky. "It grows darker and darker every day, like the light is being snuffed out more and more," Nyx let his head tip back a hair to look at the sky. "Then again, that makes sense, there's so much damn darkness in this world," Nyx said quietly, snapping again as he looked up still, his voice annoyed. "The cold war overseas that our government is too cowardly to really act on, though we know they are performing some disgusting war crimes." His fingers snapped again, more ferociously, and his eyes flickered white. "The countless deaths from that war, from collateral damage, from those who grow ill, from the children and women who get needlessly pulled into this shit because of the recessions and lack of work to put food in their stomachs..." Another snap. "All of it, it's so damn infuriating..." Nyx hissed, shaking his head as he stared up, his eyes finally going purely white. "Benjamin always asks what I wish I could be doing?! I wish I could be over there doing something to put an end to this so-called war!"

A sound like the lighting of a pack of matches going up at once as he snapped again made him look down, and his eyes went wide.

Between his fingers where he had snapped was flame. It was not a huge amount of flame, but it was a flame. Looking around in shock, he quickly stood and darted between the two buildings, noting that the windows between the university buildings were sealed and bricked off years ago.

Hunching over and making sure he was alone, he stared at the fire in his hand, making it move into his palm carefully, his head tilting to the side. With a curious look, he brought his other hand down, pointing at the fire, then grinned playfully. "What kind of witchcraft is this?!" Nyx grinned, poking at the fire, and feeling it simply curl around his finger, swirling up his hand as he laughed. "What the fuck! Playful little shit, aren't you?!" Nyx grinned, watching as the flame completely left his palm and began curling around his wrist, his eyes wide. "Fucking wild!"

Laughter in his head again, then visions. Visions that were eerily similar to what he would see before he might swerve in the road to avoid accidents on occasion, but this time, they were vivid. He saw a woman in white on the rooftops above him, her arms outstretched near some wooden crates, and she was glaring as she made them rattle towards the edge.

He felt the rocks as they came tumbling down from the ledge, shoved off by the heavy wood, and he whipped his head up just as the loud laughter echoed. The crates flew down, toppling towards him as his eyes widened, and in a moment of pure instinct, his hands went up.

Flame poured from them like a dragon, and Nyx's eyes widened in shock and awe. Panting, he watched as the flames scorched and held the crates back by their force, the heat of the flames causing the crates to begin to burn and wither.

'What in the hell is doing this?!' he thought, his eyes wide as he tried to look past the flame to see what was behind the crates. *I'm fucking hallucinating now, fantastic! Seeing shit trying to fucking kill me that's not fucking there!'* He began to relax as the crates slowed slightly, then frowned.

'Trust in your visions, Phoenyx!'

A voice, like his own but with differences in tone and accent, echoed in his head, and he refocused on the crates, which were pushing back against his flame. Someone was up there, he was sure of it. He had to trust himself.

In his head, he saw the woman again.

She laughed at the top of Ali's staircase, grinning evilly and letting loose the bindings that held the cement piping together. She smirked down as the piping rolled towards Ali, telling her goodbye, then laughing as Ali began running, her eyes wide with pure terror.

Alyson's face. Christ, her face…

He'd never seen terror like that, but he saw her eyes go wide in his vision, like she was staring death in the face as the cement got closer.

The crates began to come closer as his flame lost its power.

Her face came to his mind again, the tears in her eyes as she put up a hand, believing that she was going to die.

Whoever was trying to kill him now…

She had tried to kill his Alyson as well.

With a roar of rage, his eyes flared white, the fire from his hands growing stronger and hotter. The flames scorched the sides of the bricks, curling up the sides, up to the top, engulfed the crates.

They turned the crates to ash.

Nyx, panting, relaxed as the flames began to recede from his hands, then subsided completely. His eyes hard, he stared upwards. *'If she thinks I can still attack, she may not try again.'* Nyx muttered to himself, his eyes wide, but above, on the rooftops.

Abaddon's face was screwed together with pure worry. She had not expected Phoenyx to be able to summon his flame so adequately at this point. It usually took more time.

"They are awakening faster this time, damn it," she hissed, glancing over the edge as Nyx glared upwards, his hands up, his eyes flickering, and she shook her head. Phoenyx was always the hot-headed one. If anyone would sustain a second large attack this soon, it would be him. "Damn it." She hissed, her hand coming out to the side as she stepped into the deep gold portal, retreating, for now.

On the ground, with the silence around him, Nyx heard the tell-tale sounds of classes being let out, and he straightened, fixing his coat and hair before trotting down the alley. "Ali'll be looking for me…" he muttered, then paled. "And that bitch might come for her." He hissed, before rushing back out to the front of the buildings.

Once out front, he stared and saw Ali waving near the benches, shaking her head as he let out a relieved breath. Walking over with a grin, he smirked at her as she beamed up at him. "Nyx! Where'd you go?"

"I had some trash to take care of," Phoenyx said, going to wrap an arm around her, but she stopped him, then frowned. He blinked, then she brushed his shoulders of his leather coat off.

"Soot? Was there a fire?!" Ali asked worriedly as he shook his head, chuckling.

"No, no. No fire," Nyx said, his arm going around her waist as she blinked. "Come on, let's go get the rich boy so that you and I can get to work. He might not need to work to eat, but some of us need to earn money to put food on the table," Nyx winked as she laughed, nodding.

As they passed the alleyway, though, students chattered…

"Whoa, what happened here…"

"It looks like a bomb went off, was there some kind of fire here?!"

"This looks like there was an attack or something here…!"

Nyx, his head down, just kept his arm around Ali, and kept his eyes forward.

CHAPTER 9

Let me be your fantasy...

-ALYSON-

THE BLACK CAT WAS STARTING TO GET BUSY WHEN they finally got there, which was normal on a Thursday at five. The three quickly parked, Nyx and Ben running and getting the top and putting it on the car so that Benjamin could lock it up, then Ali grabbing her bag of clothing for later and some toiletries to wash up. The boys had offered to let her borrow their shower after her shift, which was only supposed to be until ten tonight. She had thought that she might need some time to unwind after her shift, and they had offered up the flat to her, which she had graciously accepted.

Phoenyx had darted up to the flat, pecking her cheek on his way up and telling her that he'd see her once he was out, as he was already running a hair late for his shift and needed to change into his black shirt and trousers. Ben had told her to go backstage and find Madame Devereaux, who would work her into the routines and figure out a niche for her.

Things had begun moving fast from there...

Madame Devereaux had been nothing like she had expected. Carrying a cigarette around with her wherever she went when she wasn't on-stage, she was a good twenty years older than the other dancers, but still kept the figure of a thirty-year-old at most. She had been kind but strict, running through the steps of the songs with her, telling her where to go, and what to call herself. She was not Alyson or Ali when on the stage. No, the woman had asked her a few questions about herself to learn more about her, her nature, her behavior, and then she had simply chuckled and had her put on a costume.

"No. I have it. Put this on."

She had, and the woman had smiled broadly.

"Perfect, or should I say, purr-fect."

Which was why Ali was now wearing a deep black leather corset with leather undergarments. No satin skirt piece like some of the others got, no, her piece had a small tail. Fur coated the tail and lined the leather around her breasts. Her hands were covered by long silk gloves that came up to her elbows, and she had a small headdress that she had to put on in a bit.

Cat ears.

Her name, one might ask?

Kitten.

Ali's hand fluffed the makeup brush across her breasts carefully, powdering them gently to keep them from chafing in what she knew would be a hot stage and a lot of movement. "Last thing I need is for you girls to get a rash in this get-up and then need to go dance in school too," Ali snorted, shaking her head as she set the brush down and grasped the lip brush, beginning to paint the deep plum shade across her lips.

"You're going to be our Black Cat." Madame Devereaux had smiled, her eyes devious as Ali had blinked.

"Who's in that role now?"

"No one. I haven't found anyone who could draw the eye like I needed them to do. Sweet but sultry, innocent but sexy..." Devereaux had licked her slightly wrinkled lips, tapping her cigarette and letting the ash hit the wooden floor. "No, you're perfect for it. You have the perfect doe-like eyes to draw men in. Women too." She grinned wickedly, then clapped. "Go! Get laced up! Ask one of the others to lace you into this leather corset!"

Ali set the lip brush down, her lips done nicely as she inspected herself. "Hm. The eyes could use a tad more." She frowned, then glanced over at the other table. She had left her eyeshadow brush over on the other table when she had been working on her corset. Huffing, she began to dig through what she'd brought with one hand, the other one out still, twiddling on the table as she muttered. "It'd be so much easier if you'd just float on over to me," she murmured, sighing as she bit her lip. "My life would be much simpler. Wouldn't have to dig, or get up to fetch my brushes." she groaned, shutting her bag and turning... and coming face to face with her eyeshadow brush, hovering at her nose.

She stared at the thing, then glanced in the mirror, and squeaked loudly in shock at her eyes.

White, shining eyes stared back at her, fear and surprise etched through them. Her hand came out, touching the smooth glass as she bit her lip with fright. "It's a trick," she said, nodding firmly. She pressed her hand on the glass hard, then looked over at the makeup brush, and with a gasp it came soaring to her hand, causing her to jump.

"Alyson!"

She turned, grasping the brush, and her eyes went back to their brown hue just as her fingers curled around the tool. "Y-Yes?!" she called out, mild panic laced into her tone.

"It's time! Are you ready?"

"Yeah! I'm coming!" Ali called, glancing at the mirror, and saw her normal self. Brown eyes, her brown hair pulled back fetchingly, and the makeup brush in her hand. "Tricks of the light and illusions," Ali said, shaking her head as she swept some of the eyeshadow onto the corners of her eyes, deepening the smokiness there. Then, she nodded.

Showtime.

Pulling the cat ears onto her head, she stood and moved forward, taking a breath, and letting the music take her away.

-BENJAMIN-

OUT FRONT, PHOENYX SMIRKED AT ONE OF THE MEN, sliding over a Southside and pointing to the stage as Ben came over and sat at the bar, leaning back interestedly. "Mind making me something?" he asked as Nyx nodded.

"On your tab?" he asked as Benjamin snorted.

"As always."

"What're you up for tonight?" Nyx asked, shaking his head and snickering as Ben waved his hand, sighing.

"You have time to make an Old-Fashioned?" he asked as Nyx nodded.

"For now, yes, but as we get busier, I won't," Phoenyx warned.

"Then make it now, please? I've got to talk business with Lewis later and go over numbers and I'd like to enjoy myself before then," Ben sighed as Nix nodded, moving to make the slightly complicated drink.

"Right. Is the business doing alright?" he asked as Ben nodded.

"Yes, for now. We could use a boost. I won't lie, we really couldn't afford another girl," Ben admitted as Nyx nodded, sighing. "Her pay will practically come out of my own pocket, but don't tell her that. She'd never keep the damn job," Benjamin said as Nyx frowned.

"I thought we picked up over the summer?"

"We did, but we're slumping due to the lack of tourists," Ben groused. "Damn it, I could do so much more for this place with the right promotional ability."

"What do you mean?" Nyx asked, curiosity on his face as Benjamin chuckled.

"A front-girl. Someone to slap on posters, draw in a crowd, push events around, theme around. We're in goddamn Salem, Phoenyx! Think of the mysticism we could use to draw a crowd, with tourists and locals alike!" Ben said, taking his drink as Nyx slid it to him, leaning forward to listen. "I know that the darkness of magic allures some of these people. They want into its clutches and with the right girl, we could allure them."

"Benjamin Hancott, you need to be careful. This town can still be very religious, even with the uptick of interest around Halloween." Nix said, his face worried. "You get the wrong people hearing about this..."

"No pentagrams or blood or anything demonic, but fog and beautiful, glittering black dresses. The illusion of magic." Ben said, his eyes going to the stage. "I just... I need someone to lead."

"Olivia has had her eyes on a leading position."

"Olivia is too obvious, and she's a hateful, greedy bitch," Benjamin said as Nyx snickered.

"You don't like Olivia because you two had a shitty breakup," Nyx snickered as Ben gave him a look.

"Well, when you catch the tramp in-between romps with a sewing pin poking holes in your condoms to try and get pregnant, yes, Phoenyx, that tends to sour your opinion of someone personally. But no. Business speaking, she still isn't what it takes for that role." Ben said, sighing as he sat back. "No, sex appeal comes in more than just blatantly throwing yourself at someone. It comes from that innocent woman you wouldn't expect to see as a seductress suddenly tantalizing you. Hence why I think we both find Alyson so appealing. She's not your typical woman. She's playful, innocent, but has that sultry side that we can both tell is pure..."

"...fire," Nyx finished, a grin on his face as Benjamin smirked. "Yeah. I won't lie, the idea of getting her into my bed has my cock aching."

"Mmm. Believe me, she knows her way around our anatomy." Ben groaned slightly, then shook his head. "You're on shift, though. Tame yourself for now, before you're forced to sling drinks as hard as a rock all night."

"How do you think I was the night I met the woman?" Nyx smirked, his eyebrow quirking up as Benjamin snorted. "Whole time I was behind the bar, I kept having to sneak my hand down my trousers to adjust myself when it got unbearably tight, then wash up so that I could get back to work."

"I wish I'd have been here for that conversation," Ben said regretfully. "I was sadly stuck up in Rhode Island tending to the niceties of Hancott Manor. But I would have loved to have met the girl that night."

Music started up, and the two began to pay attention to the main stage, watching as Madame Devereaux strutted out, and Nyx smirked. "Ooh. Showtime. I wonder what stage name Alyson got," Phoenyx beamed, grinning at the stage as Ben snickered.

"We'll see."

The lights dimmed, curtains rose, and the Madame began to sing. She strutted across the stage, introducing the women as the lights rose on each one, their bodies poised in various positions across the main stage.

But, to their surprise, no Alyson.

"Hm. Ali should have been in the beginning lineup. Devereaux saves the primaries for the end," Ben muttered as Nyx shrugged.

"Maybe she got cold feet," Nyx said, smiling slightly. "She can bartend with me."

"No, Nyx, Lewis will never hire a woman bartender, he doesn't believe them to be the right kind of eye candy," Benjamin shook his head as Nyx snickered, shrugging.

"I was just saying."

Devereaux got to the center of the stage, however, and both nearly fell flat as the lights came up, noting the costume Ali had been given and watching as she sauntered forward. Seconds later, Devereaux purred out her stage name, and Nyx grinned broadly, leaning forward onto his elbows on the bar as he peered at Ali, the tight leather clinging to every curve, her curls pinned in a half-up, half-down tease of a hairstyle, and the leather collar around her neck with a bell, finishing the whole look.

"Kitten, huh?" Nyx smirked, watching as she turned and kicked a fishnet-covered leg upwards, the leather gleaming in the light. "Benjamin, isn't that..."

"The Black Cat costume that I've been telling that witch to shove on a woman for months now! Yes!" Ben hissed, his eyes huge as Ali moved with the other girls. "Oh, fuck me, Nyx, I think this might be the best financial investment I've made for a business," he said, his eyes wide as she arched, his gaze going across the crowd and taking in those who were staring, almost in a trance.

"An investment?" Nyx said, his eyebrow going up as Ben rolled his eyes.

"Hiring her to the 'Cat was an investment, That's not being crass, insensitive, rude, anything. That's business," he said, his face firm. "Business and pleasure must always be kept separate, Phoenyx."

"Uh-huh." Nyx said skeptically, his eyes on the stage as she moved, swaying forward and letting her hands roam across her torso. "So, if she asked to quit right now?"

"I'd get flush on my knees and beg the woman to stay." Ben said, his eyes on the stage as Nyx snorted loudly. "But for the business aspect of it."

"Oh, of course, because it benefits the business to be paying an extra payroll out of pocket."

"Yes, look around," Ben said, his eyes darting to the other patrons as Nyx rolled his eyes, then glanced about, then straightened, his face curious. "She moves in ways the other girls do not, because..."

"She's professionally trained!" Nyx beamed, his eyes wide. "None of our other girls are! They've been coached and taught to dance, but nothing truly professional!"

"Precisely. You can see the difference in her movements, subtle, but she allures the crowd with her hips," Benjamin grinned, then blinked. His hands came up, making a rectangle shape, and Nyx stared at him.

"Benjamin? You alright?"

"I need a photographer," Ben's face lit up as he chuckled. "I know just what to take to the business meeting with Lewis." he said as Nyx got a knowing look on his face, his eyes widening.

"Benjamin, she has the starring role coming up at the university this winter, you know that. You need to ask Alyson if this is what she wants before you plan a show around her and use her to prop this broken-down barrel of a speakeasy up." Phoenyx said with a sigh as Ben waved a hand, nodding.

"She'll love it. I know she will," Ben beamed, his eyes wide as he leaned forward, watching her move. "God, just look at her. She's stunning up there."

"Ben, promise me you aren't about to do something reckless and rash." Nyx said with a groan as Ben glanced back at him, grinned deviously, then tipped his drink back. "Aw, fuck."

-PHOENYX-

ALI GLIDED ACROSS THE STAGE, HER HEELS CLICKING WITH every step, and it took her only seconds to reach the front of the stage to make eye contact with those at the table nearby, and her solo music began. Ruth Etting's *Dancing in the Moonlight* began to float through the air, and her arms wrapped around herself, her feet slowly moving as she swayed and worked the stage. At the musical cue, she began to sing, her voice carrying out over the crowd.

She walked along the stage, her hands moving along her collarbones to her neck to fluff out her curls, and at the bar, Phoenyx simply leaned forward, his eyes widening. "And she sings. Hm," He smiled, then glanced over at Benjamin, who had a look that was akin to a child in a candy store on his face. "Oh, Benjamin, do not fuck this up by treating her like a commodity and not a person," Nyx sighed, then looked back up at the stage, watching as she pirouetted on stage two or three times, spinning on her toes as those watching applauded with glee. "She's so damn hot up there. I'll admit that. But she shouldn't be forced to carry a whole damn show," Nyx said forcefully as Ali moved onstage, her face getting impish as she nodded towards the backstage.

The music, as the song ended, was quickly changed to Heart's *'Barracuda'*, and as Alyson began dancing on the stage more sensually, Phoenyx began cat-calling and applauding as energetically as he could.

With a squeal, Ali hopped off the stage, watching as people began chattering in surprise, pulling things out of her way, but she just winked and started singing a modified set of lyrics, her feet taking her across the dance floor. Exaggerating her steps, she bolted to the bar and climbed atop it as Nyx burst into laughter, watching as she began skillfully moving, her face a mixture of concentration and elation. Her feet were moving like a professional dancer would, her body spinning and twirling across the bar, and those watching her were clapping and squealing with delight.

Ali sang the last set of lyrics, turning to sit on the bar to face Phoenyx, winking at him all the while. With him between her legs, she quickly locked her legs around his waist, much to the amusement of the crowd, which broke out in catcalls. While purring out the last lines of lyrics, she arched back over the bar, her body bending onto the wood where the drinks would go, and her head draping off the edge so that she could see the crowd as she rocked her hips against his for a moment, arms locked at her breasts to keep them from falling from her top.

The song came to a close, and the applause echoed as she smiled demurely, letting one hand wave coquettishly at them before rolling herself upright, winking at Nyx again as she rolled off the bar and landing onto her feet. Her hips swayed as she headed backstage, her hand touching chairs and tables gently on her way back.

Nyx, his eyes wide, simply gaped for a moment before blinking and grinning in stunned delight at where Ali had vanished backstage off to. A few of the patrons had come over, laughing and asking him about this new girl while also getting drinks. But of course, Benjamin had come forward, beaming and wide-eyed.

"Phoenyx!" Ben grinned, locking eyes with Nyx as he took drink orders.

"Busy, Benjamin. You wanted a Screwdriver, pal?"

"Nyx! That was amazing! She worked the bar fantastically, holy shit! That settles it! I have to bring the idea to Lewis! It's too good of an idea to not bring to his attention!" Ben beamed, leaning heavily on the bar as Nyx shook his head.

"Benjamin, no. Talk to her first."

"It'll be fine."

"Ben!"

"I'm going to see how she's feeling!" Ben grinned, smacking the bar excitedly as Nyx let out a frustrated noise, calling out from around the people placing orders.

"Ugh! Benjamin Hancott, you ass!"

-BENJAMIN-

BEN, SNAKING HIS WAY BACKSTAGE, SCOOTED PAST A COUple of the girls, his eyes lit up excitedly. "Excuse me, ladies," he grinned, his black hair falling into his eyes. Blinking, he stopped, though, as a head of red hair ended up in front of him. "Oh! Hello, Olivia!"

"Benjamin, I'm bored," Olivia huffed, her hands snaking down the pockets of his trousers as he sighed. "Don't you have a few moments to sneak off to a closet?"

"No, Olivia. I don't. You need to get ready for your set," Ben said, grasping her hands and tugging them out of his pockets as she frowned.

"What?"

"You heard me. No. Go get ready, Olivia."

Olivia glared, then glanced backstage, her eyes livid. "It's the girl you hired, isn't it? The pretty little brunette you brought around the other night," she hissed as Ben gave her a look. "Benjamin, really?"

"Olivia..." Ben frowned, then pointed. "Work. Now."

She huffed, then stomped a foot angrily to the ground. "Whatever you say, Mr. Hancott," Olivia hissed, turning furiously, her eyes hardening as she crossed her arms. Sighing, Ben shook his head, then moved through the backstage, making his way to the dressing area and grinning as he came up to Ali in her vanity mirror, powdering her face once more. His arms snaked around her shoulders as she blinked, then smiled up at him serenely, her eyes soft.

"Hi, Ben."

"Hello, yourself," Ben chuckled, pecking her face, then beaming at her reflection in the mirror. "You were gorgeous out there," he said as she laughed.

"I performed. Nothing more, nothing less," she said, reaching up to stroke his face as he grinned. "That's what I was hired to do, right?"

"Absolutely."

"Were the song choices alright?" Alyson asked, her eyes going up to his as Ben gave her a toothy grin, then kissed her nose, nodding emphatically.

"More than alright, you had the crowd the most energetic than I've seen them in months!" Benjamin beamed, watching as she blushed.

"You think so?"

"I know so." He stroked her sides, then nipped her neck. "Look, I've got business to discuss with Lewis after place closes down. I won't be up until a minimum of two in the morning," Ben groaned as she sucked in a breath. "Luckily, Fridays are our off days on-campus, so we can have a bit of a lie-in. Then, I can take you to the apple festival whenever we're ready and conscious." Ben smirked as she nodded, grinning. "I've also arranged so that you and Nyx have Saturday off. But you're both on for Sunday night," he said as she grinned broadly. "You're welcome."

"Thank you!"

"Yes, yes. Now, I've got to go, and you need to mingle, my beautiful Kitten," Ben smirked, biting her shoulder slightly before grasping her breasts in the outfit and giving them a few playful squeezes as she let out a squeak, then a grin as Ben sighed wistfully. "Ugh, I wish I could tell Lewis to fuck off for the night."

Ali grinned, then shook her head, making a shooing gesture as he nodded, and with that he waved and headed back out front, leaving her to finish readying herself for the public.

-ALYSON-

THE EVENING STRODE ON, INCLUDING MULTIPLE SETS OF singing and plenty of dancing, leaving Ali plenty exhausted by her shift's end at ten in the evening. Yawning, she slipped out of the black leather corset. She hung it on what she was told would be her vanity mirror, then slid back into her leotard and skirt, but without the tights. Finally, she was ready to have a drink and go to the flat to relax.

Behind her, a pair of arms went around her neck, and a cheery voice spoke up. "You were amazing tonight!"

Ali grinned up, smiling as Delilah made eye contact with her, then pecked her lips cheekily, winking slightly. "Thanks, Lila. Five to ten in those heels, though, phew. I need to get used to it."

"You're a dancer, though." Lila grinned, her eyes on Ali as she blinked up at her. "I can tell by how you move out there, are you trained in jazz style?"

"And ballet. I'm a university student for ballet. But don't spread it around? I know how a job here could…" Ali trailed off, her face getting nervous as Delilah nodded.

"Oh, I understand. I won't say a word," she said, then grinned. "So, you're off now?"

"Yeah. I'm going to meet with Phoenyx."

"Oh! But I thought I saw you with Benjamin earlier. He was using your top as hand-warmers," Lila snickered, her eyes glittering.

Ali bit her lip, then crooked her finger at Lila, who let her eyes widen as she nodded and curled closer to listen. She didn't have many female friends, but she really liked having a girl to talk to, and Lila was someone she could get into trouble with, so to speak. Someone to gossip with, hopefully. "Uh, well, I'm actually seeing them both," Ali said as Delilah's eyes got huge. "It was a misunderstanding the other night, but we decided today that they both want to get to know me, and I really like them both, so…"

"So, you get to dip your hands in both cookie jars!" Delilah beamed, giggling as Ali squeaked. "You naughty little pussy cat!" she grinned wickedly as Ali let out a laugh. "Well, have a good time. Be careful, though, those two can get competitive."

"I can tell. I'll be fine, I can handle myself," Ali said, smiling as Delilah chuckled.

"Okay, well, I've got a set. I'll see you tomorrow?"

"Tomorrow, and then Sunday. Nyx and I have a date Saturday, so Ben helped us get Saturday off," Ali chuckled as Delilah grinned.

"Have fun with them. They can be a wild ride."

With that, Lila left her, and Ali got up, grabbed her bag, and headed out to the bar, sitting heavily in one of the seats as Nyx came over to her and beamed. "Well, hello beautiful!" he laughed, his eyes on her as she smiled brightly.

"Hello yourself. Are you good to leave yet?" she asked as he nodded.

"I am. I'm just waiting for Vince over there to catch up on orders. He's about six paces slower than I am, so it takes time," Nyx said, rolling his eyes as Ali grinned, then both cringed at the tinkling of breaking glass from down at the other end of the bar. "...and he's clumsy as fuck."

"I'm guessing so," Ali chuckled, watching as Nyx grumbled and looked down the bar.

"Vince! I'm not staying all fucking night for you, you jackass!" Nyx growled, watching as the redheaded man turned and pointed at him, his eyes fiery.

"Bite me, Phoenyx! What else do you have to do?" Vince asked as Nyx snarled, then crossed his arms and leaned on the bar next to Ali. Vince glanced over to the two, then sighed. "Oh, that figures. You're throwing an awful big fuss just so you can go get your pole damp."

"Vince..."

"I'm working on it!"

"You're as slow as a snail moving through salted piss!" Nyx hissed, then glanced over as Lewis came over, his ashen eyes lighting up. "Oh, just one moment. I can fix this. Lewis!"

"Oh, you rat bastard..." Vince's eyes got wide, about to ball up a fist. "Lewis'll have my ass if he finds out I broke more shit."

"Maybe you should be more careful then," Nyx said

casually, waving as the owner came up, his eyes surveying the grouping. Three bartenders working when there should be two and a dancer sitting at the bar patiently, though he hadn't introduced himself formally to her. "Alyson Walker, this is Lewis Gwynn, the owner of The Black Cat. Lewis, this is your new 'Kitten.'" Nyx said, smirking as Ali offered her hand. Lewis's hand came out quickly, grasping her hand and pecking it chastely as she smiled.

"Ah! Miss Walker, it's a pleasure to finally meet you in an official fashion! Benjamin sang your praises, and he was not lying, but it is still nice to be able to put a face to a description!" Lewis grinned, nodding and letting her hand go as she chuckled.

"The pleasure's all mine, Mr. Gwynn."

"Lewis. No one here calls me Mr. Gwynn," Lewis said, his nose wrinkling with distaste as Nyx snickered. "Phoenyx, what're you still doing here?"

"Your idiot can't keep it up again." Nyx said, shrugging and leaning against the back of the bar as Vince glared from the other end, serving a drink. "Did you even get your proportions right this time, limp dick?"

"Fuck you!" Vince hissed, his eyes widening as Ali giggled. "...and fuck h-" he went to say, but Nyx's eyes narrowed and his finger pointed.

"Say it and I cut off whatever small, insignificant little sausage of a penis you have and feed it to you personally with a side of goddamn eggs, you lazy shit!" Nyx hissed as Vince moved forward, slinging his towel to the ground, but Lewis got between the two of them.

"Cool off! Both of you! Phoenyx, you're supposed to be off, why are you still here?!"

"Because the bar's, fuck, eight or more fucking orders under on drinks thanks to this walking piss-stain of a bartender!" Nyx snarled as Vince jolted for him. "Do it, you ugly, pig-faced fuck!"

"Phoenyx!" Lewis snapped, then turned to Vince, who was seething. "Vince, I told you to get back to work."

"Shut his foul mouth up!"

"Vince..."

"He won't!" Nyx smirked, his ashen eyes wide with glee as Ali stared, biting her lip. "Do you know why, you saggy-assed shit?! Because I can move at three times your speed, attract both women and men to the bar, and know four times the recipes off the top of my head than you do! And I don't over-or-under-pour!" Nyx grinned toothily, his eyes delighted as he hopped slightly to make sure Vince could see him the whole time. "And do you know what I'll be doing later?"

"Fuck you, you sorry fuck!"

"I'll be up in my flat! With that beautiful woman!" Nyx sneered, gesturing at Ali like she was a prized treasure and making her blush red. "I'll make her call for every deity in the goddamn, fucking list of known deities!!!" Phoenyx said giddily, watching Vince go a cross between putrid green and reddish-purple with rage. "While you? You'll be at home tonight, fucking your hand! Again! Using your own tears as lubricant!"

Vince roared, lunging forward as Nyx darted around the bar and grinned like a child, his eyes wide. Lewis, holding the other man back, shot Nyx a look that would kill if at all possible. "If you couldn't sling drinks like you were born to do it..."

"But I can. I'll see you tomorrow night, Lewis," Nyx grinned, watching as Lewis glared, then nodded gruffly at him. Ali, her eyes huge, stood as Nyx offered his arm. "Shall we?"

"How the hell do you still have a job?!" Ali hissed as Phoenyx snickered.

"I'm talented at what I do…"

"Which is be a prick." Lewis snapped, nodding his head towards the door of the flat. "Get out of here, now."

"I'm going!"

"I-I'm sorry." Ali muttered, staring as Lewis shook his head at her.

"No, no, it's not your fault. These two bicker damn near every goddamn night, though not usually this bad. Vince, I swear if you don't stop!" Lewis hissed as Vince glared, then relaxed, shrugging him off then moving to the other end of the bar again, grousing and cursing the whole time. "Nyx hates anyone who can't even remotely keep up, and Vince is nowhere near that level," Lewis explained as Ali nodded, her eyes understanding. "I keep him because I need the help."

"Oh, I see."

"Less chatter, more upstairs. Come on, gorgeous," Nyx beamed, tugging her playfully as she let out a squeak, then huffed at him slightly. "Goodnight, Lewis!"

"Don't break my newest dancer, you bastard."

"I make no guarantees!" Nyx called gleefully, an arm snaking around her shoulders as she glanced at him, then snorted. As they reached the stairs of the flat, he pulled out his keys, grinning at her. "Hm?"

"Cocky, aren't you?" she asked as he smirked.

"Should I not be?"

CHAPTER 10

Kill the light baby...

-ALYSON-

E FLUNG THE DOOR OPEN, AND THE FAMILIAR couch and chairs greeted her, causing her to smile as she stepped in and set her bag down. Stretching, she turned towards the fireplace, her eyes slightly tired, then she blinked as she heard a small growl behind her.

Her head whipped around to see Nyx, his eyes locked on hers like a tiger going for raw meat, his shirt half undone already. Her lip went between her teeth, but she didn't make a movement to stop him as he scooped her against him and pushed her into the wall, his hands roaming hard on her skin. "P-Phoenyx?"

"I don't feel like waiting to get to a bed," he muttered, his mouth moving to her neck as she moaned. "I keep a condom in my wallet, emergency purposes," Nyx's muffled voice groaned, nipping at her neck as she nodded. His hands slid along her waist, carefully sliding the skirt she wore down off of her hips and leaving her in her leotard. "Reach into my back pocket and grab my wallet, get it out?"

Nodding, Ali's hands went around and fished into his

pockets, grabbing for his wallet as he sucked at her neck, causing her to let out a loud moan against him. "Oh, fuck…"

"Give me that," Nyx growled, grasping the wallet from her and flipping it open, quickly grabbing what he was looking for and chucking the rest against the far wall of the flat as she groaned. His free hand splayed against her leotard as he panted, the hand with the item in it tucking it away into the back waistband of his briefs for a moment.

His hardness pushed against his trousers, straining to get free, and he gave her a look that she swore could light her aflame. His lips pushed hard on hers, their tongues twining as both let out needy moans, his hips grinding on her core. Keeping her against the wall, he pulled at his shirt, shoving it over his head and giving her access to his chest. Moistness crept through her, causing her to let out another whine as her hands snaked across his collarbones and shoulders, his eyes locked on hers. "P-Please…" she moaned, her eyes on him as he grasped her hips and tugged her leotard off of her shoulders, pinning her hands to her sides as she gasped.

"Please what?" Phoenyx teased, peering at her as he pressed himself against her. Her hands went down against his stomach, then to his trousers, unbuttoning them carefully as he grinned deviously. "Please what, Alyson?"

"I already told you what to do this morning." Ali said, her eyes going to his as he smirked. "Do you have the balls, now that we're all by ourselves?" she asked firmly as he ground himself against her again, nipping at her throat once more.

"I had the balls to do it this morning." he muttered, his eyes flitting to her as she cupped at the bulge in his trousers, his eyes darting down to peer at her. "I just don't function well before

I've had a few cups of coffee and some breakfast," he said, tugging the leotard further down so that she could pull her hands out of it and exposing her breasts as she moaned. His mouth moved down to her collarbone, then to her nipple, pulling it into his mouth as she let out a loud whine. "Now, are you still naked under here?"

"Why don't you find out?" she asked, her lip going between her teeth as he glanced up at her, then grinned impishly, his hands going down and working the leotard off of her frame as she whimpered slightly. Pulling her arms free, she threw them around his neck as he tugged the cloth down her belly, then over her bottom, letting it drop down her legs as she stepped out of it. Her feet kicked it and her shoes to the side as he stepped back one step to take her in, his hands lacing in hers. His eyes grew hungry, as though he hadn't eaten in days, and he quickly pulled her back to him, pushing her back against the wall with a moan.

"Lovely," he breathed as his mouth went back to hers, his hands at his trousers to shove them down and out of the way as she panted. Fingers dipped into her slit as she let out a cry, her eyes widening slightly. Without waiting for her to open further, he coated his fingers in the dampness that had seeped up her clean slit, then searched for a moment, pressing his fingers down on her bead as soon as he found it and causing her to yelp as he smirked. Her legs spread ever so slightly, and he took the opportunity to snake his hand further down and push the coated fingers up into her, curling them and thrusting them upwards as she let out a gasp, her eyes widening as she grasped onto his neck. "Mm. Good. You're all nice and wet, Kitten." He grinned, watching as she squirmed under his touch.

Pushing back onto his fingers, Ali's eyes rolled back slightly, her body giving in to every pleasure he had to offer her. She bit her lip hard, swallowing heavily as she brought a hand down to touch and play with the little bead of flesh that he was neglecting, and blinked as he tugged her hand away. "Oh!"

"I'm not playing with your clit right now for a reason." Nyx snorted, shaking his head as his other hand thrust up roughly, causing her to arch slightly and moan. "Later for that, we have all night. Right now, my damn cock is hard as a rock," he growled, his teeth coming to her throat as she panted. "I want in you. No playing, no games, not right now. I have wanted to fuck you since I met you at the bar over a week ago," Phoenyx panted, his eyes going to her as she moaned, "...and then that fucker got his hands in my honeypot first," he hissed, sucking on a spot of flesh at her neck as she let out a loud groan. His hand released hers, feeling her wrap both hands around his neck again as he panted, grasping the foil he'd shoved in the back waistband of his briefs and pulling his hand out of her for a moment. He made a show of licking it clean in front of her, straightening and tugging his fingers to his mouth as he spoke, her eyes locked on his. "I have wanted to slip myself into you..." he purred, tugging his fingers through his mouth, then grasping the foil to rip it open, throwing the wrapper to the side as he grasped himself in one hand and pulled the sheath on with the other, "...since we spent the day together yesterday," Nyx groaned, grasping her leg as soon as he had his hands free and lifting her, her arms tightening around his neck. With one hand to guide him, he pushed at her core, then sheathed himself in her hard, her eyes widening as she moaned and grasped his hair.

"Fuck, Nyx..." she whimpered as her eyes rolled back, his firm gaze locked on her as he pushed forward in her roughly. Her back arched against the wall, curls spilling from her updo as his hand grabbed her hair comb and tugged it off, throwing it across the room before locking at her throat gently, causing her gaze to go back to his as he thrust forward, his one hand holding her leg up around his hip.

"I don't think I've ever wanted to punch my roommate..." Phoenyx growled, his eyes locked on her as she let her mouth fall open, his thumb tracing her throat carefully as he moved, "...as much as I did yesterday. It took everything in me not to throw him across the room," Nyx muttered, pushing needily into her as she let her hips rock with his, her hands locked into his hair.

"W-Why?" Ali mewled quietly as he huffed out a small chuckle, his head moving to her breasts to nip at her carefully.

"Why? Watching his cum dripping down your palm, and seeing his face flushed red? Knowing what he'd gotten to do and I hadn't?" Nyx growled, pulling a spot of skin between his lips and sucking hard as she moaned loudly. "I saw pure red..."

"W-Will... you still be angry..." she asked, feeling him thrust rougher as she let out a loud yelp of pleasure, her hands clenching on him, "...i-if... if I spend the evening with him too?"

"No." Nyx smirked, grinning up at her as he grasped her legs, then hoisted her up, thrusting harder as she let out a loud cry. "First, because that's what we three have agreed on. You'll see both of us. Date both of us, and that includes getting fucked by both of us." He said, his eyes intently watching as she let her head tip back. "...and second? Because, I know damn good and well, that even though he may be able to buy you whatever you fucking want..." Nyx smirked, his eyes getting wicked "...I can fuck you as hard as you want, and as long as you want, from dusk until dawn," He growled, then let a hand ball up into her curls as she yelped with pleasure. His hips slammed into her, his hand at her bottom holding her in place as she moaned and whined.

The doorknob jiggled in the next moment, though and Nyx glared as a voice called out. "Nyx!? Nyx, unlock the damn door! I need to get my papers for my meeting tonight with Lewis!" Ben's voice called through the door as Ali glanced over to the door, then at Phoenyx, who was fuming.

"Fuck off!" Nyx hissed, his eyes flaming as his hips pounded into her, her mouth dropping open as she bit back a moan. "Moan for me, I want to hear you, Ali."

"Nyx! Goddamn it, I need those papers!" Ben yelled, booming on the door as Nyx growled, then grabbed a nearby, leftover glass, then chucked it towards the door, about 20 feet from them, watching it shatter as Ali let out a yelp, then a loud moan as Phoenyx's thrusts grew more heated.

"Go the fuck away! I'm busy!" Nyx growled, his face furious and his dark brown curls falling into his face, then his eyes went to Ali, who was biting at her fist, her breasts heaving as she moaned. "You're so goddamn tight and wet..."

"N-Nyx!"

"You come for me," Nyx groaned, feeling her tighten up around him as he sucked in a breath. "Come on..."

His hips pushed forward, and his hardness hit one spot, and her shout echoed through the flat, her legs wrapping around him tightly as he groaned and thrust erratically into her, his eyes rolling back. Her hands balled into his hair, causing him to let out a deep moan, his thrusts slowing as he began simply pushing hard into her, then kissing her neck.

"Phoenyx..." Ali panted, her voice tired as she went to put her feet down, but he grasped her legs tightly, snorting.

"No, I'll move you towards the couches, away from the broken glass." Nyx grinned, watching as she chuckled. "Oh, you're an amazing woman, do you realize that?" he asked quietly as she simply shrugged, her eyes on him. His hands locked around her body, keeping himself sheathed in her for the moment as he carted her to the couch, then setting her down on the back of it as she smiled. Rolling around, she watched as Nyx moved to the bathroom, grabbing a bathrobe, a lovely one that was a gorgeous blue shade. "This is Benjamin's. Mine's not as nice."

"He said you were nude the other day, do you even own one?" Ali asked skeptically as Nyx grinned deviously and shrugged, tossing her the bathrobe as she squeaked, her eyes wide. He began cleaning himself up, throwing away trash and wiping himself clean, fixing his pants, then grinning as he came out, watching as she wrapped up in the robe, her eyes on him. "In case Ben comes in," she said coyly as Nyx smirked.

"Oh, so not because I'm here?"

"No. He has to work to see it." Ali said, her nose going up as Phoenyx burst into snickers, tugging her to him and curling around her on the sofa, right as the door jiggled again

-BENJAMIN-

MOMENTS BEFORE...

"Go the fuck away! I'm busy!"

Benjamin's eyes had widened at the moans he had heard after that and the pounding against the wall. Then he'd put two and two together. Alyson had been off at the same time as Phoenyx, and both had vanished from the 'Cat. He had assumed she had gone to shower, but he must have skirted her away for a romp, the lucky fucker.

"Oh, you asshole," Ben murmured, a snort leaving him as he moved to the stairs and sat, shaking his head. "Guess I should wait here a few moments." he huffed, glancing up at the door for a moment before sitting with his chin in his hand, huffing. "Knew I should have told Lewis to fuck off."

"Why should you have told Lewis to fuck off?"

Evelyn's voice rang out as she came over, her face amused as Ben snorted. "Oh, no reason. Phoenyx just being himself," he said casually, glancing at the door as the pounding against the wall intensified. "For fuck's sake."

"Sounds like he's about done." Evelyn chuckled, then shook her head. "Anyone I know?"

"Kitten." Ben snickered, his face lit up as Evelyn gave him a look.

"But I saw you with Kitten earlier in the evening."

"Yes. We're sharing. We both wanted to get to know her, and before she got her job here, she had met us. It's a really long story. She's courting us both for now, to see where it goes." Ben said, his eyes glittering as Evelyn stared, then laughed.

"You and Phoenyx have never been conventional." she chuckled, then tilted her head to the side. "I'm surprised, but pleased, that you found someone willing to give both of you a fair chance, though. Treat her well." Evelyn smiled as Ben nodded.

"Mmhmm. Of course," Ben said gently, then listened at the silence. "I suppose I should try again, I really do need those papers."

"Good night, Benjamin," Evelyn laughed, shaking her head as she headed around the corner, and he headed back up the stairs. He jiggled the handle again, then huffed at the lack of response, but moments later there was the sound of glass crunching at the door as it was unlocked, then opened, and Nyx's flushed face and upper chest greeting him as he leaned in the doorframe.

"Nyx." Ben snorted, shaking his head as he tried to duck around him, then watched as Nyx blocked him. "Oh, for the love of..."

"Give her a fucking minute," Nyx said pointedly, glancing over his shoulder, then nodding as he moved. Benjamin stepped in to see Alyson laying on their couch wrapped in his bathrobe, her eyes slightly timid as she bit her lip, and he chuckled as he waved.

"Hello, did the fucker at least do his job right and leave you satisfied, or should I step in?" Ben asked cheerily as Ali flushed, then bit her lip, her hand going to her collarbone to trace it and touching various love bites.

"No, no, he d-did his job." Ali said as Ben grinned, moving to his room and rifling through papers in it, then swearing loudly.

"Goddamn it! I know I left those papers here! I had a whole business proposal lined up, damn it!" Ben hissed, rifling through things as Nyx snorted, moving to the counter. Ali, blinking, turned to see Nyx pick up a small stack of papers that were left sitting near the sugar bowl, smirk playfully, then put them between the breadbasket and the wall of the counter as she bit back giggles, her eyes widening. "Lewis has no visual sense. He won't be able to see what I've got planned without me spelling it out for him!" Ben sighed, his eyes going through the room as Nyx straightened quickly, then moved to the refrigerator, shrugging slightly.

"Damn shame. Alyson, would you like something to eat?" Nyx asked, his eyes gleaming as she bit her lip slightly. "I know you must be starved now." Phoenyx smirked wickedly as Ben snorted, coming into the kitchen area to rummage through the cabinets, causing Nyx to glance over with a raised eyebrow. "Really, Benjamin, do you really think you put the papers with the salt, pepper, and lavender?" Nyx asked with a snort as Ben glared over at him, his eyes fuming.

"Well, it's better than simply turning in place like a top. I need the damn things now." Ben said, his eyes on Nyx as he grasped a few things, tugging down some boxed spaghetti noodles and a jar of sauce. "You're going to actually cook a full meal?!"

"I said she was probably hungry." Phoenyx shrugged as Benjamin gave him a jealous look. "If you want, I can save you a plate."

"Please?"

"Sure."

Alyson gave them a curious look as she curled into the bathrobe, leaning over the back of the couch, and Nyx grinned over at her. "I love to cook," He explained, grabbing a couple of pots and placing them on the stovetop. "Benjamin is terrible at it, so I tend to get off work and make dinner, then leave him a plate when I'm not exhausted. When I am, he orders in and gets enough for us both."

"Oh! That's nice!" Ali grinned, her eyes lit up as Nyx chuckled, nodding.

"He's good at it, too, the cocky shit." Ben snorted, shaking his head. "That bastard makes some of the best pasta I've had, outside of actually visiting Italy."

"Mm, so sit back while I take care of your growling stomach, my lovely." Nyx smirked, watching as she snuggled into the back of the couch. With a small smile, she watched him start cooking, observing as he grabbed meat from the refrigerator all while Ben moved through the flat frustratedly. Nyx rolled his eyes. "For fucks sake, Benjamin! Do you need it?!"

"Yes! I need it!"

"What would you give me if I was able to produce the papers?" Nyx smirked, throwing meat into the pot to brown it as Ben blinked, then glared.

"You have my papers?!"

"No, but I know where they are."

"Bastard! What's your price?!"

"Wine. You bring up wine later." Nyx smirked as Ben glared, then huffed, nodding as he kicked at the floor with annoyance.

"Ugh. Fine. I'd have done that if you'd have just asked."

"This just guarantees it, and I like watching you squirm," Nyx snickered, grabbing the papers from their hiding spot and handing them over as Ben blinked again, then pointed at him.

"Asshole."

"Mmhmm. I'll save you a plate."

Moving to the couch, Ben simply grasped Ali by the back of the neck, then dipped her back as he rolled her into a kiss, her eyes widening as she squeaked. His hand snaked into the robe, tweaking her nipple, his tongue twining with hers with a quiet moan, but he released her after a moment, letting her roll back to her stomach to peer up at him again as she panted. "Please do." Ben purred.

-PHOENYX-

Waving, Ben left, and Nyx shook his head as the food cooked, grabbing the dustpan and broom and beginning to sweep up the glass he'd broken as Ali bit her lip. "Ass."

"He seemed to just be in a hurry."

"No, not that." Nyx snickered, then gestured at her. "One of our agreements between us was that we wouldn't step on one another's toes. So, when one of us has earned time with you for an evening, the other stays out of the way," Nyx explained, watching as she nodded. "He was being a dick by pulling that move, not that I care. I'll have all evening to make a meal out of you and make you mine all over again," Nyx smirked, sweeping the glass into the pan and moving it to the bin as she grinned, her cheeks reddening. "Now, why don't you put on a show for me while I wash my hands and make dinner?" he grinned as Ali bit her lip, her eyes on him. "Unless that's too forward?"

"Considering you just took me against that wall like a madman..." Ali chuckled, letting the bathrobe come off as he beamed and began adding sauce to the meat. "...not too forward at all."

Downstairs, Ben bolted to the office right as Lewis got in, his eyebrow raising as Benjamin raised one hand. "Yes, yes. I apologize. I'd misplaced my papers."

"Benjamin, it's fine. Though I don't know why we're bothering," Lewis sighed, shutting the doors as he sat heavily. "We're sinking like a wrecked ship."

"I have some ideas to fix that," Ben said, sitting across from him and grinning, his eyes lit up. "Listen, I've been saying for months now that we need a girl out front."

"Yes. Olivia wants the spot," Lewis said, rolling his eyes as he glanced out of the window of his office. Women were walking around, interacting with the clientele as bartenders slung drinks, the bar at half-capacity. "If you ask me, none of our girls that we've had long-term could do it. They don't have the skills." Lewis sighed as Ben nodded fast.

"I know. Olivia is too hot-tempered for it anyhow. And greedy. She's also stolen tips according to some of the other girls, not that we can prove it. We let it go because she's pretty and garners attention, but if we could maybe replace her with better." Ben muttered, his mind thinking fast as Lewis stared.

"Hancott, what're you thinking?"

"Kitten. Alyson. Miss Walker. She's a professional dancer." Ben admitted as Lewis sputtered. "I didn't think to say anything about it before now because honestly, I did not think she'd care for the job. But she enjoyed herself tonight." Ben said, his eyes wide. "She is a natural talent, and a beauty."

"I'll say. She had the crowd eating out of her hand, and working Phoenyx into her routine was genius," Lewis snorted as Ben nodded.

"Yes. I...I think she could be the front-runner we've looked for. A star for the show," Ben said quietly as Lewis stared, then frowned.

"Have you spoken to her about this?"

Ben quieted, then spoke fast. "Yes. Of course. She was adamant that the idea was sound." he lied swiftly. *I'll have to explain that the 'Cat was close to collapse and that without this, there would be no jobs for anyone.'* he thought, his eyes firm.

"You think this will perk us back up?"

"I do," Ben said carefully. "If we promote her properly, she will be an asset that we cannot afford to lose. Think about it, Lewis. We are called The Black Cat, but there is no Black Cat. You have no show-woman, no one the men come to see as a main attraction," Benjamin's voice was quiet but confident. "Make a whole show around her. Give her songs, dances, routines. Her own outfits that are separate from the others. Photoshoots. Everything," Ben gave a firm nod as Lewis stared in surprise. "Promote her like a star and people will treat her like a star."

"Are you certain she can handle the pressure?"

"Absolutely," Ben nodded, his face firm.

"Hancott, how are you in damn medicine and not goddamn

business?" Lewis chuckled, his head shaking as he glanced over at Benjamin.

Ben snickered, then shrugged as Lewis grabbed a bottle of gin. "Because if I was in business, I'd have to be back home in Rhode Island more, and you would all miss me."

"So, what comes next?"

"Photos of Alyson dressed as our Black Cat, new costumes, I'll fund it, don't worry, and a new show. It'll be grand."

Upstairs a small time later, the smells of spaghetti floated through the flat, strained noodles off to the side and sauce cooling on the stove, but on the couch...

The two were curled around one another again, moaning and grinding on one another hungrily, Nyx tugging her hand up as she whimpered. "No, naughty girl, this is my snack," Nyx panted, pulling her hand to his lips as she huffed at him.

"B-but, I was so c-close..." Ali groaned, feeling him suck her fingers clean as she let out a moan. "That's not fair! You told me to p-put on a show! I d-did what you asked, and now you've stopped me from finishing m-myself off!"

Snorting, he let her hand go, then undid his trousers, grinning deviously at her as she bit her lip. "How about this? I get you off quickly, get myself off in the process, then we have dinner? It's a win-win situation."

Huffing playfully, she simply peered up at him, then gave him a slightly cross look. "You only had one condom on you. Are there others in the house? Maybe in Ben's room..."

"I'm not going into that rich boy's fuck den. Not even to get my own pole wet, Kitten."

"Well, then I guess dinner it is, then." Ali said as he gave her a pitiful look.

"I'm good at pulling out. I swear not to finish in you, Kitten."

Nipping at her lip, she frowned, then nodded as he gave her a wicked smirk, kicking his pants down again, then pushing in her achingly as she moaned, his hips shoving into her like a dehydrated man given a drop of water. Her hands grasped at his hair as he bit at her collarbone, then pulled out of her, her eyes widening in surprise.

"N-Nyx...?"

About to say more, she was stopped as he roughly bent her over the edge of the couch, slamming back into her at a hard, fast pace that left her mouth dropped open and her head tipped back. His hand grasped into her curls as he used them for leverage, a growl leaving his throat as he snaked a hand around to tap at and toy with her bead. Yelping, she straightened slightly, giving him access to her breasts as the hand in his hair moved around to grasp her breasts, tugging at a nipple. "I want you to come," he purred anxiously, his hips rocking forward roughly as she moaned loudly.

He brought the hand at her breast to her throat, grasping it carefully as he thrust upwards, his ashen eyes locked on her frame as she quivered and whined around him. She felt him bring his lips to her neck and suck on a spot as she moaned, his thrusts increasing, growing harder. "I-I..."

"Yes, good Kitten," Nyx moaned, his head resting on her back as he thrust up into her roughly, her core dripping around him. "...tell me exactly what you want."

"...h-harder, Phoenyx, f-fuck me harder," she groaned, getting a deep growl out of him as he pushed himself into her firmly, causing her eyes to roll back into her head and her hands to come back to go into his hair, "...l-like that! I-I'm gonna c-come!"

"Come for your Nyx, Kitten!" he hissed, bending her over the couch again and pushing his hand against her back for leverage, his hips slamming into her hard. Her head tipped back moments later as she saw stars and gasped, her core clenching around him and causing him to groan, thrusting harder...

Then with a loud, uncontrollable moan he was grasping himself and pulling from her, spurting along her backside and legs as she whimpered from the loss of touch.

Both panted, and he smirked, leaning around to peer at her impishly.

"See? I told you I'd pull out."

She whipped her head around to glance at him, snickered, then kicked her foot out as he yelped slightly, his eyes widening. "Ass."

"Hey!"

Straightening, she stretched, and he simply tilted his head to the side, admiring his handiwork as she blinked. "What are you...?" she asked, then glanced at her backside before rolling her eyes. "Oh."

"I have to say, I look great on you," Nyx smiled innocently as she shook her head, pointing to the shower. "Oh, come on, leave it until the rich prick gets home!"

"Phoenyx."

"Just a while longer!"

She simply shook her head, but as she walked, she dragged her hand through the creamy white fluid, chuckling as he flushed and twitched again, his eyes on her. With a smile, she brought it to her lips, sucking the fluid clean as he beamed. "You know, you taste pretty good yourself," she said, biting her lip as she slipped into the bathroom, her eyes lit up. She closed the door, and he grinned as he tucked himself back into his trousers once more, his eyes wide.

"Hancott can fuck himself. Literally," Nyx said, beaming at the bathroom. "I'll propose to that one. The woman's amazing and matches my every goddamn move." he grinned, turning to wash his hands at the kitchen sink before grabbing plates. "Even lapped up my damn fluids off her leg, the minx. And she's even funny. I'll marry that one. Hancott can go make little baby Hancotts with some other little princess," Nyx said, hearing the shower start. Plating up noodles and sauce, he moved to the table as he heard her voice float from the shower, his eyes softening as he peered at the bathroom. "And even if she wasn't such a sexually charged woman, she's damn beautiful, has an amazing voice, and is damn kind." Phoenyx smiled, setting plates at the small table in the kitchen area, then grabbing forks.

"Phoenyx? I brought my own bath soap, can you bring it to me?" Ali's voice called to him as he glanced up, then over to where she'd tossed her bag when she'd gotten in, right before he'd pinned her on the wall. Smirking, he knelt and rifled through the bag, grabbing at a bottle of scented bath soap and carrying it to the bathroom, knocking on the door.

"Is it this green soap?"

"Yes! It's a nice, tea-scented soap!" Ali called as he opened the door and walked in, glancing into the shower at her silhouette. She was gorgeous, but he knew that. That said, he hadn't seen her like this. Vulnerable and wet, open to him. She simply beamed at him, her hand out as he handed over the soap bottle, her eyes on him as she held up a dirty washrag. "I had to use a washrag for my makeup. I'll scrub it out, I swear."

"It's fine," Nyx chuckled, leaning on the counter as she smiled over at him, lathering her hair, then the rag. Scrubbing her body, she glanced over at him as he gave her a gentle smile. "You know, you truly are stunning."

"And you really are trying to fluff my ego," Ali laughed, shaking her head as he shook his head.

"No, you're stunning," he said, his eyes on her frame as she glanced over at him. "You have the loveliest skin I've seen. Fair, but naturally so. You take care of yourself, but you're not a princess. You have beautiful curves, and believe me, getting my hands on them was more than fun." Nyx smirked deviously, an eyebrow rising as she laughed. "How are you not married? How do you not have children?" he asked curiously, watching as she stiffened, then bit her lip. All playfulness melted off of her, her eyes getting hard, and his face softened further. "A-Alyson? Did I say something?"

"Nothing that you'd know not to say," she said quietly, smiling over at him as she finished scrubbing, her arms wrapping around herself in the water. Swallowing heavily, she looked up in the shower, letting the heat start to rinse her clean, then closed her eyes. "You don't believe women who were used without their consent are worthless, do you?" she asked carefully as he shook his head, then spoke.

"Of course not," Nyx said firmly, his eyes on her as her lip quivered. "What happens to someone outside of their control is just that. Outside of their control."

"I don't want children, Phoenyx." Alyson said, her eyes up as he blinked in surprise. "But I have a... well, what I hope is a good reason for it," She rinsed the rest of the bubbles from her hair, then turned the water off and looked over where the towels were, watching him grab two and hand them to her. "Thank you," she sighed, wrapping one into her hair, then one around her as she stepped out. Drying off her body, she grabbed Nyx's shirt that he'd hung from the other night, black and long and just sitting in the bathroom, pulling it onto her once she was dry and hanging one towel up.

Nyx's eyes watched as she went to the couch, sitting heavily as she frowned, then toweled her hair as he knelt in the floor in front of her, his eyes gentle, but curious. "Tell me?" he asked, sighing slightly at the pain that flitted across her features. "Why would you not want children?"

"It'd spoil our evening."

"If we're gonna get to know one another, this is something that we'd have to talk about." Nyx said as she sighed, then nodded, her eyes closing as she bit her lip.

"My father was... awful. He did things that no father should do," she said harshly as he paled. "It was small when it started. Little touches. Little things. Nothing obscene, at least, I didn't know it was then. I know now that it was..." She fiddled with the towel, her eyes down, her face going ashamed. "He got hard when I'd sit in his lap, and he would spend an extra long time bathing me. Little things. But as I grew older, he grew more interested in me. My mother acted as like she never really noticed, I think she was trying to hide away from it," Ali mumbled, getting up to move to the window as Nyx watched, half-holding his breath. "Even still, she was a wonderful woman. She was the one who took me to dance and encouraged me to follow that path. She loved me. She really did. But she was scared of him," Ali muttered, staring outside. "When I was sixteen, I don't know. Maybe it was what I wore for dance that day, maybe he was drunk, but he came into my room, and assaulted me. Tried to sexually assault me. And where my mother had turned a blind eye to his groping before, she wouldn't let him do that." Ali said, her eyes getting wet as she stared outside. "She attacked him. She stopped him, and I ran away that night. But I don't... I don't want children. I don't feel as though I should, or can, properly care for a child after that kind of life. I need to focus on my own life, and the people I love, without making a small child." she mumbled, shaking her head as Nyx sighed, getting up and moving over to her.

"Alyson..."

"Is that a dealbreaker?" Ali asked, glancing up at him with damp eyes as he shook his head.

"No," Nyx smiled. His hand cupped her chin, making her look up at him carefully. "If you never want a child, and we ever married, then we would never have one. I'm not a rich man. I have no name to worry about passing along. No legacy. I'm just stupid old Phoenyx Coleman. My father's long dead, and my mother..." he sighed, shaking his head slightly. "I have a feeling she's on her way," he said quietly as she stared, then grasped his free hand with hers. "That's where my money goes, Alyson. My mom's sick. I care for her with every dollar I get. I make very good money here. I could support a family of four with what I make here easily, especially with my tips, but I have to pay for her treatments," Nyx said, his own eyes getting wet as she shook her head.

"Phoenyx, I'm so sorry."

"You're sorry," he chuckled, his thumb stroking her lip gently as she peered at him. "I'm sorry. No one should have to deal with that from anyone. And you dealt with it for years upon years," he said, tugging her to him as she let her hands splay on his chest, her eyes soaked. "Your mother. Is she...?"

"I don't know." Ali said quietly. "Like I said, I ran away that night. I've never seen them since."

"Do you know how strong you have to be to run and care for yourself since you were sixteen?" Nyx peered down at her with bewilderment in his voice. "My mother would adore you. She'd think you were a spunky thing," he said as Ali choked out a laugh. "Would you want to meet her at some point?"

She blinked up at him, her eyes wide as he chuckled. "B-But..."

"We've shared more tonight than I have shared with some women that I have tried for second dates with, and I never get further than that. You are the first woman in a long time to connect with me, Alyson. I'm not saying to meet her on Saturday, she's too ill right now. But when she's feeling better, would you meet her?" Nyx asked, his voice slightly hopeful as Ali bit her lip, then nodded slightly.

"Y-Yes, alright."

"Great! She taught me to cook, I wish you could have her actual cooking. She was an amazing cook back in the day. Speaking of cooking, the food's likely cold as fuck now, but still tasty if you want it?" Nyx chuckled, pointing at the plated spaghetti as she laughed, wiping her eyes and nodding.

"Yes, I'm still starving!"

"Good! And Alyson..." Nyx said, grasping her hands as she blinked up at him, her eyes widening, "...I was serious. The actions of others don't make me think lesser of you by any means. If anything? I think you're a stronger woman for surviving through that," He kissed her hand carefully as she bit her lip, then nodded.

"T-Thank you."

"Of course. Now, let's eat, and then let me take your mind elsewhere again," he said, smiling as she flushed slightly. "If you want me to, that is."

"I absolutely want you to..."

-ALYSON-

A MEAL AND SOME SHEET-TANGLING LATER, AND THE TWO collapsed into Phoenyx's bed, both panting tiredly. Nyx rolled to the side, tiredly cleaning up as Ali stared up at the ceiling, her eyes exhausted, then locking on his as he rolled over towards her, stroking her hair. She smiled, then let out a deep sigh, her face utterly satisfied as he chuckled. "Mm, Alyson, I think I'm spent," Nyx snorted, his ashen eyes on her as she let out a snicker.

"Oh, that only took once on the wall, once on the sofa, and twice in the bed." Ali laughed, her eyes mischievous as he grinned deviously. "Not to mention when I took you down my throat..."

"God, let's not forget *that*, that was an experience in and of itself." Nyx groaned, then traced her sides carefully as he smiled at her. "I wish our time was tomorrow again, and not his," he said, lacing a hand through her hair to stroke it as she nodded. "...and I wish my stupid mouth had stayed closed rather than telling you to let us share."

She blinked, then sighed, curling into him as he kissed her forehead. "Phoenyx..."

"I know. My idea, my consequences," Nyx's voice was wry as he thought about the repercussions of his own stupid ideas, making him sigh. "It doesn't mean I like it, not after the evening we just had," he said as Ali nodded, "...and I think I'll like it less and less as we grow closer," Nyx frowned. "In trying to make sure you would still spend time with me, because most women simply didn't want to spend time with me beyond the first day or the first night, I guaranteed that I would have to give you up to him as well." Phoenyx sighed, looking up as his hand grasped onto her shoulder.

"If you would have asked that afternoon..." Ali muttered, her eyes down as Nyx groaned.

"Don't tell me you would have simply chosen me." Nyx moaned as she got quiet, then he looked down to her with wide eyes. "You aren't serious?!"

"We had a connection that day." Ali mumbled, her hand tracing his chest as he brought one hand to his forehead, slapping it exasperatedly.

"I'm an idiot," he groaned, then glanced down at her as she bit her lip hard, "...but a deal is a deal. Be fair to the rich fucker," Nyx snorted as she nodded, frowning. "I think he does care for you, but he hasn't had to really show anyone how he feels for them in a long time." Nyx said cautiously as she nodded.

"H-His family?"

"Bastards." Nyx warned her, his eyes up. "I've heard stories from him. Alyson, they're bastards. Rich, pretentious bastards who treat Benjamin like shit. He would be better off writing them all off and starting off fresh."

"Then why doesn't he?" Ali asked, her face curious as Nyx held up two fingers and rubbed them together, her face getting a look of understanding to it. "Oh."

"They control his purse strings, even though he controls the businesses. He does the work while they sit on their asses," Nyx snarled, shaking his head. "I hate those bastards. They treat him so poorly and they expect him to be nothing more than a cock to breed and produce little baby Hancotts for them to extend their line, whether he loves the mother or not."

"Are all rich people like that?"

"The extremely rich ones?" Nyx frowned, then nodded. "Yes. They want their little babies to pass on the lines, then the spouses can go play with whom they like. It's a fucked system."

"Ben..."

"Hates it with a passion. He got out. He ran after his brother died," Nyx muttered. "He told me a bit about it. His brother's name was Bartholemew. He was kind, but planned to marry to please their parents. If he did, the pressure would be off of Benjamin. Ben could do as he pleased. He was the second-born. The firstborn was what mattered." Nyx said as Ali nodded, peering at him. "Bartholemew was in an accident. Ben hasn't told me all of the details, but it was terrible. Ben wishes he had done more to save him. Now, though, the pressure is on Benjamin as the only son to provide heirs and pass the name on."

"Poor Benjamin..." Ali murmured, her eyes damp as Nyx nodded.

"I hate it for him, and I've suggested that he just live a simple life, leave the bastards and be a simple man. But he fears that without their influence and the family money, he will have no way to provide for himself or his business ventures, and for part of that, he's right. He keeps the 'Cat afloat." Nyx sighed. "He's a gifted businessman, the money is honestly his, not theirs."

"You care about Benjamin a lot." Ali said, peering up at him as he blinked, then reddened slightly.

"He's my best friend."

"He's very lucky to have such a caring best friend," Ali said, stroking his cheek as Nyx sighed, then smiled at her.

"Thank you."

After a few moments, though, Ali let out a small chuckle, her eyes growing distant. "Funny," Ali muttered, laying her head on his chest as Nyx blinked down at her. "You said that no woman would be suitable for Benjamin if they did not provide heirs for him."

"Right, his parents are adamant about children," Nyx said, sighing as she tightened up around him, stiffening slightly.

"I'm already unsuitable then," Ali said wryly, her eyes damp as Phoenyx blinked, then sat up slightly, cupping her face as he shook his head.

"No, you aren't."

"For Benjamin? Yes," she murmured, smiling as he stared. "I won't change my stance, Phoenyx. I refuse to bring a child into the world. I don't want to be a mother. I don't want to be with a man who would force that on me." Alyson said as Nyx nodded, stroking her cheek.

"He wouldn't do that."

"But he also won't stand against their whims, will he?" Ali asked as Nyx quieted, and Ali smiled slightly. "You see?"

"Get to know him before you jump to worrying about that." Nyx said quietly as Ali chuckled.

"I thought you'd be thrilled I was writing off any chance that I would have with him."

Nyx's eyes widened, then he snorted loudly, shaking his head. "Fair point, but I want you to make an honest decision, not one based on pillow talk with me," Nyx said, bringing his lips gently to hers as she sniffled. "Sleep for now."

"Will... will you..." Ali trailed off, her voice timid as he blinked.

"Yes?"

"Would you tell him?" she asked as Phoenyx stroked her hair, his eyes confused, "...that I do not want children? Gauge his reaction for me, before I go putting myself through heartbreak again?"

Nyx's eyes softened, as he had been the one to put her through that the last time, and he nodded. "Of course, my lovely Kitten..." he said, stroking her curls as she rolled into him, her hand resting on his chest. "Rest..."

CHAPTER 11

Insanity is in the blood...

-BENJAMIN-

AN HOUR OR SO LATER, THE DOOR TO THE FLAT opened back up, and Benjamin came in to dimmed lights. Glancing into the kitchen, he found the dishes washed, minus a small amount put aside for him, thank God, because he was starving.

He set the wine he had brought in on the counter, then stared into the kitchen. Moving to the plated food, he uncovered it, then began scarfing down the pasta, moaning quietly as he chewed the food and swallowed. "If the man was a woman, I'd have married him for his cooking skill, fucking amazing cook," Ben groaned, taking another bite as he glanced around the flat.

Ali's things were scattered throughout. Her bag, her clothing, her tights were dangling precociously on a chair, her leotard tossed to the side of the wall. Her hair comb was resting on the counter, and his hand snaked out and picked it up, toying with it as he chuckled. To be honest, the femininity was a nice addition to the usually overly-masculine flat.

"I love this comb, something about it..." Ben smiled, twining it into his fingers in one hand as he took another bite, swallowing again, the dangling moons and stars resting on his knuckles, "...reminds me... I don't know. But it seems perfect for her."

Sighing, he set the comb down, then peered around a bit more, finishing the plate quickly and setting it in the sink to be done in the morning. Yawning, he walked through the flat, then glanced into Phoenyx's room and got a glimpse of Nyx's bed.

Phoenyx's arm snaked around her waist, her body gently curled around him as she slept. Chuckling, he simply moved for his own bedroom, then stopped as a creak from Nyx's bed caused him to pause.

"Ben?" Nyx yawned, throwing his trousers on as Benjamin nodded, his eyes gentle.

"Yes. Sorry to wake you, I brought that wine, but it looks like I got in too late." Ben snorted, glancing in at Ali as she slept. "Go back to bed."

"No, no." Nyx muttered, closing his door slightly behind him as Ben blinked, frowning at the look on Phoenyx's face. "She told me what she told you," He said quietly, his eyes down as Ben sighed.

"Ah..."

"Benjamin, you should know..." he muttered, then stopped and sighed.

"What?"

"She doesn't plan to be a mother." Nyx said seriously, his eyes going to Ben's as Ben frowned.

"What? What do you mean?" Ben asked, peering at Nyx as he moved to the window, making Ben follow.

"Just what I said, Benjamin. She has no intentions of motherhood. She'll tell you that in her own time, but don't pressure that on her, for the love of God," Nyx hissed, his eyes hard. "She's pretty firm on the fact that she doesn't want kids, ever. She's very upfront and honest about that." he said as Ben sighed, looking out the window.

"Fuck."

"Yeah..."

"I...I don't know what that would mean for me," Benjamin admitted, his eyes focusing outside as Nyx nodded. "My parents expect heirs, Phoenyx. Even if I didn't love the damn woman, they want little brats. They expect me to bring home a woman I can fuck and impregnate, to extend their line."

"Benjamin, you have to decide if you want to marry a woman you love or marry a woman to breed with. Do you want a woman for her heart or her womb?" Nyx asked, his eyes on Ben as he ran a hand through his hair. "Alyson is willing to give us both a chance, but we shouldn't waste her time if we're not interested in someone who isn't willing to give us a child," he said as Benjamin stared at him.

"And you?"

"I don't need a child for happiness." Nyx chuckled. "I've been poor as fuck my whole life, Benjamin. I know how fast one can fall into debt, how fast you can end up broke as a joke, and how hard it is to raise a kid in that. I had to watch Mom struggle to feed me, and half the time, she didn't even eat. I can't help but think that if she hadn't skipped so many meals, she wouldn't be so sick now. No, honestly, thinking about it. I might be in the same line with her. As much as I'd love to have a baby, for her to have my baby..." he said, his eyes slightly wistful as he stared out of the window, "...I don't want to risk throwing a child into the hell I grew up in any more than she does. Growing up eating out of garbage cans some nights because we couldn't find dinner for a week. No, Benjamin. You don't really understand, you are an upper-class man. You can simply decide to have children. Throw away your condoms, your birth control, and find a woman," Phoenyx said, his eyes on Ben as Benjamin stared.

"Phoenyx…"

"No, let me finish." Nyx said, his eyes firm. "You have that choice. You can just do that. But for me, if I did that, I'd bring a child into a world of nothingness. A world where they'd be adored and loved, yeah, but still, a child I can't support. Alyson? She'd bring a child into the world that she can't be sure that she would be mentally fit to care for properly, and I understand that, believe me," Nyx said, his eyes wide. "She admits her flaws. She knows that she was scarred as a child, and she's terrified of having a child of her own."

"Why are you telling me this?" Ben hissed, his eyes on Nyx as Phoenyx stared at him, then looked out of the window.

"Because I told her I would. She said she would as well, in her own time, but she asked me to say it first because she wanted to avoid more heartbreak like she got the other day. After that hell that I put her through, I absolutely agreed to tell you." Nyx watched as Ben recoiled slightly. "We grew a lot closer tonight, Benjamin. We didn't just sit up here and fuck the whole time."

"I won't lie, I was really hoping that was all you did."

"No. You'll have your chance, I won't take that from you. But she and I did connect tonight," Nyx said, looking outside as Ben stared. "Did you do it?"

"Yes."

"Goddamn it."

"I swear, I'll tell her tomorrow." Ben said quickly as Nyx glared at him.

"You should have asked her first!" Phoenyx snarled, then ran a hand through his hair. "You're not even with her a full day and you're already making a fuck up! Do you realize how much stress you're gonna put her through?"

"She'll be fine!"

Ali's face, groggy and confused, popped out of Nyx's room, and the two quieted as she peered at them. "...'s everything ok?" she asked tiredly as Ben nodded fast.

"Yes, my dear," he said, smiling at her standing there in Nyx's shirt. She came over quietly, rubbing her eyes, and Nyx sighed, his face worried. He watched as Ben's face softened, pecking her cheek as she came up to him. "I promise, it's all fine. Go to bed. We have a long day tomorrow."

Alyson nodded, then glanced at Phoenyx, who wrapped an arm around her. "I'm coming. Benjamin, I'll see you in the morning." he said, then he gave him a look that spoke volumes as he led her back into his bedroom.

'Tell her, goddamn it, or I will.'

Ben frowned, then yawned with exhaustion from the long night, plodding across the floor to the bathroom that was between the two bedrooms. Stripping himself of the dirty, grimy-feeling clothing that was covering his body, he relieved himself first, then got the shower started as he ruffled his own hair and scratched his head tiredly. As soon as the spray was going, he stepped in, sighing in utter relief as the water went over his body, rinsing away the overnight grime.

"Fuck me, that's better." Ben chuckled, his head going into the water as he sputtered slightly. He carefully began washing his arms, peering up thoughtfully, his thoughts going to a dream he'd had the previous night. It had been a dream of a fight between himself, Nyx, and Ali, though their names were changed. In it, he'd thought he had caught Ali cheating on him with Phoenyx. But in actuality, he'd been caught by her doing that very thing, something that had made him cringe thinking about it. Phoenyx had been understandably livid with him, comforting Ali, and she had been... powerful. So, so powerful. Shuddering, Ben took a breath as he scrubbed, lost in thought.

As the water ran over him, he allowed his eyes to drift shut. His mind wandered back to his dream, how his dream had shifted, moved into something else. He had been walking down the street, one hand out, and a small orb of water hovering in his palm, then swirling around his arm before moving back to his palm. He'd been concentrating, trying to control the water, which was moving at his command. Every thought had controlled the orb, causing it to move and swirl.

He opened his eyes to see the water of the shower slowing slightly. He stared in shock, his hand raising up to touch the droplets. Multiple drops of water gathered, like a star imploding, being gathered to one core. He couldn't see his eyes, but he could swear it had gotten a bit brighter in the room.

His eyes glowed brilliantly, the water rippling, then curling around his arm as he jumped. "Hell!" he yelped, nearly slipping in the shower from shock. The water began to flow around his body gently, causing him to take a shuddering breath. "I never woke up this morning, did I? That must be it, I'm still sleeping," he said, then frowned and pinched his own hand. He hissed slightly, the pain stinging and causing him to swallow heavily. "Not a dream, then."

His hand went forward a bit, the water zooming from his body to hover above his palm. He watched as the water coming from the shower head slowed to almost a crawl, seeming to hover in the air. He swallowed heavily once more, then tilted his head to the side, his hand going out as if he were throwing something invisible. Water shot across the room as he sputtered with shock, his eyes widening as it bounced off the door and splashed on half of the room, including the toilet paper and dry towels. The water began to seep below the door, and a voice called out worriedly.

"Ben? Are you alright? There's water coming out here like a small river! Did a pipe burst?"

Ali's voice rang out as he jumped, his focus wavering, causing the water to fall as gravity regained its hold on the liquid that was in the shower itself. It splashed around him, causing him to slip and fall, barely recovering before knocking himself stupid, then sitting up quickly.

"Ben?! That sounded awful, are you ok?!"

'Think of an excuse, think of an excuse.' he thought quickly, his eyes wide. "Yes, Alyson! I thought you were going back to bed!" he said fast, staring at the door as she spoke once more.

"I had to use the bathroom. Nyx told me there's just the one bathroom in the apartment, so I was waiting on you to finish up."

"I'm so sorry you had to wait, Alyson! I-I'm fine! I just... I slipped and fell!" he called out, clearing his throat. *'Come up with something else! Make it more believable, you fool!'* his mind hissed at him. "I-I was... Um, I was taking care of... personal matters! You were already soothed by Phoenyx earlier, but I saw you all wrapped up like a lovely present and ended up hard as a stone! I t-took care of that and lost my balance!" he lied smoothly, groaning inwardly. The best he could come up with was that he was getting off?

"O-Oh! Um, okay! Sorry to h-have bothered you, then!" she squeaked, causing him to shake his head.

"Quite alright! I appreciate your concern, Ali!" he called, then took a deep breath to steady himself. "I'll be out of your hair in a moment!" he called again, then turned off the running water, his eyes wide as he took in the chaos around him.

Water was dripping down the walls, causing streaks of moisture to puddle at the floor. It flowed across the tiles to settle into every crack and crevice, going under the door as Alyson had said. He reddened, then shakily stood, stepping out of the tub and watching the water around him. His hand came out once more and he focused, then stared in shock as the water seemed to flow backwards, coming back towards him rather than going in the opposing direction. It flowed up his legs, his hand twisting and coaxing the water back up, back into an orb that hovered above his palm. He sucked in a rough breath, then let his hand go limp, watching as the water splashed back into the tub.

The floor was now damp rather than soaked, and he glanced around before grabbing the towel in the room, which was now just as lightly damp as everything else. He wrapped it around his waist, then moved to the door, peeking out to come face to face with Ali, who was blinking at him curiously.

"Are you alright, Ben? You seemed to be having trouble."

"Just fine, unless you want to help me that is." He grinned, wiggling his eyebrows at her as she leaned away giggling.

"Ben!" she squeaked, then bit her lip as she smiled. "As much as I'd love to, and believe me, I would, Phoenyx kind of wore me out," she said, her eyes almost sad as he smiled.

"Are you sure? Because I promise you, I can do things that Nyx couldn't dream of doing," He leaned against the door frame as she bit her lip. "Come on, honey, say yes. Please," he purred, leaning closer again as she flushed. "I want to treat you like the temple you are. I want to cherish you, worship at your feet and work my way up to all of the other places," he said, his eyes staying on her as she sucked in a breath. "Be my goddess for the night, love. Please."

She swallowed heavily, then nodded slowly as he smiled. He moved out of the way for her, watching as she ducked under him and closed the door to the bathroom. "Meet me in my room," he said, hearing her squeak in response. With a small smirk, he headed for his room, leaving the door open for her as he lay across the bed like a wolf in his den.

CHAPTER 12

We belong to the shadows of the night...

-PHOENYX AND ALYSON-
GLASTONBURY, ENGLAND
457 A.D.

ALYSON, NO, YOU SIMPLY DON'T UNDERSTAND!"

Giggling and chuckling echoed through the hut at this, as it often did when Phoenyx and Alyson were left alone while Benjamin went to go on a mission of mercy to the villages. As usual, he lay in the hut shirtless in just his leather trousers, because Phoenyx simply grew annoyed with too many layers of clothing on. Then again, that made sense, as it would be rather annoying if your shirts always caught aflame when you tried practicing with your elemental ability and slightly miscalculated even a hair.

"I understand completely!" Alyson laughed, her eyes on him as she lay on the fur rug on the hut, her eyes wide. "You wish to practice your flames on me! Use me as your test subject!"

"I'll make it enjoyable for you, my goddess!" Phoenyx said, his eyes wide as she kicked at him, laughing. "Hey!"

"You'll turn me into dinner!"

"Never!"

"Phoenyx!"

His fingers snapped and a flame appeared between them, causing her to squeak and curl up, her white and light green dress shining in the light of his flame. "My goddess! Look!" Phoenyx chuckled, then grasped her hand as she beamed, her eyes wide. He blew at the flame, sending a small bit to swirl around her wrist as she bit her lip nervously. His eyes were lit white, and his face was focused as he kept the heat low enough to not burn her skin, causing her to be able to experience the flames on her body without being harmed. "You see? I won't let them hurt you, my love. I control them. They're my toys."

Alyson nodded as he twitched his fingers, summoning the flames back towards him carefully. "I know. It still frightens me, though." She muttered, watching as he let the flames spiral through his fingers. "It can scorch and singe skin away. I have seen it do so, Phoenyx."

"Only when I command it to do so," Phoenyx's voice was firm, his white-eyed gaze going to her as she bit her lip. "Benjamin's water, it can drown and overwhelm the lungs, killing in moments if he chose it to do so, and in the direst of circumstances, he has had to do so," Phoenyx said as she sighed. "His water can push with the force of a raging storm, cutting away skin like a blade..." he smiled. "...and it can be gentle, like a stream going over your skin." He traced her cheek with his hand as her eyes fluttered. "If his gifts can be gentle, why can mine not be as well?"

"Flame and water are not the same, Phoenyx," Alyson sighed, her eyes on him as he frowned, then smiled slightly.

"Let me prove it."

"What?"

"Let me prove to you that my flames can be as gentle as his water," Phoenyx said, sending his flames away for a moment as his hands went to her dress. She peered at him carefully, her eyes curious as he grinned. "We have played, we always play, but we don't truly explore what my gifts can do, aside from heating my own body's temperature, and while I know you enjoy that..." Phoenyx grinned, watching as she flushed slightly, "...I swear, I have more to offer."

Alyson's fingers traced her dress, then she nodded, her hands going to the lace at the center that held the green fabric of her dress on. "Alright, but Phoenyx..." she warned, her eyes stern as he grinned playfully. "One burnt hair and I wallop you with a stone."

"Yes, my beautiful goddess!" Phoenyx beamed, watching as she snorted, her hands unlacing the dress and letting it slip open. Her shoulders came bare, letting her shimmy herself from the rest of the dress and set it to the side as he smiled, his eyes on her bare form as she lay back, shaking her head. "You always look like such a stunning creature. Like a doe, resting in the chilly winter's forest..."

"And you always like to fluff my ego." Alyson smiled, then sucked in a breath as his eyes went white. His hands twitched, causing flames to swirl onto her like snakes, slithering into every nook and cranny as she gasped. "Phoenyx!"

"Yes?" Phoenyx beamed, his eyes on hers as she panted nervously, refusing to move. "Relax, my love. I won't burn you."

"Your flames are sliding along me like... like serpents!" Alyson said frantically, her eyes wide as Phoenyx chuckled.

"Does it feel bad?" Phoenyx asked as she bit her lip, then shook her head, taking a breath.

"N-No. It... It feels strange, though," Alyson said as Phoenyx nodded.

"You're used to his water is all," Phoenyx said, his warm hands stroking her skin as she watched him. "You can move, Alyson.

Touch them. Go ahead," Phoenyx encouraged, his eyes on her as she let her hand come up to his, where he still had a small ball of flame lit alight within his palm. Slowly, she brought her fingers to his palm, reaching to the flames, then snaking them into them, her hand trembling slightly.

No pain, but warmth.

It was like running her hands through silk.

She blinked in surprise, feeling as she swiped his palm, and he chuckled in amusement as he grinned. "You see? I won't let anything happen to you, my love." Phoenyx beamed, his eyes on hers as she tilted her head curiously, his hand lacing with hers and the flame in it moving to swirl with the rest of the flames along her body.

Letting herself sit up, Alyson swallowed and took in the designs that Phoenyx was making along her body, then snorted as he grinned cheekily. The flames swirled around her nipples and breasts, creating little designs and patterns as she bit her lip, then chuckled. Down along her mound, the same thing; the flame had swirled into an intricate, beautiful pattern that she honestly wished she could have made into clothing.

"I wish I could wear this as a chemise, to be honest," Alyson smiled softly as he raised an eyebrow, then laughed quietly.

"It's an old family crest." Phoenyx said softly as she peered at him, her eyes widening. "I modified it to match the occasion, but yes. We would get it on red dresses, back when ladies in my family had money," Phoenyx sighed as Alyson nodded.

"It's lovely..." she said, letting her hand go down into the design as he watched, intrigued at her fingers tracing the patterns. "What was your family like..." Alyson's face shifted into intrigue as Phoenyx blinked, then smiled, "...if you don't mind my asking..."

"No, no, I don't mind at all, Ali." Phoenyx smiled, his hand coming up to trace her shoulder. "We were proud lords, much like the water sprite and his line." Phoenyx murmured, his eyes gentle. "We weren't always destitute, with nothing to our name but the flames in our hearts." Phoenyx sighed, then let his hand come down to stroke her hip. "We had lords and ladies in our courts. Beautiful castles to live in with feasts to fill our bellies."

"What happened?" Alyson asked, frowning as Phoenyx growled slightly.

"The Order." he hissed. "We were drawn into the conflict when it began so long ago. We were mages, and as such, we gladly came to arms against the necromancers, trying to put a stop to their dark magic. But those before me were cocky, too cocky." Phoenyx sighed, his hand stroking down her thigh as she nodded. "Where we knew alchemy and were fire elementals, calling hellfire itself to our aid, we were weak elsewhere. But we refused to admit it," he said, his face serious. "It is why I always admit my flaws. At least, I attempt to."

"Sometimes you do." Alyson chuckled as he grinned.

"There are not many left in my line. The seraphim have seen to that. We have to renew and rebuild our line." Phoenyx brought his lips to her shoulder as she shivered, then smiled. "To be honest, I was hoping that someday, I could ask you to do me that honor," he muttered as she bit her lip. "I realize that the water sprite has likely already asked, and I would not ask you to be a breeding mare. But I would truly wish to have a child with you," he said quietly as she smiled softly.

"If we ever finish this," Alyson sighed, then nodded. "I would not be adverse to bearing you a child. I wouldn't gate having a whole herd of babies from the three of us, to be truthful."

"Do you mean that, my angel?"

"I do, though Benjamin does not seem to understand my reasoning for waiting. He wishes for children now." Alyson sighed as Phoenyx rolled his eyes.

"Benjamin is a dodo," Phoenyx huffed as Alyson snorted, shaking her head. "What?! The spoiled little shite hated the idea of the three of us sharing in the first place! When you expressed that you had feelings for me, he wanted to blast me with his water into a stone wall!" he said, pointing at her as she snickered. "He huffed and stamped until you literally told him that you had fallen in love with us both and that it was hurting you to not be with us, and then the spoiled shite caved and allowed for you to be with us both."

"To be fair..." Alyson sighed, her eyes going down as Phoenyx smiled gently, "...we should not have gone behind his back initially."

"He had told you that he was interested in bringing another woman into your fold, but not another man, knowing you had no interest in that. He had seen the way we had spoken with one another and was trying to keep us apart. He was simply being a shite," Phoenyx said pointedly as Alyson sighed heavily. "He was the one to make a move on another first, you literally caught him with that wench from that coven."

"She was trying to build power for a spell, her whole coven was."

"He could have called you for that." Phoenyx said, his eyes firm. "He chose otherwise. Even if it was merely for a single spell, to enhance the sexual energies in the atmosphere, you know damn good and well that one can get one's own sexual energy to its peak and achieve the same result as with having intercourse."

She remembered that confrontation between the three of them. Benjamin had returned from his meeting with that coven with his face frustrated, and had found her and Phoenyx. Not intimate, they were not having intercourse, but Phoenyx was comforting her, telling her that Benjamin was a shite for what he had been caught doing.

Benjamin had exploded.

"Why the fuck are you here?!" he'd yelled, pointing into the hut furiously as Alyson had jumped, then stood, her eyes soaked, watching as Phoenyx had simply stood and snarled.

"Comforting your woman since you're too busy shoving your cock down another woman's hole!" Phoenyx hissed, his eyes going white, and Benjamin had paled white, then looked to Alyson, who was wet-eyed and frowning.

"You literally scold me for getting close to Phoenyx..." Alyson muttered, her eyes at the floor as her lips trembled, "...when you snuck off to another coven to fuck another witch."

"That is not fair," Benjamin said, his eyes wide as Phoenyx scoffed. "It isn't! Their coven was performing a spell! They were using sexual energy... I did not know until I was there!"

"And you could not summon your 'beloved'?" Phoenyx snarled, his eyes narrowed as Benjamin visibly cringed, looking down. "You're ashamed. You know damn good and well that what you did with that coven was wrong. You could have used your own sexual energy for that spell without fucking another witch."

"Why is it your concern?!" Benjamin snarled, his eyes going white as he summoned up a ball of water, about to toss it at Phoenyx, and Alyson darted between the two, her eyes wide.

"No!" she yelped, shaking her head. "Benjamin, no!"

"You're taking his side?"

"I saw you." Alyson said quietly, her eyes going to his as his face fell. "You had forgotten your wormwood. You'd said you needed it, so I followed to bring it to you," she said, a tear slipping down her face. "When I got there, and got through their maze of huts, I saw their little ritual, and saw you happily participating with that witch. So, I came back. I was stunned… in a daze…"

"She was fucking attacked," Phoenyx snapped, his eyes furious as Benjamin paled further. "She was in shock from seeing your stupid arse. Necromancers set a horde of creatures after her. I'd seen it, I came. I found her and fought them off," he said gently as she bit her lip and nodded.

"Phoenyx saved my life, Benjamin," Alyson said quietly, her eyes on his as Benjamin's eyes went back to blue, his face stunned shock. "If it were not for Phoenyx, I would not be alive to be crying at you right now."

"She has wounds," Phoenyx muttered, his eyes on Benjamin as the other male's eyes widened and he came forward. Alyson backed up, shaking her head slightly and Benjamin's face grew hurt. "Yes, see, I've been telling her lovely, yet stubborn arse to allow you to at least heal her since I saw that the damn things had gnashed her."

"G-Gnashed her?!" Benjamin panicked, his eyes wide as Alyson bit her lip, then lifted her dress, showing her thigh, which had a deep gash in it as he stared in shock. "B-But, you are not in pain, there's no bleeding!"

"I'm an alchemist," Phoenyx explained, watching as Benjamin's face grew understanding, a sigh leaving his lips. "I got her to my workshop, gave her tonics for pain, bleeding, infection, but I cannot close the wound," he said, his face worried. "I bandaged it, but it seeps through, so at this point she has been keeping those off, says they slip down her thighs…"

"And since what you would have seen was merely a couple of days ago..." Benjamin muttered, his eyes down as he brought a hand up to trace her wound, her face frowning.

"It has been like this since she was attacked, which was a little over a day ago now." Phoenyx nodded as Alyson scowled.

"It is my business."

"Those kinds of wounds do not heal naturally, Alyson! You can tell by the edges, there's a venom that prevents natural healing!" Phoenyx scolded, his eyes firm as Benjamin peered at the two, then nodded, his eyes gentle.

"He's right." Benjamin said carefully, sighing. "The slashes will not heal on their own. You need a healer."

"There are others," Alyson said quietly as Benjamin stared, his eyes on her.

"You'd risk losing the limb to spite me?"

"You risked losing your cock to spite me," Alyson spat out as Phoenyx coughed slightly, his eyes widening. "You offered to bring another woman into our bedroom as soon as I grew interested in another male. I do not have interest in other women, Benjamin! Not at the moment! You cannot simply shove another fuck friend at me to placate me!" Alyson hissed as Benjamin backed up a hair, his eyes widening in surprise and the ground beginning to shake. "I merely wanted a friend at first! You grew so jealous that you pushed me closer to him! And then you...!" her finger went up as a few of her plants began sprouting icy-cold vines.

"Alyson..." Phoenyx warned, his eyes darting to the side as she angrily shook.

"You started sneaking off to that shitty little coven! I knew they were up to that kind of shite, but I said nothing. I let it go. I trusted you. My Benjamin would never do that, not after the fuss he's put up about Phoenyx..." Alyson hissed, her eyes huge as Benjamin backed a few more steps back. "But no! I find him rutting around with some whore of a witch from another coven!"

"*Alyson!*" Benjamin yelped, his eyes huge as the floor shook and a few things fell from their shelves. "I'm sorry!" he cried out, staring at her in shock.

Phoenyx's body dodged as her plants lashed out, vines whipping from them violently as she grew more chaotic and unbalanced. "Alyson! Enough!" Phoenyx yelled, his eyes wide as she continued her tirade, her eyes leaking tears.

"You distrusted me, but I have never once been intimate with Phoenyx! And believe me, he has asked!" Alyson hissed as Benjamin whipped his head to the fire starter, who gave him a defiant glare, panting as he found a safe spot away from her plants. "Has he kissed me? Yes!"

"Did you enjoy it?" Benjamin asked carefully as Alyson's anger calmed, and her eyes went back to brown. Her plants found peace, the vines creeping along the floor as Phoenyx looked to the heavens in relief. She sighed, then spoke again.

"Yes, Benjamin..." she said, swallowing heavily as his shoulders drooped. "...but you act as though that means I cannot love you as well..."

"You love him, then?" Benjamin muttered, sitting defeatedly on the floor as she sighed again, then nodded, cupping his face.

"I love you both." Alyson said firmly, watching him frown up at her. "I love you both equally. And having to choose is ripping me in half," she murmured as Phoenyx glanced over at them, then nodded.

"We could always both have her."

Benjamin's face went to one of anger, then Alyson's eyes got curious. "Explain."

"The water fool comes from a line of lords and ladies, right?" Phoenyx asked as Benjamin frowned, then nodded. "You should already know exactly what I mean, just in reverse. In your culture, men are allowed many lovers, right?" he asked as Benjamin blinked, then got a surprised look on his face.

"Y-Yes, that's actually rather common. Lords, kings, they have a wife, and many lovers and concubines." Benjamin murmured, watching as Phoenyx snickered.

"A similar concept, but one of equality. She says she wishes to have us both equally, so let her have us equally."

Benjamin frowned, then took a breath. "You suggest that everything I have been doing with her, you would as well?"

"Yes." Phoenyx said firmly, his eyes locked on Benjamin's. "It is what she wishes. If she wishes to share a bed with one of us one night, then the other the next..." Phoenyx murmured, watching as she cringed at the moment, "...or if she needs time away from one for a bit..." he watched as Benjamin sucked in a breath, "...the other can be there for her. But both are equal, and neither takes the place of the other," Phoenyx sighed as Alyson gave him a grateful look. "This is what you want, isn't it?"

"...How did you know..."

"I have the gift of foresight." Phoenyx smiled, sighing. "And sometimes it takes me further into the future than I would like."

Benjamin quieted more at that, then ran a hand through his black hair. "Do I have a choice?"

"Always." Alyson said quietly as Benjamin nodded. "But after this, I do not know if I would stay with you alone."

Benjamin glanced over at her, then Phoenyx, and he nodded. "As you wish, then. I suppose, after my actions, that this is more than fair," he said, his eyes glancing down.

"Is there more that I did not see?" Alyson asked quietly as Benjamin peered at her, his eyes glassy.

"Do you truly wish to know?"

Alyson's eyes grew blank at that, then she nodded. "Yes. I want to know every dirty piece of shite that you got up to with that damnable coven," she hissed, her eyes on him as he nodded, staring down. "And then you are to stay the fuck away from them!"

"Agreed." Benjamin had nodded, his face dull.

Phoenyx had needed to support her back for some of the things that they'd tried doing, the rituals that Benjamin and that coven had attempted in their own attempts to 'stop the necromancers'. He had fallen in line with those who practice the dark arts, and he had not even seen it. The last straw for him was when they had convinced him to betray his lover, but by then it was too late. He had performed their dark occultist rituals.

Benjamin had been lucky. Phoenyx had been able to cleanse him of the tainted energies with tonics, though it had taken weeks. But it had been a trying time for them all, and catching him in the first place had shocked her to her core.

"It would not have been much better..." Alyson admitted, biting her lip as she frowned. "But I admit, it would have been better to find him stroking himself with that woman and her coven as she pleasured herself rather than him screwing her for the sexual energy needed for an accursed spell. One that did not even work anyhow," Alyson groused as Phoenyx nodded.

"Exactly. So do not let yourself feel guilty that your heart

Ben you to more than one partner..." Phoenyx said, his eyes on her as she frowned. "That is what I mean by Benjamin being a spoiled shite. He believes he can do as he pleases, but those he is with must do as he asks."

"He was raised as a nobleman..." Alyson sighed, moving to curl into Phoenyx's side as the male grumbled slightly. "He is having to relearn how to act around those not of the nobility."

"Fuck him," Phoenyx snapped, feeling Alyson's head whip up and her eyes widen.

"Phoenyx!"

"Well! He's a right arsehole half the time!" Phoenyx hissed, glancing at her in defiance as she huffed. "I can't stand his uppity behavior! He acts like a damn lord on a horse! Like I should be carrying his bags! 'Phoenyx, why the devil are you doing that?! That's not the proper way of grinding herbs! Come, let me show you how I was taught at the Academy...' I swear, Alyson," Phoenyx snarled, his eyes wide as Alyson bit her lip, "one more impromptu lesson on how to use my mortar and pestle, and that smarmy fuck will be walking with a limp for a week, trying to fish my pestle out of his arsehole!"

Alyson burst into giggles at that visual, her eyes widening as she curled into his side. Around them, as Alyson's eyes began to faintly glow, her blossoms began to bloom in her pots that she kept, her mirth overwhelming her own elemental magic. "P-Phoenyx! You will waste a perfectly good pestle!" Alyson laughed as Phoenyx blinked, then grinned wickedly.

"How do you know I don't already have one put aside for that purpose?" he asked as she squeaked. The heat of his flames got a hair warmer as she sucked in a breath, her eyes latched on his carefully.

"Your fire is growing warmer, Phoenyx," Alyson warned as he nodded.

"I'm aware."

He peered down at her at that, then nuzzled her neck as she let out a small whine. "Your breath is so warm..." she muttered, feeling him breathing heat along her collarbone as he pressed his lips along her throat. "Like a dragon, breathing fire along my body, except you don't plan to scorch me..."

Phoenyx simply kissed along her throat, letting his warm breath out along her skin as she moaned. "I am a dragon. I come after beautiful things, claim them..." Phoenyx murmured, pulling her against him as she whimpered quietly, "...keep them as my own..." he said, then he grinned, his eyes flashing at her as he snorted out a soft, warm flame from his nose at her, her eyes widening as she burst into giggles.

"Oh!" Alyson laughed, feeling him curl around her softly, the warm flames wrapping around them, then dissipating as they lay there. "Such an imp!" she squealed, watching as he let out a playful roar, then blew out more flame from his nose, making her giggle again. "Or perhaps you are a dragon! Will you devour me?!" she squeaked, rolling away as he blinked, then smirked, rolling to crawl towards her, his eyes devious.

"As I said, my goddess..." Phoenyx growled slightly, showing his teeth as she scooted backwards, her eyes widening. "I am a dragon, and I plan to keep you as mine, in my lair, and have you when I please." Phoenyx darted forward at that, grasping her legs as she squeaked and rolled to her belly, trying to scrabble away as he playfully tugged her to him, his trousers beginning to tent out. He snaked his hands to her thighs, stroking up to her bottom as she bit her lip and glanced back at him, then rolled back around, her eyes wide.

"What do you plan to do with me then, dragon?" she asked innocently, her hair splaying across the floor as he undid his trousers, smirking at her.

"Oh, fair maiden..." Phoenyx growled playfully, kicking the leather trousers to the side and crawling over her, his swelling hardness freed from the constraints as he moved atop her. "I plan to devour you..." he grinned, letting his bare body press on hers as she bit her lip and peered up at him, her eyes gentle. "I plan to engulf you in my flame..." he purred, his lips on the hollow of her throat as he spread her legs and nudged at her entrance, his eyes growing more needy. "...and I plan to make you mine in every sense of the word," Phoenyx murmured, pushing into her with a groan, holding her legs upwards...

Then he got a look at her eyes... and the devious grin on her face.

His head tilted to the side and her lips moved subtly, muttering a spell under her breath. He yelped as his hands and legs were gripped by chilled vines on both sides, tugging him off of her. She waved a hand, making the vines pull him to his back as he wriggled, his eyes on her as she stood and began to raise an eyebrow. "My, my, how fast the tables turn, Sir Dragon," Alyson chuckled wickedly as Phoenyx tugged at the vines, his eyes wide.

"I'll burn these things..." he warned as Alyson pointed at him harshly.

"You burn my babies and I'll kick you up the arse! Do you know how hard it is to find plants that grow without hesitation in the cold of winter?! Every time I touch the other vines in the area, they wither from the cold." she scolded, watching as he frowned. "Now..." Alyson began walking around him, her eyes on him as she smiled deviously. "I rather like you in this position, Phoenyx," she smirked, biting her lip as he glared slightly. "What?! You two pin me like this all the time!"

"Because when you orgasm, you tend to levitate, Alyson!" Phoenyx said, watching as she knelt next to him and chuckled, her fingers tracing up his leg to his hardness. With a smile, she wrapped a hand around him and stroked, watching as his head came up and his eyes locked on hers. "Goddess..."

"I never said I planned to be mean, my love." Alyson laughed, shaking her head as she moved her hand, causing him to let out a frustrated noise at her abrupt stop to her ministrations. However, the groan of pleasure he made moments later when she sank herself onto him more than made up for that, his eyes locking on her as she began rocking her hips on him and panting. "...I wanted to take my pleasure for myself..." Alyson moaned, her hands coming down to rest on his chest as her vines locked his limbs away, forcing him from being able to move.

"And you call me wicked." Phoenyx growled up at her, his eyes locked on her movements.

"At times, you are." Alyson panted, grinning deviously as she lifted her hips onto him, pushing roughly down as both let out cries of pleasure. "R-right now? I want to be wicked..."

"I believe I am rubbing off on you too much..." Phoenyx murmured, watching as she dripped around his hardness and base. "Not that that is a bad thing."

"Of course it is not." Alyson grinned, leaning down and wrapping her arms around his neck, her tongue twining with his as their lips met. She grasped his hair, getting a hiss, then a moan of pleasure from him as her hips pushed forward roughly, hungrily, her eyes staring heatedly at him. His temperature began to rise, his eyes lit white as Alyson moaned loudly, peering at him.

"P-Phoenyx!"

"Yes, beloved?"

"You are growing warmer!" Alyson yelped, clutching him to her as he grinned wickedly.

"I am. Always seems to happen when someone's doing a good job of fucking me." Phoenyx smirked, watching as she whimpered and slammed herself on him harder, her back arching as he groaned and roughly thrust his hips up the best he could, trying to match her movements. "Damn you, woman, allow me my movement!" Phoenyx hissed, his eyes on her as she shook her head, her eyes rolling back.

"No. I enjoy having some control for once!" Alyson said, panting and grasping at his chest. "B-Benjamin always... always pins me, uses his water to hold me, or his hands. I so rarely get to move freely! And you... You allow me more movement, but you always place me on my h-hands and knees, or against a wall. You d-do not give me the freedom to truly have control!" Alyson said fiercely as Phoenyx scowled at her.

"T-Then I shall allow you to have control more, but I grow weary of your vines." Phoenyx growled as she bit her lip, then slowed.

"Will you roll me to my back?" Alyson groused, crossing her arms as Phoenyx snorted, shaking his head.

"No. If you wished to ride me like a stallion, you merely had to ask, beloved." Phoenyx snickered as she grinned slightly.

"I thought capturing you was more fun."

"It was amusing. For a bit." Phoenyx admitted, then growled playfully. "Then it grew frustrating. Now, my hands and legs?"

Alyson's eyes went white again as she flicked her wrist, the vines retracting as he chuckled, shaking his head. "Better?"

"Much." He said, then grasped her waist as she squeaked, her eyes widening. Her hand swatted his chest as she gasped, a frown coming to her face.

"You promised!" Alyson scowled as Phoenyx nodded.

"And I am not going against my word!" Phoenyx said, his hands rocking her on him carefully as her eyes rolled back, her head tipping back. Her hands cupped her own breasts as he groaned, thrusting upwards as she gasped out and whined. "...Yes, my goddess. You see how much better it is when we work in unison?" Phoenyx purred, his eyes on her movements.

"I-I know..." Alyson whined, feeling as he pushed up harder into her, his hands cupping her bottom to hold her where he needed her. "...P-Phoenyx..."

"There's my goddess..." Phoenyx muttered, panting heavily as his stomach muscles tightened up, "...come on..."

Her body arched pleasingly as she yelped with pleasure, wrapping her arms around herself and letting him roughly move her onto his member as he panted roughly. With a heavy cry, he shuddered moments later, curling into her as he filled her with his intense heat, his eyes latching with hers.

As they rest, the two panted, catching their breaths. "My b-beloved..." Phoenyx murmured, his hand coming up to stroke her cheek as she smiled, "...I love you."

"And I love you," Alyson smiled, watching as he cupped her chin and pressed their lips together in a less heated, but no less passionate kiss.

"How long was the idiot supposed to be gone for?" Phoenyx asked as Alyson sighed.

"Benjamin could be gone another day or more. It depends on how ill the villagers are. Why?" she asked curiously, feeling him curl into her side and smile.

"Because, I want you all to myself a little while longer, my love." Phoenyx beamed, pecking at her as the two spooned on the fur rug, still refusing to allow himself to slip out of her.

Alyson just smiled, letting their hands lace as his kisses moved to her shoulders, and both enjoyed the quiet.

Which was soon replaced by chirping birds and the ringing of an alarm clock.

CHAPTER 13

-ALYSON-

MANY WEEKS HAD PASSED SINCE ALYSON's chance meeting of Phoenyx and Benjamin. The three had grown close in that time, working together almost daily and spending their evenings wrapped in either Ben or Nyx's sheets. The pair had done wonders at keeping her relaxed, even after the worst of days.

Unfortunately, it was doing nothing to stop the unrelenting nightmares.

Every night, it was another strange dream involving her, Phoenyx, and Ben. Each one was in a different period in time, and each one was more vivid than the last. In one, she had been riding on a horse through what she could only describe as the Wild West. In another, she was in France, a mage working with two musketeers who used magic themselves, all three trying to save the king from those wishing to do him harm. Each one felt so real, and after waking she could remember every detail.

She ran her hands through her hair, walking to the door of her apartment. It was hours before Halloween, so the 'Cat had been extremely busy preparing for the next day. Phoenyx had needed to stay past his shifts because they'd been so busy, none of the other bartenders keeping up with him. Ben had been discussing things with Lewis, trying to come up with more for her to do in the speakeasy.

Her keys stopped in the door as she thought about that, her chest heaving as she inhaled deeply. She was so overwhelmed, her mind never resting. With the dreams, her work, and school, she truly felt like she would never be able to get her head above water, not even with a life jacket. It was like she was on the Titanic, sinking into the depths.

"Ben! Can you stop it?!"

"T-The hull... it's too much water, Ali! I can stave it off, try and buy time, but..."

"There's not nearly enough lifeboats! Goddamn Abaddon, she knew if she did this, that so many would die!

"Nyx, you need to try and do something to reinforce the hull if you can!"

"Ali, if I add any heat to this floating coffin, it'll make it worse! B-Ben's the only one who can do anything to stave this off..."

"I'll hold it as long as I can. Try and help get people to safety. Try and get off the ship yourselves!"

"I will not leave you!"

The voices echoed in her head as she stumbled into the now open door, her eyes widening. She gripped the frame to keep herself upright, her eyes wide as she looked at the floor, panting. These hallucinations were coming so much more frequently, and they felt so real. She could smell the salt, hear the rushing water, feel the cold hitting her body. She moved through the room quickly, her eyes wide as she rushed for the kitchen to get a glass of water, the door remaining open.

"Turn around! Beware! You are in danger, Alyson!"

A voice, similar to her own but with a different accent, caused her to whip around, her eyes widening in shock as she stared into the dark room. She could make out shadowy figures, each one watching her with eyes that shone through the darkness, glowing a pale blue with a white halo around each iris.

'Are they... their eyes are so beautiful...'

"Do not look at their eyes! They will deceive you! Alyson!"

She tried to pull her eyes from their gaze, her mind growing cloudy, foggy. It was like trying to see through a haze, one that caused her movements to freeze. *'They look like angels...'*

"They are not what they seem! Look away! Now!"

She took a soft breath, then watched as their eyes began to glow brighter. She felt like she was surrounded in warmth, her mouth gently hanging open as she kept her gaze on them, unable to pull away. *'It's warm, like sitting in front of a fireplace, and harder to breathe...'*

She heard the voice yell once more, then shielded her eyes as the light flashed at her. She wanted to let out a scream, suddenly filled with unexplainable terror, but instead she just closed her eyes and tried to curl up.

When she opened them, she stared in shock.

She was in a dirty little cabin that felt more familiar to her than foreign. Pentacles and crystals adorned the walls, and a petite woman in a Puritan dress of a pale blue shade moved around the room with a feeling of urgency. Her hair was falling from a bun on her head, her hands hastily going across a bookshelf as she muttered to herself.

"Where is it? I have to hide it, hide our cavern..."

Ali watched her, a feel of familiar dread washing over her whole body. She stepped closer, moving up to the figure as if trying to inspect her, trying to see something that was missing, something important.

As soon as the figure turned, she realized what that important thing was.

She was looking at herself, though a version of herself from a time long ago. This young woman was a little older than she currently was, with eyes that had seen horrors beyond imagination. She was grasping a book triumphantly, flipping it open, then raising one hand as she muttered under her breath. "Oculis occultis, abdita mente. Te mane luceat lux et te abscondat a volentibus te perdere."

A small hatch camouflaged in the floorboards seemed to shimmer with power, then faded from plain sight as Ali gasped softly. She watched as the book was hastily shoved down into the hatch, then sealed with another set of words. Ali knelt, a hand carefully tracing the seam where the book had been shoved, her eyes locked on the familiar wood.

"Open up, you demon!"

"Witch!"

Ali's head whipped around as her counterpart turned, her eyes widening with fear. "They're here to kill me, all in the name of their false God," she hissed, shaking her head and straightening. "If they wish to kill me, they will have to truly fight to do so."

Her hands raised, her eyes beginning to glow a bright white, then a pale blue hue. Plants in the house rose like they were sentient, curling around at her feet as she touched one flower gently. "I need your help, my babies. They wish to kill me, and I do not wish to die. I also do not wish to harm them. Restrain, my babies. Give me the time I need to flee," she murmured, then raised her hand once more. The cold vines crept across the floor as the door was kicked open, whipping forward and grasping the intruders by the legs. The men let out shouts, some being held upside down as the vines moved around them, giving Ali's counterpart time to turn and flee, ducking past them with her dress hiked up to allow her to move more freely. Ali's eyes widened as she darted after her, following her every step.

Her counterpart ducked further into the woods, glancing behind her as she dodged past a tree. She came to a halt, however, when a figure appeared in front of her.

The woman was beautiful. Her long, curly blonde hair seemed to give off an ethereal glow, a shine coming from her very skin. Her eyes were rimmed with white halos, and with a start Ali realized that she recognized the woman. She'd seen her minutes before actually, her eyes glowing just as brightly in Ali's apartment.

Ali raised a hand furiously, her eyes narrowing, but the woman simply shook her head and raised her own hand. Her counterpart was sent flying backwards, her head whipping up to stare at the woman in anger. "Abaddon, you wretched creature!"

"You are still too weak, child of the light. On top of that, your lovers are out hunting me. By the time they discover that the trail I have left them was false, you will be nothing more than a cinder."

Ali's eyes went wider still as a blast of white left the hand of the beautiful woman, shielding her eyes as her world went white.

When she pulled them down, she was in the back of a crowd, looking up in horror at the woman tied to the pike. She was stubborn, even as a torch was brought closer to her, ready to light the wood under her feet. "Do you repent, child of Satan?" A priest near to her called, causing the woman to glare at him nastily.

"Your god is a false one! He kills innocent women and

children for his own amusement, allows for and encourages the rape of women, and even impregnated an already married woman who was still but a child! He killed his own son! He is not the god you claim he is! He is darkness and horror!" she yelled angrily, her eyes forward as the men near her yelled obscenities at her. "I will never submit to a god who would murder innocents for their own whimsy!"

"Blasphemer!" The priest shouted, his face reddening with anger as he took a step forward. "Wicked devil of a woman! Even as you face the flames, you refuse to repent, to give your heart to the Lord, our Savior!"

"Not my Savior. You forget, priest, your ideals are your own. You cannot force everyone into following your views. Your precious god gave everyone free will, remember? That means that you are free to make your own choices. Why would you be forced to follow his teachings if you had free will? Is freedom only a gift given to those who believe? Again, that's not a god I want to believe in."

She stared down the priest, who was panting with rage, his eyes flitting up to lock with hers as the torch was brought closer. The priest snatched it from the man carrying it, then thrust it at her feet as she held her breath. Ali's shriek of fear echoed as she tried pushing through the crowd, trying to get to the woman. She was holding her head high, even as the flames licked at the hem of her dress. Ali panted, shoving people aside and stumbling closer to the pyre, tripping and falling to her knees at the base of the fire. Her fingers gripped into the dirt, grabbing a handful of damp mud and squeezing it roughly.

"Look up, Alyson."

She blinked in shock as the woman spoke to her, her head whipping up in surprise. Even as burns appeared on her body, the woman maintained eye contact with her, her hair whipping in the wind and smoke. "Y-You..."

"You have to awaken, Alyson. They plan to smite you, wipe you from this plane of existence," she said as Ali stood, staring up at her in shock.

"L-Let me get you loose first!"

"I am nothing more than an echo of what once was. A shadow destined to be with you as you grow into your destiny. Listen to me. Do not be fooled by their beauty. They are not what they seem, Alyson. They are darkness, not light. They want to end you, your lovers, and everything you hold dear," she warned, the flames beginning to lick at her face as Ali's eyes widened.

"W-What do you mean?!"

"Armageddon, Alyson. Their goal is Armageddon. The end of life as you know it. You must stop them. All of you must do so together."

The fire began to engulf her, swirling violently into the air as her skin burned and charred, though not causing her pain. Her hair crisped, filling the air with an acrid scent that had Alyson biting back vomit. She put a hand over her mouth, her face screwing up as she gave her a dark look.

"Awaken from this vision! Stop them! Put an end to their madness!" she yelled. Ali's eyes went to the edge of the trees, widening as a familiar pair of heads came out, their eyes filled with devastation and rage as they raised their hands. "Awaken! Now!"

Ali sucked in a breath at the bright, white light that engulfed her again, pulling her back to the present. Her eyes opened, her head whipping to the side as the hooded figures took a step back in surprise.

"She pulled out of the visions." One of them spoke softly, their eyes still glowing as another stepped forward, her eyes furious.

"Continue anyway! We won't get another opportunity!"

"But, Abaddon..."

"Do it!"

Ali's eyes rolled back as the force of their abilities knocked the wind from her, pushing more visions into her head in an attempt to lock her away, keep her from gaining control. She could feel power at her fingertips that, until now, she had believed was a trick of the light and her imagination. Her mind swirled, memories seeming to flood into her brain like a supernova. Each memory had Nyx and Ben, and whether they were fighting side by side, or making love, one thing was very clear: the bond they all had with one another.

With a furious yell, she let her hands raise up, her eyes flashing and staying a brilliant white shade. The cloaked ones flew back, hitting the back wall of her apartment and sending things flying across the floor. Her head turned as she swung her arm to the side, causing a large shelf to topple onto one of the figures with a shout. Her whole body was on fire, tingling and almost itching with pent-up power that she needed to release, like a dam after a flood. She could see many of the figures creating portals and leaving, shooting her looks that ranged from indifferent to frightened, as though she were a demon, a dark entity that needed to be contained.

She felt something lock onto her wrist and her eyes darted down to see a band snaking around her skin, locking the power away once more. Her upper lip curled with anger as she locked eyes with the owner of the band, the one she'd called Abaddon in her vision of the past. She was giving Alyson a nasty smile, causing the metal to burn as it laced around her flesh. "Enough games," she nodded, balling her fist as the metal hardened.

Ali felt instantly weaker, almost dropping to her knees as she sucked in a breath. She tried pulling her wrist back, feeling it held in place by Abaddon, who was using the band on her body to leech her power from her. "S-Stop..."

"No. It's time we end this, Alyson," Abaddon said firmly, her eyes glowing brighter even as Ali weakened. Her hand went to her head, pushing some of her curls from her face as she broke out in a sweat, staring at Abaddon with wide eyes.

"I...I said stop!"

Ali's yell echoed as her eyes went a shining white, the power flaring from her and pushing into the band hungrily, causing it to crackle. Abaddon's face went from smug to confused, staring as the band chipped away. Ali's face scrunched up as she let out a scream of white-hot rage, causing the band to shatter into burning-hot pieces that flung themselves across the room. The pieces sizzled as they hit furniture and fabric, a scent of burn and char beginning to float through the air. One of the larger pieces flew onto the couch, hissing as the spot began to smoke, then caught aflame. Fire whipped up across the piece of furniture, causing an orange glow to fill the apartment. Abaddon hissed, then jerked herself back, her eyes narrowing as Ali stared her down.

"This is not over, Alyson," Abaddon snarled, then snapped a finger. Magic looped across the openings of the apartment, sealing her in as Ali frowned. "You will burn tonight, witch, whether it be by my hand, or your own."

With that, Abaddon summoned a pale blue portal and stepped through it, the others with her doing the same, and the light in the apartment fled as fast as it had come in. She collapsed to the floor exhaustedly, her eyes going to the flames that were now dancing across most of the furniture in the small living room of her apartment. She shakily stood, then moved unsteadily to the door, grasping the handle and trying to turn the knob, then sucking in a breath when the knob refused to turn.

"N-No... open, come on!"

She whined slightly as the flames crackled around her, her eyes flitting over to the bedroom on the other side of the apartment and the window that was just waiting for her in there. Moving quickly across the room, she rushed over to the window and let her hands grasp on the latch, shaking it roughly and letting out a small yell as it refused to budge. Her eyes grew wide at the snapping of wood, the scent of charred wood and burning fabric, and the heat that was growing around her. She couldn't get back to the door. The fire had grown, crossing the room and engulfing everything between her and potential freedom in flames.

She had no options, no way out.

Curling into a ball, she sank next to her bed and tried feebly to push the power she'd felt before out of her again, make it push the fire away, but she felt weak, like she'd been drained of everything. Her body shook as she let out a small sob, her knees going to her chest. She let out another whimper, then closed her eyes as she cried out.

"P-Phoenyx, Benjamin, Help me!"

-PHOENYX-

"Phoenyx, Benjamin, Help me!"

Nyx's head moved fretfully on his pillow, sweat dripping down his brow. Nightmares had plagued him that night, visions of a burning woman from another time going through his mind. He'd followed along, watching while doppelgangers of himself and Ben tracked a trail in the woods, trying to find a woman that had been eluding them for a while. He'd overheard as his doppelganger had sucked in a breath and told Ben's doppelganger to stop. He'd seen something wrong, something amiss, and he'd mentioned a woman... that she was in danger. The two had turned and rushed back towards a village, daylight slowly creeping over the horizon.

He'd stared in shock as they'd reached the edge of the village and seen who they were desperately trying to save... and realized that they were moments too late.

A woman on a pike, who looked almost exactly like Alyson, was limp and charring, her hair burnt to her scalp and her clothing seared off of her body, or, in other places, fused to her melting and peeling skin. She'd been horrifically wounded, and nothing they could do would fix the damage done to her form. He'd then stared in shock as Phoenyx and Benjamin had raised their hands angrily, their eyes flashing in red and blue respectively. Fire and water rushed from them as they let out unholy howls of emotional agony, the pair beginning to lay waste to the village as the people rushed off with fright.

Phoenyx's eyes widened, then he jumped as he felt a hand on his shoulder. He whipped around and came face to face with... himself.

"Y-You..."

"Phoenix, you need to awaken," his doppelganger said firmly, his face streaked with mud and blood. Nix stared, then went to touch the filth on his doppelganger's face, his breath catching as his wrist was grasped by the doppelganger.

"Blood..."

"They killed her, Phoenix," his doppelganger said firmly, his eyes hard. "They killed so many innocents. Salem's puritans panicked at the idea of witchcraft in their midst, brought so many women, men, and even children to their trials. They burned them, drowned them... Alyson was the last. We vowed that they wouldn't harm another soul, and we saw to it that no one with the power to do so was left alive," he said softly, his eyebrows furrowing with thought.

"Alyson, she looks like..."

"She is one-third of a whole. Three parts, three souls, that combine to form one. Destined to find one another for all eternity," his doppelganger said, nodding. "She has had many names, as have we. She has always found us, though, and we have always found them. We always will. It's why we were given the gift of foresight, Phoenix."

"Foresight..." Phoenyx frowned, then ran a hand through his curls. He looked down, his eyes widening as Phoenyx nodded.

"Yes. Actually, calling it foresight is an understatement. We can see things as they happen. We can view the past and we can see paths of possibility. We can see what may happen and what is happening. We can see it all. It is a gift and a curse, but it is ours to bear."

Phoenyx looked forward, then frowned as the scene before him changed.

Trees shifted like smoke in the wind, turning into a familiar apartment. A voice cried out, calling for help, one that he was very familiar with. He squinted, watching as orange flickered against the walls and the scent of smoke filled his lungs. He heard the voice calling once more, then inhaled sharply as the scenery seemed to rush past him, putting Alyson's face into his view.

Soot and smoke residue were smeared across her face, one hand feebly out as though she were reaching out for help. Her eyes flashed a bright white, then flickered green before sputtering out. "A-Ali?"

"One part of our whole. Our conduit," his doppelganger nodded, glancing to Alison before focusing on Phoenix once more. "We are her protector, fire and water both made into her shield. We are destined to find her and keep her safe, help her power blossom and grow, and love her eternally. Right now, she is in danger."

"Danger how?!"

"Mortal peril. We can all perish, and thus would be forced to seek one another out again. We are at our weakest when one of us has been killed, Phoenyx. Their goal is to remove one of us from the equation to allow the rest of us to be taken easier."

Nyx frowned, then blinked as time seemed to slow. He looked to his doppelganger, who had no shock on his face from the action surprisingly. "Taken by who, exactly?"

"The 'angelic' ones."

Nyx's face paled slightly as his eyes widened, surprise etching across his features. "A-Angelic ones?! Like... Angels?"

"Humanity has given them many names, but yes, one of those names is 'angels'. We prefer to call them 'seraphim'. I would explain this all to you more, but time is short. Alyson is in danger, Phoenyx. The fire you see is happening as we speak. They came to her, tried to smite her. They failed. They awoke her power instead, but it weakened her. She cannot defend herself any longer. They trapped her within the confines of her home, warded it from being opened from the inside. You can get in, though. The warding does not prevent others from coming to her. You and Benjamin must get to her as fast as you can. Now, awaken Phoenyx! Awaken!"

Phoenyx's eyes opened wide as he shot up in bed, his sheets quickly flung off of him as he leaned forward and panted heavily. He could still smell the smoke and hear her screams for him and Ben in his ears. He stumbled forward, not bothering to throw a shirt on with his boxers and moved across the hall towards Ben's room. He could see Ben tossing and turning fretfully as well, mumbling something in his sleep. The name 'Phoenyx' slipped from his lips, causing Nyx to blink, then shake his head at the words from his vision. She cannot defend herself any longer.

Alyson needed them, and she needed them right now.

He bolted to Ben's bed and shook his shoulder, causing Ben's eyes to fly open as he sucked in air and let out a yelp. "W-Wait, what do you mean?!"

"Benjamin, it's Nyx. Look at me," Nyx said firmly, getting Ben to sit up and look at him, a mixture of confusion and worry on his face. "We need to go. She's..."

"She's in danger."

Ben's words had Phoenyx pausing with surprise, his eyes widening as Ben nodded. "I saw her, and us. It was really weird, Nyx. A dream, but so vivid. I could smell smoke and feel the rage we had. Ali was there, but not as Ali. She was Alyson... she was d-dead. Burnt to death. You were Phoenyx, and I was someone named Benjamin. He spoke to me, actually, said that she needed us. That she was calling to us."

Nyx nodded, his eyes locking on Ben's in the dark. "We had abilities in my vision."

"Mine too. I controlled water."

"And I was a pyrokinetic, I controlled fire. It's not the first time, either," Nyx said, then shook his head. "Ben, this has to wait. Alyson's in danger, there's a fire."

"Her apartment!" Ben sat upright, his eyes wide as he threw his covers off. "Nyx, I think there's a fire in her apartment!"

Nyx nodded, then moved to the doorway quickly, rushing across the room. "We need to get dressed! We'll take my bike, it's faster than your car!"

The pair quickly threw on clothes and shoes, moving down the loft and out to Nyx's parked bike. Traffic and the night air zipped past them as they rushed towards the apartment, both smelling smoke the closer they got to Alyson's place. Fire engines could be heard in the background, heading from across the town but nowhere near their destination, as though something was holding them up from their goal.

They skidded to a halt in front of the building, and both tore through the main doors, their eyes widening at the smoke billowing from the windows of Ali's apartment. Rushing up the stairs, both stopped in front of Ali's apartment door while Ben reached down for the knob, hissing and drawing his hand back quickly from the heat searing across his palm. Nyx frowned, his hand hesitating at the knob.

'Grasp it! Your hand won't burn, Phoenyx! Fire is our plaything. We command it, not the other way around!'

His eyes hardened as he grasped the knob firmly, Ben at first trying to make him let go, then staring as Nyx turned the knob. They felt a rush of energy leave the door, like a rope being cut after being held tight for too long. Nyx shoved the door open, then took a step back at the wave of heat that exploded out at them. Their hands came up to shield themselves, but Nyx's eyes went bright red, his brow furrowing as he let his fingers move like a puppet master. The flames twisted around them, avoiding them by inches as Ben cringed away from the heat. As the flames subsided both leaned forward, hearing terrified sobbing. They exchanged a glance, then moved into the heat and flame, squinting in the light to try to find Ali.

"Alyson?! Where are you?!"

"Ali! Tell us you're alive!"

Both cried out to her, holding their breaths until they heard a whimpered yell call back to them. "N-Nyx?! Ben?!"

"We're here! We're coming, Ali!" Ben yelled, then looked to the side, his eyes taking the room in, memorizing all of the details: where the couches were, the tables, the sink. He held his breath, one hand coming out as he felt something within him thrum with energy. He let his fingers twitch, his eyes focusing, then he hesitated, glancing at Phoenyx worriedly.

'Let go, Benjamin! You have to, or you'll lose her!'

Ben's voice echoed in his ears, and with a small nod, Ben let his mind focus. He felt the water in the pipes, willing it towards him, coaxing it out of the faucets and leaks in the pipes. His eyes let off a blue glow, the light in them covering his entire iris and pupil and leaving him with a shining blue that could be seen in the darkest night.

The water drops surrounded him, growing into a mass of liquid as Ben let out a strained grunt. Though he'd been playing around with his abilities over the last weeks, he hadn't fully mastered them yet, so the amount of power he was using was tiring him quickly. He panted lightly, then thrust his hand out in front of him roughly. The gathered water splashed and sizzled on the flames, quenching some of them and making a path to Ali's room, giving them a visual of her curled up near the window, her face smeared with black and her knees at her chest. They tore across the room, both reaching her about the same time and skidding down to her, their eyes wide as she scrabbled over to them, grasping at them desperately.

"D-Ben! N-Nyx! You came!"

"Of course we did," Ben said gently, then glanced around at the flames that were beginning to flare back to life, gaining traction as the water he'd flung evaporated off of the scorched furniture. Nyx frowned, his eyes hardening as the flames flared, climbing a curtain near them. Ali shook her head quickly, her eyes watering as she clutched at them.

"W-We'll burn in here," she whimpered, her eyes closing as Ben shushed her, his own eyes getting wide with concern.

'You can stop this, Phoenyx...'

Nyx's eyes widened at the voice in his own head, causing him to look up as he raised one hand upwards, his fingers outstretched towards the flames. His eyes flickered white, then a brilliant, bright red as he began to take deep breaths. He could feel the heat surrounding him, but unlike the others, he found it to be like a friend's warm embrace rather than an enemy. He glanced over his shoulder to Ben, who was staring at him. "Go! Get her out of here!"

"B-But we can't leave you!" Ali cried out, trying to grasp at his shirt as Ben tugged her.

"Come on! He can handle this!"

"No!"

Nyx pulled himself away from them, nodding at the door as the glow in his eyes intensified. "Get to my bike!" he said firmly, his other hand coming out to grasp at his extended wrist. "I'll be right behind you!"

Ben tugged at Ali, getting her to her feet as she gave Nyx a frightened look. "Alyson, anything you need, and I mean need, tell us where it is!"

"N-Nothing! I don't have anything that can't be replaced!" her head shook as Ben nodded and pulled her, grasping her hand

and leading her from the burning apartment as Nyx got to his feet. He took a step behind them, his eyes wide as some of the flames came to his feet, encircling him and engulfing him in warmth. He could feel them snaking up his legs, tickling his skin gently and giving him a focus point to concentrate on.

With every ounce of strength he had, he willed the flames back, forcing them to bend to his control. What was a rampaging fire quickly tamed, growing calmer as the sounds of fire engines finally grew closer. Nyx's eyes went upwards as he listened for others in the building, making sure that anyone else who had been inside had already evacuated. He didn't hear anyone else, no footsteps and no other cries for help.

Turning, Phoenyx let his hand drop, the glow dimming in his eyes as he moved for the door. His control of the flames wavered, tiredness taking over his body. With one last glance towards the burning apartment, he quickly went out the door, the edges of his shirt worse for wear and holes burnt into his clothing, but his actual body was completely unharmed. Not a hair on his body was even singed.

He quickly rushed down the stairs, nearly slipping as he reached the ground level and bolted out of the doors, his eyes glancing around through the now-gathered crowd to find Ben and Ali and spotting them hovering around his bike where he'd told them to go. He glanced up as the fire broke the windows of the apartment, concentrated to that one part of the building in an unnatural way.

His hands grasped at Ali, taking in her frightened state and her shaking frame. She looked into his eyes, taking a shuddering breath to try and ground herself. Phoenyx tugged her to him as he glanced back at the burning apartment, which was now a raging flame once more. "We need to get out of here. The people who did this, they might come back," he said softly as Ali's head whipped up, her eyes widening.

"How did you know someone did this?!"

"I saw it. It's hard to explain..." Nyx sighed, then frowned as the surroundings shifted in his sight once more. He blinked as faces came into view, beautiful faces with glowing eyes. He saw their hands raising, followed their line of sight, and jerked back to see the three of them, at this exact moment in time. Without a sound he grasped Ali's shoulders and moved her quickly to the side right as his vision came back to that current second in time, his eyes darting to the trees. A small rune appeared under where Ali had been standing, the area under it turning a sickly shade of grey before crackling, leaving a small hole as the magic sucked the life from that spot. Ben's hand went up towards the trees angrily, his eyes widening, but Nyx grasped his arm and shook his head.

"We're exposed out here Ben, and there's too many people. Someone could be hurt." he said, guiding Ali onto his bike carefully before hopping on quickly and revving the engine. "Get on. Let's take this..."

Ali's arms grasped around his waist as her eyes glowed once more. "I... I know where to go," she said, nestling her head into Nyx's back as he glanced at her curiously. "I don't know how I know, but I do. I can't describe it. It's in the Salem woods, but it feels like home."

'That's because it is home. Find us, Phoenyx. You have to learn more about your past in order to move forward. Until you do so, you are vulnerable to them. They have an advantage. Take their advantage away! Open your eyes!'

Phoenyx revved the bike once more, letting the tires spin in the dirt as Ben hopped onto the very back of the seat, balancing on the edge as his arms went around Alyson's waist. Instead of aiming for the road, Nyx turned the bike towards the trees. "Nyx?"

"Yeah, Ben?"

"Do you know how to ride this thing in the dirt..."

"Can't be much harder than riding it on the pavement." Nyx smirked as Ben groaned.

"That's what I was scared you'd say!"

Ben let out a shout as the motorcycle zoomed forward, his arms tightening around Ali's waist as he closed his eyes tightly. "I hate this stupid fucking thing!" Ben yelled, curling around Ali as she glanced back at him and finally cracked a small smile. The bike zipped around trees as Nyx leaned forward, easily balancing and, for once, not fighting the foresight that was coming to him. Whereas before, he would try and shake off the strange visions of obstacles that weren't there, writing it off as road dementia or something, instead he embraced it, using it like another sense and letting his reflexes work with the sight. He dodged to the side before even seeing a tree that they'd have smashed into, curving the bike to the side to avoid a root that it was too dark to notice, but he was seeing this behind his own vision, like a mirage, catching enough of a glimpse to twist and dodge.

A crackle of power went past them, causing all of them to duck down as the energy hit a tree and snapped it down the middle like lightning. Phoenyx glanced behind them, staring at the motorcycles that had seemed to materialize from nothing to follow them. He gave the bike gas, letting it lurch forward and adding some distance between them even as Ali turned and stared. "Nyx..."

"I saw." Nyx nodded, glancing around at his surroundings with a furrowed brow.

"So, can we maybe take the next exit?" Ben yelped as Nyx snorted, then glanced at a tree that was set in a high upwards slant. It'd make a perfect ramp...

"Hey Ben?"

"What the hell is it, Nyx?"

"Have you ever wanted to fly?"

Ben's eyes opened wide as Nyx turned and went straight for the tree, the bike's front wheel skidding slightly as it hit the bark and caught traction. "Phoenyx, I hate you!"

"Love you too!" Nyx smirked, then leaned forward to give it more speed as Ali bit back a yell and clung to him tightly. She closed her eyes, holding her breath as they went up the tree, then left the ground.

'Alyson, use your abilities! Your magic! Push the bike along through the air and soften the landing!'

Behind her eyes, she could see her doppelganger again, her eyes lit up with concern and excitement, as though this were something she would have lived for. Ali's eyes opened once more, then her hand left Nyx's waist as she bit her lip, then her fingers splayed. Her hand went in front of them, around Phoenyx's back, and he simply blinked and glanced at her as her eyes went a brilliant white. She could feel the earth below them, the waves of power flowing through the very dirt, and with wide eyes she realized what exactly she was feeling. Magnetism. Waves of magnetic pull within the earth itself. It was like this ability worked in tandem with nature, with the control over the plants of winter and the ice that she had seen in her vision. It was a form of telekinesis, something separate.

She shuddered as she used her ability to slow the bike's descent back to the ground, the jolt of the tire hitting the dirt causing her to inhale sharply. She glanced behind them, noting that they'd put a lot of distance between them and their followers, but they were beginning to catch up again. She frowned, then swung her leg to turn herself. Ben sputtered as her legs went around his waist, her arms going around his neck as he scrabbled closer to wrap his arms around both her and Phoenyx. "A-Ali, what the hell?!"

"Keep me steady." She said, taking a couple of deep breaths and closing her eyes, then snapping them open, a brilliant icy-blue hue flashing from them. She extended both hands, her eyes narrowing as she spoke. "Surgat terra, crescat vites. Absorbeant inimici mei natura ipsa, et lumen extrahat tenebras, easque in ima profunda trahat!"

The words came to her naturally, leaving her lips as if she'd been singing a lullaby. Her eyes flashed brightly as she uttered the last word, the earth seeming to tremble, and seconds later, the ground itself seemed to roar. Pale, frosted vines whipped across the ground, hitting the bikes following them and causing them to vanish in puffs of smoke, their riders flung to the ground. The ground began to crackle and shake, and like the snap of a finger, cracked open below their feet. The figures were pulled into the dirt, their eyes wide as they vanished from sight, hands up as though they were grasping at anything that might save them.

With a groan, Ali's hands snapped and curled upwards, causing the ground to close in seconds. Nyx glanced behind him, then skidded the bike to a stop. He looked at the empty space where their pursuers had been, his eyes making sure that none had been missed, and though he knew he should feel more remorse for the loss of life, something in him told him that there hadn't been much lost.

-BENJAMIN-

BEN'S HANDS WRAPPED AROUND ALI AS SHE LEANED FOR-
ward heavily, then he straightened. *'Benjamin. Forward. You
know where it is.'* The voice he'd been hearing all night spoke
once more, causing him to rise off the bike. The others looked up
at him in confusion, and he simply turned towards a long-aban-
doned path, now overgrown with ivy and morning glories. "This
way." He said quietly, moving down the path as leaves crunched
under his feet. Nyx helped Ali from the bike, then the pair followed behind him, Nyx's arm wrapping around a slightly shivering Alyson.

"Where are we?"

"...this area is familiar to me..." Ben murmured, turning to a
tree... and blinking as he ran his hand across the scratched and
carved bark. An A swirled into a B, which swirled into a P. Three
that swirled into one.... As his fingers traced the markings, he
turned towards an old building, long since fallen apart.

Ali stepped forward at this point, her eyes soft as she moved
past the trees, into the hut. She couldn't make out anything, it
was so dark, but a flash of light from the fireplace had her head
whipping around, her eyes locking at a figure in the door with
glowing eyes laced with red. Phoenyx was staring at them, his
eyes seeming to burn a hole right through her, though it didn't
scare her.

Nyx's hand went down, his eyes looking up at the various
things hanging from the damaged roof. He traced his hand along
the wood, murmuring to himself. "This was home."

"This IS home..." Ali said, stepping forward once more, then
pausing at a spot in the floor. It was disguised. She could feel it,
and she could see how it had been hidden from the world, frozen

in time. Her hand came up as Ben came in behind them, his eyes taking everything in as she spoke. "Tua secreta revela... introitum nobis concede. Veniamus in domum nostram..."

"What are you saying, Ali?" Nyx asked, watching as Ben stared, then ran a hand through his hair.

"I recognize it, but I can't place it."

The air seemed to grow heavier around them, then an energy snapped free. A trap door revealed itself to the three, dusty and caked in mud, dirt, and leaves, but safe. Nyx moved forward and grasped the large iron handle to the trap door, then looked up at Ben and Ali, both of whom nodded as Ali spoke.

"Do it."

He gave them a small nod in response, and with the light of the moon shining in on them, he pulled open the trap door, and for the first time since the days of the witch trials, the three felt a sense of home.

Without hesitation, all three moved into the darkness within the passageway, going down the stone stairs that led to their destiny.

CHAPTER 14

Let my light bring you home tonight...

-PHOENYX-

THE CHILL OF THE BRICKS IN THE PASSAGEWAY HAD them shivering lightly, each one touching the wall to guide them through the darkness. They could feel the dampness that clung to the stonework, the moss that had grown up over the years.

Nyx's hand extended as he summoned flame to his fingers, illuminating the stairs that they were going down. Cobwebs and the scent of the earth filled their senses, the small flames giving them enough light to ensure that they didn't fall.

Down they went, further and further into the depths. It almost seemed unending, and the entrance above them was a speck of moonlight now, barely visible in the blanket of night.

Phoenyx's foot hit the bottom, causing the creak of wood to echo through the large space. He paused, then held the flickering flames up to get his bearings. Small torches and candles lined the walls, meant to provide light in the darkness of the night. He knelt, then closed his eyes to let instinct take over for him. "Luce tenebras, flamma perennis. Ignis qui numquam extinguitur," he muttered, his eyes flashing brightly as the flames from his hand erupted around the room like a firework. Each candle and torch flared to life, illuminating the room as Ali and Ben both jumped in surprise.

All of them stared in awe at the books that rested on the shelves in the room. Different tomes of magic sat between various rough-cut crystals, each now glittering in the light of the fire. Vines grew unchecked along the walls, poking their way into the stones that made up the structure of the large area. Each area seemed to be tooled to a specific person, the room split into three separate areas that pooled into one at the center, like a large triskele.

To one side was a large, beautiful pool of water that looked endless. Ben's eyes widened as he took a look at it, moving towards the water as though drawn towards it by an unseen force. A waterfall fell at the back of the pool, through a small, dark cavernous area. Quartz crystals of varying sizes and shapes stuck out from between the rocks of the archway leading to the waterfall, glimmering in the flickering light. His hand dipped into the pool of water, feeling as the liquid flowed up his hand and arm, swirling around him and greeting him like an old friend.

Another side was laden with books and frosty vines. It had a large pouf made of soft grass, moss, and flowers. Each plant was a breed that would grow and thrive in the chill of winter, with berries growing down where the person sitting could simply reach up and pluck a snack free. Ali moved towards the cold pouf with a smile, her hand reaching up to touch the vines and beaming as they flared back to life, a pale blue glow blossoming throughout the plants that made up the area. The books, stacked along the wall and perched precariously, were balanced only by the vines that were holding them in place. They called to her, causing her eyes to drift towards them. With a smile, she flung herself onto the pouf, wriggling contentedly into the plants as she inhaled deeply, taking in the scent of the flowers, ivy, fruit, and ice.

The final area was hot, very hot. Fire flickered within a forge, looking almost as though it hadn't gone out at all in the last 100 years. There were half-finished weapons hanging out of the forge, resting in time and untouched from the last time their creator had worked on them. Other weapons hung along the walls of the area: a bow, swords, daggers, each adorned with gem work and with intricate patterns etched into the metal. Beside that was a large kettle of sorts, with various glass bottles and ingredients on the shelves on the walls nearest to the kettle. Nyx moved to the forge, his hand coming out as he grasped one of the half-finished swords and pulled it from the coals. Sparks went into the air, drifting down to the ground as he stared at the red-hot metal. His hand shone and the blade heated further, a grin on his face. He set the blade back down, then looked towards the vials and bottles. His hand moved to graze one, caressing it like a long-lost friend. "...I know what these are..."

'Phoenyx... Alyson... Benjamin...'

-ALYSON-

ALL OF THEM TURNED QUICKLY TO FACE THE FINAL corridor, small and unseen prior to that moment. The candles along the narrow hall flared to life, the floor now adorned with glowing candles that made a path for them to follow, guiding them forward. All three froze for a moment, then moved carefully into the corridor, watching as the final room in the cavern came into view.

The center of the room was filled with three large crystals, each one over 11 feet tall and 3 feet wide. They looked like large quartz crystals, with streaks of shining light going through them like cracks. In fact, the closer they got to the crystals, the more the cracks seemed to shine.

The crystals seemed to have something in the center of them, blurred from their vision due to a small layer of condensation that had formed on the outside of each one. Ali's head tipped to the side as she stepped closer, her hand coming to the center crystal and swiping it across the condensation curiously, then yelping in shock as her eyes met the figure within the crystal.

Mortally wounded and streaked with blood, her figure twisted in an unnatural way and her wrists slashed, Alyson saw... herself. She was nude, giving her a view of every broken bone, every way her body was twisted and cracked in the wrong direction. Phoenyx rushed forward and swiped one of the other crystals, his eyes widening as his own form was revealed, his hair matted with blood and his wrists and throat slashed open. Ben shakily wiped away the last crystal, his eyes widening at his broken form, run through with a deep wound that went in one side of his body and out the other, blood dried on his corpse. Their lips were purple, their skin a pallid white. They'd been dead a long, long time...

Ali's hand pressed against the crystal as a whisper echoed in her ears, her eyes fluttering closed as the room filled with a warm, comforting light...

Her eyes reopened after a moment, and before her stood herself, though older, from a time so very long ago. Their surroundings were gone, and the forms before them were corporeal, but also ethereal. They gave off no warmth, left no footprint or shadow, as though they were spirits.

"You've finally found us..." the one that looked like her in the center said with a smile, her hands clasping together as her pale blue dress seemed to flutter around her lightly. "We knew you would, when the time was right."

Alyson's eyes widened, but her voice was gone. Instead, Phoenyx spoke, his eyes locked on his own form. "Who are you?"

"We are you." His doppelganger said with a small, crooked grin. "I am Phoenyx Blackburne, this beautiful nymph is Alyson Wintreheim, and this noble fool is Benjamin Highbrooke," Phoenyx smiled as the other two with him nodded their heads in a greeting. "Our time ended many moons ago, but it also has continued throughout the years."

Ben swallowed heavily, his eyes locking on Benjamin, who was smiling warmly at him. "You... you're all from..."

"A time when magic was the norm," Benjamin nodded, watching as Alyson stepped forward with a smile.

"If you have found us, then you have awakened enough to know everything, to learn the truth about our pasts," she said, watching as Ali wrapped her arms around herself. "Do not be afraid, Alyson Walker. This is your destiny, our destiny. It has been our destiny since the beginning of time itself, some have said."

"Why do we look like you?" Ali asked, watching as Alyson nodded.

"Because you are us. We are but a whisper of memory now. We hold a power that has been locked away for decades, awaiting the right time to break free. We are humanity's defense," Alyson said. "Many decades ago, the three of us were as one on the field of battle."

"We each had our specialties, our skills that gave us an advantage in some situations. Alyson was the scholar, the strongest spellcaster among us, and the telekinetic. She could move things with her very will alone, and her illusions were topped by none. She also had a command over cold of winter and everything ruled by it, including the plants that thrive in the cold, ice, and snow. Phoenyx forged our weapons and brewed our tonics. He was a very skilled alchemist. He was also gifted with foresight, and with the ability to control the hottest of flame, and even the blood of the earth itself, the magma within its core," Benjamin said, moving in front of Ben as he winced a bit. "We, Benjamin, are healers. We can use healing magic like no one else to mend wounds. We also have chronal abilities, letting us slow or speed up time to our advantage, and a joyful partnership with the waters that gives life, and takes it when the occasion calls upon it. The water is our sanctuary, our safe place."

"As the Order of the Light fell, we realized that there was a powerful chance that we could lose one another. We could not have this happen," Phoenyx said, his eyes locking on Nyx's. "I could not lose them, Phoenyx. It would have been like losing my own life. They were the heart that beat in my chest. Though they were not both my lovers, they were still my world. So..."

"We cast a spell to allow for our souls to always find one another, so that we could battle the darkness. We would always be soul bound and would forever seek each other out. For lifetimes, more than I can count now, we have done this. We have sought one another out, over and over." Alyson nodded, her eyes on them. "We have saved many because of this."

"W-Why are you in crystals? Not here, but in the cave?" Ali asked as Alyson nodded once more.

"These were our first mortal forms. We were once more than these mortal lives, but to try to anchor ourselves to our elements, we tied ourselves to the mortal plane. After our lives were ended, our power remained, our souls, eternal as they are, lived. It was a part of the spell that we cast so many moons ago, but also part of our core being. Our souls sought forms to take corporeal form, and we found them in the form of the lifeless, babes that had not formed souls of their own, or whom were predestined to death before taking their first cries. We gave life to the lifeless, became them, and our souls dictated the shape that the figures took as we grew, always allowing us to maintain the same features. The people who gave us physical life and birthed us over the decades were not our true parents." Alyson said. "As for the crystals... I am a conduit, I always have been, and they stored much power within themselves, even in their corpses. To keep that power out of the hands of the darkness, we cast a spell from the afterlife before moving on to the plane of reincarnation. The spell brought our bodies together in our cavern and encased us in crystal. We would remain there until our full potential was needed once more, and then we would call to ourselves..."

"What the hell do you mean? Call to yourselves to do what?" Nyx asked as Phoenyx spoke.

"To fully awaken. The spell we cast to find one another was incomplete and broken. We did not remember to add that we should remember one another when we found each other, and as such a large part of our power was always locked away. This was fine and we managed until now. Now, Abaddon has once more begun the Armageddon rituals."

Alyson, Phoenyx, and Benjamin all exchanged a look, their faces paling slightly. "Armageddon? As in, the end of the world?" Ali asked, her eyes wide.

"Yes. It has been their goal for as long as I can remember. We have always tried to stop them, to save humanity from the death that they want so desperately to inflict upon them," Phoenyx said firmly. "She will continue to try to kill you, all of you. You are all that stands in her way, the only obstacles to stop her from summoning the Archangels, the strongest of the seraphim, and kick-starting Armageddon itself."

"How do we stop her?" Phoenyx asked, his eyes locking on his former self as Phoenyx nodded.

"Her ritual will take two parts to complete. First is the summoning of the Archangels... Michael, the warrior, Gabriel, the left hand, and Raphael, the healer. They are our opposite..."

"If they are allowed to meet, to come together... they will be a struggle to stop. They are currently sealed away, locked within their own crystals, sealed there by the deities themselves, to give humanity a chance."

The cavern began to shake, a rumble echoing through the underground halls. All of them glanced around, their eyes widening as the three former selves got worried looks on their faces.

"They have followed you here, and without the wards, they will now be able to enter." Alyson said, looking to Ali as she inhaled sharply. "You must take your power, your memories..."

"You must become one. One with your powers, and one with each other." Benjamin nodded. "You won't survive elsewise. They will have sent Abaddon herself after you. She will have come to end you."

"If you do not stop her now, she will summon the archangels, and though it may take decades, they will rise if her rituals succeed. And if they rise, then Armageddon will begin," Phoenyx said with a shake of his head.

"Ragnarok. The end battle, the end times," Alyson nodded, her eyes emitting a faint glow.

"Apokálypsis, the revelation." Benjamin stood firm, then watched as light began to surround them. "We are out of time. Remember, take your power, stop Abaddon!"

"How?!" Ben asked frantically, shaking his head. "How do we take our power?!"

"You will know how, like water flowing towards an ocean. It will be natural to you." Benjamin smiled as the light began to blind them all. "Remember to lift one another! Without one another…"

"…you are at your weakest…" Alyson nodded, grasping both of their hands.

"…you are vulnerable," Phoenyx said, his voice fading into nothing as a hum began to fill their ears. The shaking around them increased, the light burned behind their eyes…

-BENJAMIN-

THEIR EYES OPENED ONCE MORE, STARING UP AT THE crystals with their previous forms entombed within them. The ground was trembling beneath them, the entrance booming as something hit the trap door they had come down roughly. Ali stood quickly, her eyes wide as she took a small step back. "What do we do?"

Nyx looked to the crystals, then back to the entrance. "We're stuck down here. We'll have to fight our way out," he muttered.

"Oh, fantastic," Ben groaned, taking a step back. "How the hell do we fight them?! I can barely summon enough water to put out a campfire!" Ben growled, watching as Nyx's head whipped over towards him.

"I'm exhausted too, Ben! I don't think I could light a match if I tried!" Nyx hissed, his eyes narrowing as he took a step closer to Ben. "You don't hear me bitching!"

"It's not bitching!"

"It's bitching, Ben. You're whining more than a fucking dog that had its nose rubbed in its piss puddle!"

"Fuck you!"

The pair bickered, growing closer to each other as their fists balled up, but Ali simply stared at the crystals. She took a deep breath, her hand coming out to press against the crystal holding her own pale corpse. Her eyes went up, her face pained as she shook her head gently. "We don't know what to do..." she murmured. The shaking increased, dirt falling from the roof of the cavern and crumbling at their feet. Ali's eyes closed as her head tipped down, her voice quiet as she spoke. "It already feels like we're one in a way..." she said as the light in the crystal grew, "...like a memory at the edge of my consciousness, waiting for me to pluck it free..."

Wind gushed into the cavern, moving around Alyson in a spiral. Her hair went upwards, her curls whipping up as she frowned, her head moving to press on the crystal. Nyx gazed at her, his quarrel with Ben momentarily forgotten, and he let both hands touch the crystal, his body pressing forward against the warmth radiating from the core. It was like a fire, waiting to break free. Heat rose, the flicker of flame rushing from the ground and sputtering upwards, like a flint sparking against dry straw. The cracks in his crystal grew, heat flowing from it like a firepit.

Ben stared up at his own crystal, then let a balled-up fist come forward, striking it right over the chest of his former corpse. "You're expecting us to just know what to do! You didn't even know what to do! You were killed because of your stupidity!" He snarled, flashes of memory coming to life behind his eyes. He could see his former self sending away Phoenyx and Alyson, moving into battle on his own. "You broke your own damn rule!

You left them alone, left them to die!" he yelled, his eyes locked on his previous form. Water droplets pulled forward, tugged from the dirt and the crystals in the cavern. They flowed around him, swirling at his feet and being pulled into the air to orbit him. "She killed them because of you! You started this damn roller coaster of death and rebirth by leaving them alone, making them weaker! Maybe we're tired of coming back to life over and over, forgetting each other every stupid time!" he yelled angrily. A single tear slid down the eye of his corpse, flowing down his cheek and gathering at a crack in the crystal, slowly seeping towards the edge. Memories rushed forward, causing him to bite back a choked sob as he saw himself with Nyx and Ali over and over, lifetime after lifetime. His head drooped down as he let his forehead rest on the smooth surface of the crystal, near the cracks. "I'm sick of always losing the ones I love every time I have to come back..."

The cracking intensified, light pouring from the crevices. All three opened their eyes at the same time as the crystals shook violently, then shattered in a flash of light. At the entrance to the cavern, figures were blocking the light from their eyes, the blinding whiteness filling every crack and crevice.

Within seconds the light was gone, leaving the whole cavern in the dark. Every candle and torch had been extinguished by a sudden gust of wind, the air growing chill with the darkness.

"They've disappeared!" One of the intruders spoke, going further into the staircase that led into the cavern as another hissed angrily at him.

"They're here somewhere! Be alert!"

A slam caught their attention as the trap door they'd taken crashed shut behind them. Two of the intruders moved to the opening and shook the handle, paling as the hinges stayed firmly shut. "It won't budge!"

Laughing echoed from the fourth chamber, the room where the crystals had rest moments before. Three voices called out into the echoing cavern, their voices dark with anger.

"Poor, pitiful souls..." Ali's voice reverberated in the air, hanging over them like a mist. "What a mistake you made..."

"You didn't trap us in here with you..." Ben snickered, footsteps echoing with his voice as he spoke. "...no..."

"...you're fucking trapped in here with us," Nyx snarled.

-PHOENYX-

THE CRACKLE OF A FLAME HAD THE INTRUDERS STARING down the corridor to the crystal room, watching as a flame flared to life rapidly. Eyes began glowing an orange-red shade, a head tilting to the side, almost curiously, then with a thrust of an arm, the fire was sent rushing down the corridor, engulfing the intruders at the front of the entrance and sending them howling backwards. The figure with the red eyes stepped forward, having followed the flame through the corridor, and he swept his hand around once.

Every candle was relit, brighter than before. The laughter of souls could be heard surrounding them, a darkness cast through the cavern. Before them was Nyx, though different than before. His eyes, glowing brightly red, were cast in shadows and darkness that made the top of his head look inky black, like an abyss. Behind his eyes, it was like magma itself flowed, and his forehead sported two small, yet sharp horns. He let out another laugh before sweeping his arm once more, the flames flowing through the room as though trying to snuff out the intruders. The two he had engulfed were unable to move or speak, and the others were shielding the fire back, though they were struggling.

"Demon!" A shielding intruder, this one a woman, hissed at Nyx, who gave her a broad smirk.

"My dad won't be fucking happy to hear you say that, he hates that god damn word. At least, coming from your mouth he does..." Nyx snarled, his voice seeming to echo through the chamber once more. "Enjoy the taste of hellfire, bitch."

The plume of flame pushed forward once more, even as one of the intruders cast a blast of dark magic at him. It struck his chest, causing him to stumble back even as Alyson moved forward. Her eyes were glowing a brilliant pale blue, shining in the light. Icy pale ivy had grown across her hair in a crown, creeping down to frame her face. Blonde streaks went through her curls, accentuating the periwinkle hue of her eyes. She tilted her head to the side, her hand coming forward as they flinched away from her, then frowned at the lack of attack. She simply smiled, then beckoned forward a shadowy, four-legged creature from the entrance, which had been flung open once more.

A beautiful white wolf crept into the cavern, moving past the intruders and coming straight to her. She knelt, caressing its fur lovingly, then murmured into the animal's ear. "...go my beauty. Show them your power," she purred, watching as the wolf turned and stalked forward towards the intruders. With a heavy growl, it lunged.

She chuckled as the intruders began to fight off the wolf, her hands clasping in front of her as she let her head tilt to the side. "Nature... beautiful and deadly all at once," she said, beaming as Nyx snorted at her.

"Never change, my love," he said, straightening and coming over to her as she turned to face him. Amidst the screaming of the intruders, he grasped her waist and brought her closer. Before that night, Alyson would have pulled away with fear from his appearance now. His glowing red eyes and horns looked as though he'd eat her if given the chance. Now, though, she leaned into his arms, her eyes going to his even as her wolf got ahold of an intruder and tore open its arm, causing the man to let out an unholy howl. Another flailed a leg, as Nyx's fire caught his pants aflame and refused to go out.

"Here. Let me help you with that."

A rush of water flowed from the cavern, going between the two embracing and hitting the flailing man square in the chest. The man fell, his leg growing soaking wet and his eyes wide with fear. The third and final figure emerged from the corridor, his eyes a brilliant pale blue. Small blue and teal scales adorned the sides of his face, going down his neck and, if one could see it, down his chest and sides. Around the scales, his skin was tinted a teal shade.

"Ben, who the hell told you that you were allowed to put out my fucking fire?!" Nyx asked with a huff, annoyed that he'd been moved from Alyson even as she chuckled with amusement.

"I did, you hotheaded asshole. These are just men and women... mortals. They're blinded by the promise of a utopia that those halo-headed bastards never plan to make good on," Ben said with a pointed look, even as one intruder shook his head.

"When the Rapture comes, they will take us with them! We have earned our place!" a woman shrieked as Alyson shook her head.

"How is murder and sacrifice a ticket to your 'Rapture'?" Ali asked, her eyes on the woman. "Do you truly believe a righteous god would require that of you?"

The woman looked down, trying to think of a rebuttal when one of the men spoke. "Shut your whore mouth, blasphemous witch!"

"You shut your fucking mouth before I shut it for you!" Nyx hissed, his eyes brightening as the heat in the cavern rose once more. "Talk to her like that again, you bastard..."

Ben frowned, shaking his head as he looked across at the intruders. "They need to be subdued but left alive. Don't you feel the air? The heaviness of darkness?" he said as Ali shivered and nodded.

"She's here."

-ALYSON-

Nyx glared, his head turning in each direction. "Oh, fuck no, where's that ugly bitch?!" he hissed, his eyes glowing brighter as Ali shook her head.

"She's their puppet master, Phoenyx, can't you feel it? The strings of coercion tugging at their minds? They may believe as she does, but she is intensifying their hate, calling them to this rage-filled behavior," she said as Nyx took a breath, his eyes narrowing.

"...Ben, do you mind? My power isn't the best for knocking out while leaving them alive," Nyx said with a frown as Ben nodded, a small chuckle leaving his lips.

"Absolutely," he said, then raised one hand. Water rose like a tidal wave, streaming from the pool at his side of the cavern and flowing around towards the intruders. Ali's wolf darted back out the door, letting go of the intruder it had attacked, but not killed, giving the rapids the space to do what they needed to do.

The water hit with the force of a battering ram, throwing the intruders back and causing them to go limp. Another turn of

Ben's hand had the water receding, flowing back into the pool, and the intruders soundlessly fell to the ground, gently being helped down by Ali's vines, as she twisted her hand and gave her fingers a small wriggle, almost like a dance.

The three moved forward out of the cavern, climbing the stairwell to exit through the trap door once more. Looking around, each of them stood within the withering cabin, seeing it from a new light.

Ali's head turned, a nagging feeling at the back of her head tugging her into the woods. "I can feel her..." Ali murmured, moving carefully forward and allowing herself to pick up speed.

"Wait for us, damn it!" Nyx said quickly, moving to follow her as Ben scrambled to keep up.

"Slow down, Ali!" Ben called. He tripped on a vine, nearly falling as Nyx snickered.

"Keep up, fish-boy," Nyx grinned, getting an ever-so-polite middle finger from Benjamin as he straightened.

"Go to hell."

"Sure thing, as long as you come with me." Nyx smirked, then stopped as he caught up to Ali. She was standing in a clearing, looking up at a figure who was hovering over the center, darkness surrounding her.

"Come down, Abaddon. Or are you going to make me come up to you?" Ali called, her hands twisting slightly as the pale vines around her curled and twisted, raising her off the ground to match Abaddon's altitude. The air around them chilled, causing their breath to come out in small puffs of frost and vapor.

"I don't have the time for you, witch. There are other, more important things to do this Samhain night. I have to release the seals, set Michael, Gabriel, and Raphael free of their bindings," Abaddon glared, her hands coming up to let the darkness swirl around her arms, gathering in her palms. With a snarl, Abaddon's hands thrust forward, sending darkness at Alyson with a force that had her stumbling back, then thrusting a gust of ice and snow towards her enemy. Nyx's hand raised, his eyes brightening as he summoned up a blast of hellfire and sent it at Abaddon, who dodged it deftly, then ducked at a blast of water from Benjamin. Both men were glaring angrily, itching to join Alyson up with Abaddon, but knowing that they would be unable to keep their footing on the vines like Ali could. Ali also didn't have the energy to keep them up using the vines along with herself and also attack. She'd be left open to an attack.

"Ben, come on. We can at least chant protection spells for Ali," Nyx said firmly as Ben nodded. As they went to take a step forward, to get beneath Ali and surround her in warmth, they felt a heavy weight wrap around their torsos. They struggled as Abaddon's darkness took physical form, turning into a sludge that kept them locked in place, bound tighter than any rope would.

Ali glared, her hand going up angrily. "Aren't you supposed to be all 'holier than thou'?! Fight fair, Abaddon!" Ali hissed, her eyes livid.

"That is fair. They do not need to be free. You and I can fight, Alyson... Alyson Wintreheim." Abaddon said, her back straight. Dark, inky wings were receding as Ali moved and let a vine whip out, striking Abaddon in the face. She let out a hiss of anger, her eyes flashing even as Ali sent another attack at her back. Abaddon sent a blast of darkness towards Ali as she hit the ground, watching as Ali let herself be lowered to the earth once more and sent a blast of light magic back at her.

The two exchanged blasts of magic as Ben and Nyx struggled against their bindings. Both were growing frantic, their eyes wide as Alyson and Abaddon moved through the clearing and sent blasts of power from their palms at one another. They circled each other, Ali's eyes darting to Phoenyx and Benjamin once more before she gave Abaddon an angry glare.

"Release them, bitch!" Ali snarled, watching as Abaddon simply let another blast race towards Alyson, who deftly dodged and brought a hand up. Vines snared Abaddon's legs, twining them and tugging her back as she glared furiously.

"At least one of them was mine before he was yours... the son of the fallen. He was my apprentice before you were even a whisper in the wind to him. Perhaps I am simply reclaiming what was originally mine."

"Nyx will never be yours, Abaddon!" Alyson yelled with rage, lunging and leaving herself wide open to attack.

Abaddon's eyes narrowed, and she glanced past the clearing towards the long drop behind the three, leading to the abyss of a lake forgotten by mortals and utilized by those who practiced the occult. Though the seraphim tended to hate the sacred places of those who followed the pagan deities, she had to admit, the lake itself, with its darkness, its vast depth that looked as though one would be swallowed whole... it would make for a perfect resting place for the three.

Starting with the woman.

Abaddon's eyes flared once more, her hand rising as she sent shadows and darkness towards Ali at full force. It was a fair chunk of her power, but if she could take one out, the others would fall at her feet easily. Ali's eyes widened as the blast hit her square in the chest, causing her power to be snuffed out before their eyes. The others struggled harder against the dark bindings that held them, watching anxiously as Ali brought her hands up, trying to physically block the next attack that threw her backwards and sent her flying through the air. She felt the wind knocked out of her body as she went downwards, her hands coming up to reach desperately for her lovers.

-PHOENYX-

ALI DROPPED OUT OF SIGHT, SPLASHING INTO THE LAKE, and Abaddon's head whipped over at the rage-filled screams that filled the clearing. Nyx's body shook, his muscle mass increasing and his teeth sharpening as he pushed against the dark bindings that trapped him, then broke them loose, to her shock. A black crown of obsidian and oNyx went across his forehead, snaking behind his now-pointed ears and around his horns. Rushing to the edge of the water, he stared over the side, begging the powers that be that he would find her, and instead seeing nothing. There was just a heavy mist and inky black water, a fog so thick that the brightest flame wouldn't be able to clear it. His head whipped back around, his voice warped to more of an animalistic tone as he crouched, then lunged at Abaddon, his magic mostly forgotten. His hands plunged down at the ground as he moved, ripping tears into the rock and pulling magma to the surface. From the heat of the molten stone his hands pulled up two blades, the hilts made of smooth oNyx and the blades themselves a glistening gold, like the brightest fires of hell.

"...Prince of Hell. Demon-seed. Plague," Abaddon hissed at him, watching as his hands whipped the blades in front of him and his mouth curled into a snarl once more.

"Your kind are the fucking plague, always have been," he snapped, moving fast and bringing the blade to Ben's bindings, causing the darkness to release him as he shook.

"You did not call me a plague before, child of the fallen. I was teaching you the light, do you remember? I sent you to them to gain their favor, and you betrayed me. But I can still forgive you. Cast out the mages, the abominations, and come back to my side. I can find a place for you in His kingdom, I swear it." Abaddon cooed, her eyes on Nyx as he panted, then snarled.

"I left your side because you were fucking insane. They taught me true love, true power. You taught me to lie, to cheat my way through life. They taught me to embrace what comes, to use it to my advantage and blaze my own way through life. They are my life now. You are a skid-mark of a memory in the underwear of life." He snapped, heat flaring from him once more, stronger than before.

"P-Phoenyx... is she there?" Ben asked, pleading with Nyx wordlessly to tell him that she lived, but Nyx's eyes spoke volumes. Ben crumpled, his head shaking as he stared at the ground. His hands balled into fists, his body shook with anguish and anger. Water pulled from around him, from the streams and lakes near to him, and encircled him carefully. His eyes closed as tears slipped down his cheeks, the water rushing to him and flowing up like a waterfall in reverse. Abaddon's hands went up, her eyes widening as the water zipped past her to grow into one mass, covering Ben's body. She let out a small hiss as one stream nicked her arm, and she stared in shock as blood dripped down her arm.

"We do not bleed." Abaddon said in surprise.

"You do now," Nyx hissed furiously, bringing his blades in front of him and crossing them. "And trust me, when I'm done, you're going to fucking bleed buckets..."

He swung wildly, her arm coming up as darkness swirled around her arms and turned into gauntlets, protecting her from the blades. Nyx snarled, ducking and bringing a hand up as hellfire swirled around them, trapping Abaddon in the clearing with them even as she eyeballed her way out. He sneered, watching as her eyes shot to him with worry. Nyx's blades ripped through the air once more, moving to tear her flesh from her body. His focus was her death, revenge for what she'd done, what she'd done so many times over the decades.

A blast of water shot Abaddon back, throwing her into a tree and snapping it in the middle as it broke and fell to the ground. She looked up in shock, her eyes locked on Ben.

Benjamin's eyes glowed brightly, a hand gripping a silver trident. He was standing straight, one hand up and aimed at her. The scales had grown, increasing in their amount on his face, and his ears had pointed more, though not as much as Phoenyx's. His back was straight, his posture poised. "Prince of Atlantis," Abaddon said, moving backwards with worry as he took a step forward, "...keeper of the oceans..."

"This is over. We're done. You're done. No more end times. No more destruction. Just peace from this point out," Ben said carefully as Abaddon snorted.

"You do not seem to understand. Humanity is war. It is hate and destruction. It has self-destructed and killed itself over and over, time and time again. They have earned their sentence, son of Atlantis. Their fate is their own."

"Not with you deciding their fate for them. Innocent, good people don't deserve to be punished for the sins of the few," Ben said firmly as Abaddon stood once more.

"She can't be reasoned with, Ben. She never could be! She's always believed that humans deserve fucking death, that all of them should be purged from the realms!" Nyx snarled, shaking his head.

"They should. They do not deserve life, nor do they deserve hope! They have done nothing to deserve the gifts they have been given!" Abaddon glared.

"Gifts?! Humans go through hell! Have you heard of taxes? Or how about just surviving? With every advancement they have made, they also have created more hardship for themselves! But they thrive and survive!" Nyx yelled angrily.

"They thrive based on deceit! They lie and cheat to get ahead in life," Abaddon hissed, her hands coming up quickly and sending a blast of darkness at them. The two blocked her attacks, each bringing their weapons up and grunting from the force of the dark waves sent their way, bouncing off their weaponry and hitting the nearby trees and plant life.

"N-Nyx..." Ben glanced over at him, both shaking slightly from the attacks.

"Shitty timing, Ben. What the fuck do you want?"

"A-Alyson would be pissed that we were hitting her ice plants," Ben chuckled, his eyes damp as Nyx snorted. "She always said it was hard to find plants that grew in the cold..."

"She can kick my ass when we all end up together again." Nyx said firmly, however, his blades crossed once more to divert her attacks more towards the stones and dirt even as Ben smiled slightly, then glared over at Abaddon.

A blast from the ravine shot her back, her eyes widening with surprise and shock.

The two stumbled as the attack was abruptly cut off, their heads whipping around as runes began to light up the sky. The forest became alive with the sounds of chittering, as though nature itself was rising with a rage never before seen. Snow began to fall from the sky, falling like a blizzard as the temperature dropped fast. The glitter of eyes was visible through the trees, reflecting the light of the full moon.

Hair flowing around her like a halo of sorts, her arms out at her sides and one leg bent, Alyson rose from the ravine, fury on her features. The finest golden gauntlets inscribed with runes encircled her wrists, leaving her hands free but giving her arms another level of protection that circled her body like a blanket. Her eyes flashed a bright, yet pale periwinkle blue, more blond creeping up her hair.

"...You live. You're like your father, deceitful." Abaddon snarled, coming back to a stand as Ali moved forward and landed gently between the two men, both of which had visible relief on their faces.

"My father is tricky, not deceitful," Ali shook her head, glancing across at the furious being before her. "Your kind are deceitful. You entice and enchant these humans into believing in you, in your creator, with the hope of rapture and eternal celebration, eternal peace. You offer death in exchange. Your rapture is nothing more than the destruction of their souls. You are deceit. Pestilence. Plague. You are the ones who deserve eradication, not us," she said with a shake of her head.

The two beside her let their hands touch her gently, one stroking her hair and the other her arm, both keeping their eyes on her form.

"Let's end this." Ben said hoarsely, emotion in his voice.

"Yeah, I'm hungry." Nyx smirked.

Ali glanced between the pair of them and giggled slightly, then nodded. "It's time. Humanity has earned another chance, a chance to determine their own fate."

"And if they fuck up, we can help set them straight again," Nyx said casually as Ali snorted.

"That too."

All three moved closer to Abaddon, Nyx's eyes flashing as sigils etched themselves into the ground beneath Abaddon's feet in blue hellfire. She went to move but found herself frozen in place. Her eyes went down, and she sucked in a breath, spotting Ben's Atlantean waters encircling her feet and pinning them in place, rooting her to the spot. The three surrounded her, then brought their hands out and grasped one another, latching their hands into a circle. Ali's head tipped down as they rose, toes leaving the ground as they began to chant.

"Light of the Morning Star, we call upon thee. By the moon of Samhain, we request your aid. Give us your power, your strength..."

The glow in their eyes increased in their brilliance as Abaddon struggled against the water pinning her to the spot. This was a predicament she had never foreseen. She never imagined that the three would ever defeat her. He had always told her that it was impossible. He would never allow it, but he had apparently forsaken her.

"Da nobis tuam protectionem, gratiam tuam, Luciferum..." they murmured, the ground flashing a brilliant blue hue from the spell. "Imitatores sumus lucis sidus. Has tenebras, hanc pestem purga."

"Dípla sta Nerá tis Atlantídas, afíste to skotádi sas na katapieí stin ávysso," Ben hissed, his eyes locked on Abaddon's form.

"Per ignes inferni te ab hoc regno proicimus," Nyx snarled, his eyes flashing brightly as he spoke.

Ali's words sealed her fate, her eyes flashing a brilliant green as light filled the circle. "Með protectionrinn ór divine,inn vér kastþúr út!"

"Ad nihilum te obligamus, obligamus ad cecitatem. Vincula solve huic regno et abito!" The three finished the chant loudly, their eyes flashing once more as the light at the bottom of the circle shot up like a beacon. Abaddon let out a scream, her hands coming up to feebly try and protect herself as she spoke.

"Armageddon is still coming, creatures! You have stopped nothing! You have only delayed the inevitable, for He has already given us the power to set into motion their release and we have already used that power to unlock their bonds!"

The final words echoed among them as the fire ate away at her form, snapping her threads of immortality and causing her to burn away. Her ash fell to the ground in the circle of fire, taken by the wind moments later.

All three came down to the ground, panting tiredly as the light left their eyes and their bodies shifted back to their normal, mortal forms. Nyx glanced at the others, then grinned. "We did it! Fucking finally! She's dead!"

"Didn't you hear her, you hot head?!" Ben hissed, his eyes narrowing. "We failed! It's in motion already! The end times are coming, we didn't stop her!"

His emotions caused the air around them to grow heavy as Ali's head shook, her hand touching his arm gently. "Ben, we'll find out what she meant. We'll stop it."

"We can't stop it if she's already done it!" Ben said furiously, angry with himself. "I screwed up!"

"How the hells do you figure that?!" Nyx asked, his arms crossing stubbornly.

"If I hadn't sent you away that day, we could have stopped them then! We could have stopped them from ever setting the rituals into motion! Instead, because I sent you two to fight alone, she got the upper hand and killed you both, and it set into motion the cycle of resurrection and death that you two have been forced to go through every time!"

"Ben, Phoenyx had seen us all fall that day. You tried to give us a chance to change our fate, but we fell. We were destined to fall that day, just like we were destined to find one another each time," Ali said softly, stroking his cheek with her hand.

"You fucking know that those stupid visions would have come to pass. They always did! We had more time to prepare because of you," Nyx snapped, shaking his head as Ben closed his eyes tiredly.

"I can't help but think that... that if I hadn't messed up, that if we'd stayed together, maybe we could have stopped her sooner and prevented their coming. Once they rise, that's it. We lose." Ben's eyes grew damp once more as Ali cupped his face.

"That isn't true! If they rise, we'll stop them, my love! Their hate will not overpower our love!" she said, her eyes staying on his. Around them the wind seemed to slow, dust hovering in the air along with leaves.

Time was standing still.

Nyx straightened, his eyes widening as he looked around at the area around them and the way time had seemed to slow to nothing. "Alyson, we have to calm him down."

"I'm trying, Nyx! He's scared, worried..."

"He's losing control!" Nyx snapped as Ali's eyes widened, her hand coming out to stroke Ben's face.

"Ben, you need to breathe, control yourself, slow the sands of time..." she said softly as Ben's head shook, his eyes widening as they grew brighter.

"I can't! I can't stop!"

Nyx moved forward, gripping Ben's shoulder to try and ground him just as the world seemed to fast forward around them. Animals went by at a breakneck speed, bugs did the same. The seasons shifted within moments, going from fall to winter, then back to spring and summer. Over and over the world changed. Trees grew taller, plants grew thicker. Rain fell and the sun shined down over them.

It all spun so fast, so out of control, that it left Ali and Nyx reeling even as Ben panted with exertion. If they let him simply go until he tired, they'd be waiting forever for the world to slow.

Instead, Ali leaned forward, gently cupping his face in her hands once more, and pulled him down to her, their lips meeting. He took a focusing breath, his eyes fluttering closed as she deepened the kiss, letting his tongue move with hers with more force. His hand came up and pulled her closer, wrapping around her waist as time began to slow once more. The seasons and their shifting came less frequently, the growth of the plants less rapid.

"Slow down, damn it," Nyx muttered. "We aren't going anywhere, and we're going to fix this..."

Ben whimpered slightly against Ali's mouth, then let her pull back as time came to a halt around them. It left Ali and Nyx both reeling, though they hid it from Ben to keep him from feeling even more guilty.

They glanced around. They could see through the trees. What had been a forest behind the clearing had changed and was now a tourist attraction. People were moving around from building to building, chattering excitedly as children brought candy buckets with them.

Halloween... Samhain. It was Samhain.

Magic had guarded them, kept the world from stumbling in on them as they'd remained seemingly frozen in time. The area under their feet was now covered in moss.

Nyx frowned, taking the first step from where they'd been standing. The world was shaky, his head swimming, but he was still forcing his body to move. He stepped through the trees, hearing the others follow him. Ben was muttering how sorry he was, over and over, while Alyson simply told him it would be ok, that he hadn't done anything they couldn't fix. Nyx stepped onto the path, his head tipping to the side, and he blinked as someone walked into his side, bumping him.

"Whoa, sorry man! Hey, nice 80s costume!" the girl grinned, then pulled a device back up to her ear and spoke. "Hey, Angie! Yeah, I accidentally bumped into this hot guy, he's got such an authentic 80s costume on!" she said, chattering away as she walked off, her voice growing quieter the farther away she got.

Ali's eyes widened as she looked around, holding her breath at the way things looked, the technology. Cars looked different and even the styles for decorations were different. She grasped onto Benjamin's arm tightly, her eyes growing more concerned, and Nyx's eyes went up, drawn to a billboard, one like he had never seen before.

A moving picture played on the billboard, and down a small driveway was a fairly decent-sized mall. The billboard was showing off advertising for all of the different stores, each one with bright, flashy lights. He stepped back, feeling Ali grasp his arm tightly as well.

"What fucking year is it?!"

To be Continued...

MUSIC IS MAGIC...
The Songs that Inspired *Awakened*

Shadows of the Night – Pat Benatar

Barracuda – Heart

Crazy on You – Heart

Magic Man – Heart

Love is a Battlefield – Pat Benatar

Invincible – Pat Benatar

Heartbreaker – Pat Benatar

Fire and Ice – Pat Benatar

We Belong – Pat Benatar

Control – Halsey

Gasoline – Halsey

Young Gods – Halsey

Strange Magic – Electric Light Orchestra

Stay the Night – Zedd ft. Hayley Williams

Find You – Zedd ft. Matthew Koma & Miriam Bryant

Only You – Yazoo

The End of the Innocence – Don Henley

Waiting for a Star to Fall – Boy Meets Girl